THE CHAMPION'S DESIRE

MARIE LIPSCOMB

Second edition.

ISBN 978-1-957313-12-2

Cover: Najla Qamber of Qamber Designs and Media

Editing: Ali Williams

Formatting: Jack Harbon

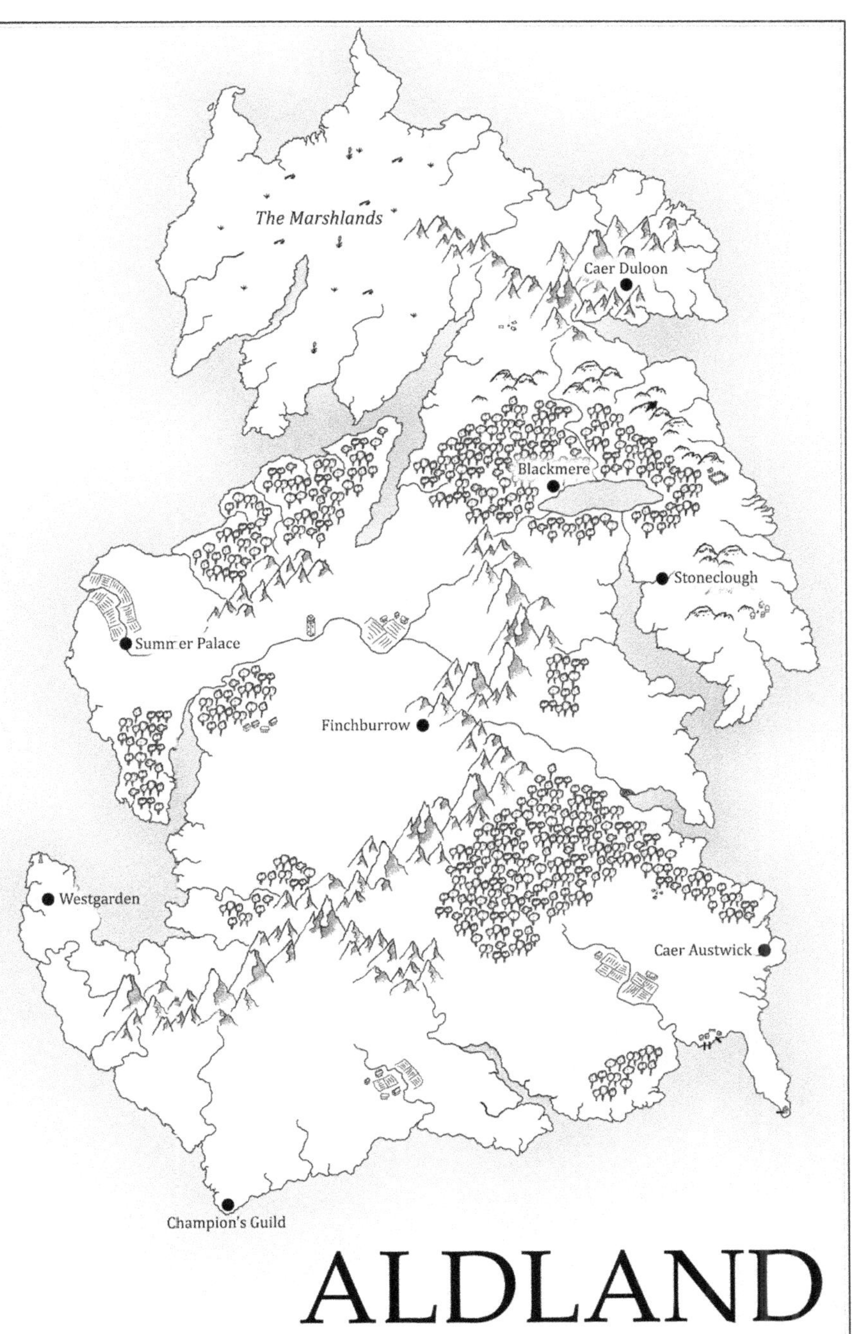

The Marshlands
Caer Duloon
Blackmere
Stoneclough
Summer Palace
Finchburrow
Westgarden
Caer Austwick
Champion's Guild
ALDLAND

To everyone who has ever been made to believe that they aren't enough.

You are. You always have been. You always will be.

THE CHAMPION'S DESIRE

PROLOGUE

For centuries, the champions protected the people of Aldland from their foes. Anyone who could prove their strength and courage could join the order and be remembered throughout history as a guardian of the people. To join their ranks was an honor.

As the world changed, so did the Guild, and with peace came new purpose. Instead of protection, they dedicated their lives to entertainment.

But even when Aldland was at peace, the hearts of men were rarely as tranquil. After travelling the land and returning each time to find their castle was overrun by thieves and brigands, the champions decided they needed a leader.

Thus, the position of Guild Master was forged. Under the watchful eye of the strongest and wisest champion of them all, the Champion's Guild flourished. The leader's purpose was to remain within the keep, mold the champions into legends, and arrange their events.

Built upon a foundation of tradition and honor, the Champion's Guild remained a respected order, reminding all who witnessed them, that anyone with strength, courage, and determination, might someday become a champion.

CHAPTER

ONE

The clatter of galloping hoofbeats stilled Natalie's heart. Her feet pounded the floorboards as she hurried across the room and peered from the window, hope and fear battling for dominance. A rider thundered along the road towards her; a messenger, dressed in red. Brandon was late, and daylight was fading fast.

"Oh, Goddess no." She held her breath, willing him to keep riding. Whatever message he carried had clearly come with the instruction not to spare the horse. If it was from Brandon, it was not good news.

Mercifully, the messenger passed below the window in a flurry of chestnut and flowing crimson, a cloud of dust billowing in his wake as he sped up the road.

Natalie found herself able to breathe again.

Hours earlier she might have entertained herself by attempting to guess where the rider was going and what tidings he brought, but she was only capable of dark thoughts now. She wrapped her arms around herself and fought off a shiver.

"Where are you?" Her question rode on a puff of vapor, out into the rosy-skied evening.

Closing the window, she turned back to the room. After a month of fruitless searching, shivering through the night in wet clothes and drafty tents, foraging for meagre meals, the small, simple room in the roadside inn was practically palatial.

Brandon's armor gleamed in the corner of the room, laid out so Natalie could learn the names of all the pieces. Eager to excel at her new role as squire, she had polished and re-polished it that morning until her arm ached and he had teased that she would wear through the steel.

How she wished he had worn it when he rode out to meet the other champions who were joining their hunting party.

Their quarry was one of their own, Henry Percille, the Dragon, the champion who had organized the bandit attack on Blackmere and fled before his secret was discovered.

There had been no sign of Henry since, but even so, Natalie worried. Every clatter of hoofbeats, every raised voice coming from the bar below, spiked her pulse. Skilled, vicious, and fueled by ambition, Henry Percille was as dangerous as he was cunning.

As Natalie set about straightening the worn grey bed sheets for what might well have been the twentieth time, a sharp knock on the door turned her lungs to iron. She bolted across the room and flung open the door.

"He's not back yet then?" Genevieve asked in lieu of a

greeting. Natalie shook her head. The champion's expression remained neutral as she gave a casual one-shouldered shrug. "The Bear never does anything quickly."

Natalie stepped aside to allow Genevieve into the room and closed the door behind her. The champion strode towards the bed, her boots thumping on the wooden boards. She peered down her nose at the sheets, as though assessing whether they were clean enough for her to sit. "I hate this inn."

Natalie fought back a grin. "Not as nice as Blackmere's tavern, is it?"

"No. No it isn't."

Since the day they had set off from Blackmere, Genevieve's temper had grown sourer and sourer. Natalie knew the cause. She knew why the champion's sullen gaze drifted to the east whenever she thought no one was looking, and why her expression hardened at the end of every unproductive day.

Genevieve, the indomitable warrior known in the arena as the Thorn of The Rose, was in love, and the woman she longed to be with was more than one hundred miles away; a barmaid, working in the tavern in distant Blackmere.

Compared to Genevieve's heartache, Natalie's anguish at being away from Brandon for a day seemed pitiful.

The bed squawked as Genevieve sat upon it. "I need help writing Jenny a letter." She braced her elbows on her thighs and let her hands dangle between her knees "I want to tell her we're still searching for Henry but have found nothing, and that I think about her every day. I don't want her to think I've forgotten her."

Natalie could not help but smile. "I don't think you need to worry about that, but I'll help write it."

Genevieve buried her face in her hands and released a weary breath. When she raised her head again, her eyes were glazed. "Do not tell anyone."

"Of course. Your heart's icy reputation is safe with me."

The champion narrowed her eyes. "I'm serious. When the other champions arrive, you can't mention it, and you mustn't let them see you and Brandon together. Don't even let them suspect. If the Guild finds out about Jenny and I, or you and Brandon...There's a lot at stake. Sex is fine... encouraged, even, but only outside the Guild. Relationships are forbidden. They want us focused on the fight, on training, not our hearts."

"Viv, it'll be fine. Brandon's warned me a hundred times already." Natalie sat on the bed beside the champion. Her heart fluttered as she caught Brandon's scent tangled amongst the bed sheets. She glanced back towards the window, to the darkening evening sky. "Goddess, I hope he's safe."

"The Bear's a big boy, he can look after himself. Besides, Henry will be miles away, fleeing for his life after all he did." Genevieve rolled her eyes and leaned back on her hands. "Don't fret. Darius is among the champions that the Bear is meeting, so most likely they're wrestling on a roadside, or drunk... or drunk *and* wrestling."

Natalie chuckled and fidgeted with the ram's head brooch on the collar of her dark green padded gambeson. Being away from Blackmere was both a blessing and a constant source of anguish. The brooch was a persistent reminder that her time with the champions was only temporary. "I hope so. I can't wait to meet them."

An awkward hum sounded at the back of Genevieve's throat. "Just try not to act like a noble around the other champions."

"How can I—?" The slow, steady rhythm of walking horses silenced Natalie.

She pressed her lips together, suppressing the urge to run to the window. Every hoofbeat coiled a spring inside her, winding tighter, until she felt as though her excitement would burst and send her leaping through the inn's roof.

Genevieve's eyes bore into her, a single eyebrow cocked in mock despair. "You want to see if that's him, don't you?"

Natalie released a strained breath and swallowed. "Not at all. I'm sure it's nothing."

"You're a terrible liar."

"I had you believing I was a barmaid, didn't I?"

"Not for a moment." Genevieve laughed and shook her head. "You were far too haughty. Rest your noble bottom, my sweet, delicate lady. I'll check the window." The champion stood, casually stretched her long, muscular limbs, and sauntered towards the window. Every step was torturously slow. She threw a grin over her shoulder, enjoying every second of Natalie's squirming.

Finally, Genevieve reached the far side of the room. "Ah-ha."

Natalie sat tall. "It's him?"

"Oh, forgive me, I was looking at my reflection in the glass. I thought I had something in my teeth…"

"Viv."

"...I didn't though."

"You're terrible." Natalie stood and craned her neck to peer at the road below. Genevieve turned, blocking the little window with her broad, well-built shoulders and gripped Natalie by her upper arms.

"Do you want me to check *your* teeth?" The champion teased as the hoofbeats grew louder and came to a halt on the road beneath them.

"It's him, isn't it?"

"Perhaps," Genevieve shrugged. "There *is* a big hairy man out there, riding a big grey horse."

Natalie's heart fluttered against her ribs, and her stomach flopped like a landed fish. She stood straight, checked the fastenings on her gambeson and brushed the seat of her trousers. "I'm nervous. Goddess, why am I nervous?"

"Because you are a fool, and you're in love, which is why I'm worried." Genevieve smiled and picked an invisible spot of dirt from Natalie's coat. "Before you go running down there and throw yourself into his embrace, remember what I said."

"I won't let them know we're together. It's alright. Stop worrying."

"Don't even let them suspect it." The champion's face hardened, and any trace of amusement vanished. "His family depends on it."

Genevieve's words were anchored in the back of Natalie's mind as she made her way through the top floor of the inn.

One false move could have him banished from the Guild, and people would suffer.

His mother was afflicted with back pain so severe and constant, that for years she had been unable to work, and his father was nearing seventy years of age. Brandon's salary and any prize money he received were sent directly to them, to pay for healers, medicine to relieve the pain, their noble's tax, and the cost of food and housing. Losing his position at the Guild would mean Brandon could no longer support his family.

Natalie side-eyed one of the bedroom doors as she passed. It had been reserved for her, though she had barely set foot in it since their arrival the day before. She wiped her sweating palms against her hips and ran over the formal greeting she had prepared. "Well met, Sir Brandon."

As far as the other champions knew, she was simply aiding them in their quest to track down Henry and squiring to repay Brandon for his services to Blackmere.

At the top of the wooden staircase she heard Brandon's deep, thundering laughter cutting through the humming chatter below. She stood for a moment and closed her eyes as her heart skipped along her ribs.

"Well met, Sir Brandon. Well met, Sir Brandon." She whispered the greeting like an incantation, cementing it in her memory. The formality was paramount. Too informal and the champions may suspect their relationship. "Any news regarding our quarry?"

The heat of a deep pink blush crawled up her neck as she forced a slow breath. Lightly curling her fingers around the stair rail, she ventured down one of the steps. Her soft leather boots padded upon the wood.

"Well met, Sir Brandon. Greetings, Sir Brandon? No... well met."

Candlelight flickered above her head as she passed, casting a squat flickering shadow across the stairs. Brandon's laughter spurred her heart into a gallop as it rumbled from below, accompanied by raised, excited voices.

The voices of champions.

Natalie's head spun. All her life she dreamed of meeting those heroes, renowned across Aldland for their prowess in battle and their beauty. Now she was to live among them, and work alongside them, for an entire year. Even though their task was less than pleasant, she could not suppress her excitement. A giddy smile spread across her lips as she reached the bottom of the stairs, and stepped into the dense swarm of tavern patrons, crammed into the tiny bar.

"Pardon me. Pardon me!" She grimaced as she wedged herself between two chattering men and began picking her way through the crowd. "Excuse me, sirs."

The air was thick with conversation and the sour reek of ale and sweat. Warm bodies pressed against her, unyielding to her requests to pass. She squeezed through, holding her breath as she passed beneath clouds of curling blue pipe smoke. By the time she reached the center of the crowd, she was exhausted, and there was still no sign of Brandon.

She stood on her tiptoes and craned her neck to find him, wondering how it was possible to lose a man so large.

"Can I help you find someone, my lady?"

Her heart leapt, and her breath froze at the sound of his voice. Every word fluttered against the back of her neck, sparking a fire in the pit of her belly.

She whirred around to face him. His dark eyes widened a little, as though he sensed her desire to fall into his arms, and the danger they faced if she gave in to her urge. Instead she offered him a friendly smile.

Brandon towered above everyone else and took up so much space with his broad frame that the air around him seemed clearer than the rest of the inn. No matter how many times she saw him she would always be in awe of his strength, the raw, brutal power of his arms, and the tenderness with which he held her when they were alone.

As Natalie composed herself, the lines around his eyes deepened, and a gentle smile curled beneath the shadow of his thick, silver-flecked beard.

"Well...uh... well met, Sir Brandon." She felt as though she was glowing when she looked at him, all strength and softness, a hardened exterior disguising a gentle heart. "How was your ride?"

"Too long." He took a step closer and lowered his head towards her. A thrill coursed through her at his familiarity. His eyes drifted down towards her lips, as though he could barely contain his desire to kiss her.

Heat crept across her cheeks. "You must be pleased to be back."

"Aye." His eyes trailed across her face. "I can't wait to be back in bed."

She sank her teeth into her lower lip to suppress her

grin. His voice was deep and dark and full of promise. This flirtation was a dangerous game to play.

"But first, I have friends for you to meet," he said at last, hooking his arm around her shoulders. The companionable gesture snapped her from his spell.

They made their way across the tavern as people parted to let them pass. Every pair of eyes was drawn towards Brandon, trailing up and down his body as though they could not quite believe his size. A few people turned to whisper to their companions, but no one said anything directly to him. No one would dare.

Though those who knew him knew he was kind and gentle, Brandon looked intimidating. He was a hulking mass of scar and muscle, renowned all over the land for his fighting skill. His glory days in the Tourney were years behind him, but word of his brave defense of Blackmere seemed to ride ahead of them wherever they went.

An ache rolled through Natalie's body as she pressed her side against him. She longed to steal him away, even if just for a moment.

She was burning up as they reached the far corner of the tavern.

"There he is!" A man held out his arm to Brandon and clapped him on the back, pulling him into the fray.

He was young and strikingly handsome, with warm brown skin, long, black dreadlocks, and kind, dark eyes which sparkled with excitement as he talked. "We thought you were lost forever."

Natalie's heart swelled as she looked around the small gathering. There was no denying they were champions. It was obvious from their stunning appearance, strong physiques, and the confidence with which they carried themselves. They were chosen because they were as beautiful as they were brutal.

"I hope you didn't miss me too much, Darius." Brandon's cheeks grew round as he gestured towards Natalie. "May I introduce you to Natalie, my new squire."

"A squire?" Darius's eyes lit up. "You have a squire this year? Goddess, you must be taking it seriously."

"Darius?" Natalie's breath hitched as she held out her hand. "You're the Storm, aren't you?"

"Why, yes I—" The smile dropped from the man's lips. His eyes narrowed as they fixed on the brooch at her throat, a glare so fleeting Natalie might have missed it were she not hanging on his response. Her pulse fluttered anxiously as he stiffened and tucked his arm behind his back. "Lady Blackmere." The slight was so subtle that Brandon did not notice. He gestured to a young woman, whose pale white skin, prematurely silver hair, and slender, muscular frame made her seem as though she was a statue carved from ice. "This is Sara."

Natalie bowed her head, restraining her enthusiasm. She knew the young woman as the Snow Fox. Both she and Darius were fresh out of their debut season and riding high on a wave of expectation. They had not qualified for the Grand Tourney held that year at Blackmere, but hopes were high for the following year.

Sara's features hardened as she looked down at Natalie. "Brandon told us about what happened at Blackmere."

"Oh," Natalie felt herself redden. She wondered how

much Brandon had told them. Her stomach coiled at the thought that they might know about her deceit, and her failure to prevent the attack. "Yes, it was truly terrible. I'm so sorry for what happened."

Darius raked his eyes across her face, leaving behind a trail of blazing heat. "We lost good people."

Shame weighed heavy in Natalie's chest as she searched for something to say. It was her carelessness which had led to the deaths of champions and squires. Among the list of the dead was Robert Trevaryn, a man beloved by Brandon, his best friend. His death still stung.

There had been many nights she noticed Brandon staring into the flames of their campfire, his dark eyes glazed with unspilled tears.

Now the eyes of all the champions were on her, burning into her, as though they could see the weakness of her heart, and the stain of death on her soul.

"Aye, it was a tragedy." Brandon's voice came as a relief. His arm brushed against Natalie's elbow as he shifted his weight, grounding her once more. "I'll introduce you to everyone else later, when it's less noisy. What say we share a drink?"

"I knew there was a reason I liked you," Darius's wide smile spread across his face. His eyes creased into a grateful smile as he turned his back on Brandon and Natalie, and his dreadlocks swung behind him like a pendulum. "I'll find somewhere to sit and you get them in."

CHAPTER

TWO

"I don't think they like me." Natalie rested her elbows on the bar as they waited for the barkeep to return.

Brandon stood beside her, tense, deliberately keeping his distance. His eyes scanned the rows of bottles and casks behind the bar. "Who?"

"Darius and Sara. All of them."

"They do. They just take a while to warm up around new people. Especially people with noble titles."

Natalie caught the eye of the red-faced bartender and beckoned him over. "Now for that, I can't blame them."

"You're doing well," Brandon assured her. He smiled and clapped her on the back. His touch lingered a fraction longer than proper as he swept his broad palm between her shoulder blades. An invisible binding around her chest tugged tighter.

"What'll it be?" the bartender huffed.

"Your finest honeyed wine," Natalie said, pulling her

15

purse from her pocket. She tipped the contents into the man's outstretched palm. "Six bottles of it. And six roast chickens. Will that cover it?"

The bartender's eyes widened as he counted the silver in his hand. "Aye. It will. I'll have to go down to the cellar to get the good stuff. Be with you in a minute."

Natalie bowed her thanks and turned to Brandon. "Goddess, I hope that's enough."

"You needn't do that." Brandon lowered his head to her, as though leaning into a kiss. It took all of Natalie's restraint not to raise up onto the tips of her toes and meet his lips. She heard his breath catch in his throat. "And you overpaid."

Natalie shrugged. "What need do I have of money when we are out travelling the road again? It's just an invitation to robbers. Better to spend it now." She let her eyes trail across his body and felt her hunger for him deepen. "And besides, I have everything I need already."

Brandon's cheeks blossomed above the dark hair of his beard. He lowered his voice and turned back to face the bar. "Charmer."

The barkeep returned with six bottles filled with amber wine, before running back into the kitchens, promising to bring the food over to the champions' table. "It'll just be a few minutes," he panted as he returned, wiping the back of his neck with a cloth. "We're busy today. Seems word got out that your lot were heading here and everyone came to look. Wish we'd known you were coming. We would've prepared better."

Natalie tucked a bottle at the crook of each of her

elbows and bowed her thanks. She began hooking her fingers through the handles of as many cups as she could carry.

Brandon loaded his arms with the remaining bottles, wincing a little as he gripped each one with his maimed hand, a constant reminder of the battle for Blackmere. The bandits had severed the middle finger of his left hand at the first knuckle, and the wound was not yet fully healed. "You're doing a fine job, my man. It's a wonderful little inn."

"Oh!" The bartender bowed his head. "Thank you, Brandon. Sorry, *Sir* Brandon, if news from Blackmere's to be believed."

"Just Brandon's fine. Thank you."

Natalie beamed as they stepped away from the bar. "Seems your reputation follows you wherever you go."

"Aye," Brandon released a sigh, clanking the bottles he cradled against his chest. He followed close behind her. "That does tend to happen."

Pride swelled in Natalie's heart as she walked in step with him. Brandon was a good man, and he was hers.

They were almost back at the table when a woman approached. Her shimmering waves of abyss-black hair were pulled over her shoulder, revealing the sloping, soft skin of her throat. Her full lips pulled back, into a warm and stunning smile. "Goddess preserve me, is that Brandon? I thought I saw you."

Brandon's throat twitched as he stared straight ahead.

She cocked her head to the side. "Don't you remember me?"

He made an uncomfortable sound at the back of his

throat and clutched the wine close. The lady turned her gaze to Natalie, and clearly found in her an unworthy opponent. Without a word she darted her ice blue eyes to the side. A clear dismissal, and one Natalie had grown accustomed to living in her mother's castle.

Instinctively, Natalie backed away a pace.

White teeth shone against the woman's soft pink lips. "We met back in Westgarden, perhaps... Goddess, it would've been five years ago now."

The muscle in Brandon's cheek leapt as he lowered his head. "Katryn..."

"You do remember me!" She smiled and took a step closer, placing herself between Natalie and Brandon. The flowing pink silk of her skirt brushed against Natalie's hip. "I had a feeling I'd left an impression."

Natalie's chest hollowed. Brandon was renowned for more than just his prowess in the arena. Standing there in her padded jacket and trousers, several inches shorter than Katryn and more than a foot shorter than Brandon, Natalie became painfully aware of her lack of elegance and grace.

"You'll have to forgive me," Brandon smiled cordially. "I'm dining with friends tonight."

"We're friends, aren't we?" Katryn grinned. "Besides, I'll wager I know you far better than they do."

Brandon rolled his eyes and resumed his walk back to the table. The dark-haired woman followed at his heels.

Heat crawled along Natalie's throat, burning her ears, as she made her own way towards the table. She weaved between patrons, squeezing through muffled conversations and irritated glances as she found herself parted from Brandon. Ale spattered on her boots as she sidled past a pair of disgruntled drinkers.

At last, she found the table in the furthest corner of the tavern, which the champions had laid claim to.

"Look who I found!" Darius cried out, pointing enthusiastically to Genevieve, who sat stone-faced beside him. "Viv finally decided to join us!"

Genevieve lifted her eyes towards Brandon, looking between him and Katryn. Natalie's chest tightened as she noticed Katryn's arm was hooked through Brandon's. She tossed her head back, her black waves shimmering in the candlelight.

Natalie dared not look towards them as she clunked the tankards on the table, passing them between the champions.

"Thank you, Squire," Genevieve muttered, her eyebrow cocked as she peered into the empty cup.

"Natalie's treating us tonight," Brandon said. He maneuvered his arm so that Katryn had no choice but to let go of him and placed the six bottles on the table. "The finest honeyed wine. And there are roast chickens on the way."

"It's the least I can do, to thank you all for being here." Natalie forced a smile.

Genevieve snatched one of the bottles and pulled the cork out, sniffing the contents and nodding in approval.

Natalie perched on an empty stool opposite Genevieve. Beside her Sara shifted a little further away, as though her very presence at the table contaminated the air.

"This must've cost a fortune." Darius arched an eyebrow.

Natalie shook her head dismissively and smiled. "It's nothing, really."

"Sadly, fancy things never sit happily in my stomach." He stood and sidled past his companions, heading towards the bar. "I'll get my own drink."

As she watched him stride through the crowd, Natalie's stomach lurched. He knew. He knew what she had done, or failed to do, in Blackmere. She had wronged people close to him, and her mistakes had cost lives. A solid mass formed in her throat, and her eyes burned with tears.

"It was nice to see you, Katryn," Brandon said firmly. "But I'm afraid I have things to discuss with my companions."

"Come now, are there any secrets between us?" She purred against his ear.

Natalie bit back the acid rising in her throat. This woman was beautiful, elegant, the type of woman a champion was expected to share a bed with. Brandon shivered as Katryn raked her fingernails through his hair.

A smile curved the corner of the woman's lips. "If you're ever in Westgarden, look for me."

Brandon's eyes were dark as Blackmere's waters. "Enjoy your evening."

Natalie found herself breathing a little easier as Brandon sat at the table, squeezing into a space between Sara and a young man with fiery auburn curls. He raised his eyebrows and blew the air out from his cheeks.

"You've still got it, old man," Sara smirked.

"I don't want it," Brandon grimaced as he filled his cup

with wine. He cast a sideways glance towards Natalie and raised his drink. "Thank you, my lady."

As evening drew on, and the plump roast chickens were reduced to nothing but bone and gristle, Natalie found herself swept along in conversations without context. She laughed along, afraid to ask for clarification, feeling more out of place than ever before. Even Darius seemed to relax a little after he finished his first pint of ale.

"So, Brandon," he grinned, pouring from one of the wine bottles. "We hear you're a knight now?"

"Aye, apparently so," Brandon chuckled. His lids hung heavy over his eyes. "Whatever that means."

"Knighted by Lady Austwick," Sara announced. She turned to Natalie and raked her eyes across her features. "Isn't she your mother?"

Natalie straightened her back. The sudden turn in conversation brought the tavern into sharp focus. Most of the patrons had left, and the champions far outnumbered the stragglers.

"She is," Natalie said, taking a sip from her cup. The honeyed wine, which had once tasted divine, was now sickly and thickened her tongue. She clenched her jaw as a yawn swelled in the back of her throat.

"Favoritism." Genevieve shook her head in jest. "I was there, actually fighting in the streets of Blackmere, while he was sauntering around the castle."

"Sod off," Brandon chuckled. "You were locked away in the tavern when we found you. I'll bet you spent the whole evening in there."

He tried to duck, as Genevieve flicked a chicken bone at his head, muttering a curse beneath her breath.

Natalie smiled. In some ways, the battle for Blackmere seemed like it had happened years ago. But the fear, the panic, even the passion she and Brandon shared, was as raw as if it had happened only that morning.

Darius grinned over his cup. "So, Bear, what happened to your finger?"

Brandon held out his hand and admired the bandage around the remaining half of his middle digit. "I got it into my head I could take on forty men by myself. I was, of course, swiftly captured." He paused to let the other champions chuckles die down. "The leader of the bandits asked me a question, and my finger answered for me."

Darius's laughter exploded through the air, cracking against Natalie's eardrum. "Good man."

"Does it hurt?" Sara asked, her voice laced with more curiosity than concern. She had barely sipped her drink, and sat forward, leaning her elbows on the table.

Brandon shrugged a shoulder. "I'd lost more than a finger that week."

Natalie's chest grew tight as the atmosphere around the table darkened.

"Aye." Sara lifted her glass. "To our fallen Brothers and Sisters."

As Natalie raised her glass, she felt their eyes burning into her. She lowered her head beneath the weight of their gaze.

Brandon cleared his throat and shook his head slowly. "No matter where Henry is, I will find him. I won't stop searching until he answers for what happened at Blackmere."

"Brandon," Darius leaned forward. His eyes darted to Sara, who nodded sharply. "Henry's already at the Guild."

The sudden thud of Brandon's cup slamming the table sent a jolt though Natalie. She looked up, scanning the faces of the champions.

Brandon's eyes darted between his sheepish companions. "You couldn't have told me sooner?"

Sara took a deep breath. "He arrived the day before your letter did, and he informed the Guild Master of what had happened. He believed you to be dead, until we heard from you."

"I guarantee he didn't tell you all that happened," Brandon growled. "The conniving little shit."

Sara arched an eyebrow. "He seems devastated, especially about Robert."

"Do you believe him?" The question left Natalie's lips before she could stop it.

Darius's eyes snapped to her. "I don't know what to believe. But I'm not picking sides until I know all there is to know. We're family, and as far as I'm concerned, we all deserve the right to be heard."

Brandon's jaw twitched as he nodded.

The Storm exhaled sharply, as his shoulders dropped an inch. "I think the best thing to do is rest tonight and we'll head to the Guild tomorrow to settle it." He groaned as he stood and swayed a little. "I think it's time for bed."

"I agree," Sara sighed, pushing her cup away from her as she rose from her seat. "We've a long ride tomorrow."

"Goodnight, sweet Bear." Darius bowed his head to Brandon and headed off towards the stairs.

Brandon stared ahead in stunned silence. Natalie could only watch as his lips twitched, forming around half-planned, unspoken words. She longed to move closer to him and to wrap him in her arms, to comfort him.

Finally, Genevieve broke the heavy silence. "We should go to the Guild and let them know your side of what happened."

Brandon nodded, defeated, and released a broken sigh. "It's all we can do. Let's just go to bed. There's little to be done before tomorrow."

Natalie remained seated as the table emptied. A nagging doubt clawed at her mind, that Henry's only crime was to place trust in the bandits. He had not meant for them to kill, or for them to remain in Blackmere with their hostages. If anything, she was just as guilty as he was.

With the champions gone, the full extent of the table's clutter became apparent. She scraped the chicken bones onto a single platter and stacked the greasy plates on top of each other. It gave her comfort to know that there was at least something she could set right.

When she was done, she turned towards the stairs, where Brandon stood waiting. He raked his fingers through his tousled brown hair, skimming across the silver at his temples.

How she longed to curl beside him, to have his arms wrapped around her, shielding her from all the world. As she approached, she dared not hope to sleep in his embrace.

The inn was crawling with champions and any one of them could walk into his room when the sun rose.

"My lady," he greeted her, his voice barely a whisper. Emboldened by the wine, he held out a hand, and pressed his lips to her knuckles. Her breaths turned shallow as his lips lingered "I know it's a risk, but I need to be with you tonight."

His words shattered her willpower as she threaded her fingers with his. Yes, he needed her, but as he followed her up the stairs, she knew she needed him just as badly.

CHAPTER

THREE

The bed was far too short for Brandon. He bent his knees, trapping Natalie's calves between his sturdy, hairy thighs. They held each other on top of the threadbare bedsheets, their naked bodies pressed together in casual, comforting intimacy. Weak candlelight danced across their bodies, bathing them in a faint amber glow.

Brandon's smile was fleeting and shallow.

"They'll believe us," Natalie assured him, though even as she spoke, she doubted her words. It was every bit as likely that the Guild might shift the blame from Henry onto her. She had failed in her duties as Lady of Blackmere, and though she knew Brandon did not blame her for the deaths of his friends, there was no guarantee the other champions would accept that. Fear swelled inside her, constricting her chest and blurring her vision.

"Something's worrying you." Brandon brushed his lips

between her eyebrows and wound his arm tighter around her waist. "You have that look."

She forced a smile. "I'm just so glad you're back. I missed you today." There was no need to burden him with her concerns about the Guild. "I started to worry something awful had happened to you." Her heart fluttered as he gently brushed strands of her hair back behind her ears.

"I'm safe, and I'm here with you. There's no better place in the world." He ran his fingers along her back, sending chills throughout her body. "Do you want to talk about Katryn?"

"We don't have to. Not if it makes you uncomfortable."

In truth, she had come to terms with the fact that to love a champion was to accept that she followed in the footsteps of many others, especially a champion as experienced as Brandon. It was expected for champions to enjoy sex after their contests, and plenty of it. They were made infertile by the Guild, unable to bear children. Sex was purely for pleasure, a prize for their victories, a reward for their dedication to the contests, but it was not permitted within the walls of the Guild.

Brandon and Genevieve had warned her daily that as far as the Guild Master was concerned, intimacy and love between champions and the few squires who were of age, was punishable by banishment. Romantic relationships fogged the mind, led champions to act irrationally, forgoing their senses. A jilted warrior harboring resentment or avenging a wounded heart was dangerous.

Besides, the promise of fleeting, simple intimacy gave them something else to fight for, a reason beyond gold and fame. Every Tourney ended with a swarm of admirers following the champions in the hopes they might be picked to spend the night warming their beds.

As a younger man, when his victories in the Tourneys were almost guaranteed, the bards and troubadours sang of bonny Brandon's reputation as a philanderer.

"She was very pretty," Natalie whispered.

"Aye, and that's where her list of good qualities ends."

A small laugh made its way past Natalie's lips. "You can tell me about her if you like." It could be no worse than she was imagining.

"Remember what I told you that night, in your room at Blackmere?" Brandon took a deep breath and traced his fingertips across her bare shoulder. The sensation sent tingles across her skin. "I told you that some of the women in my past had expressed their disappointment that I didn't live up to their expectations. Katryn was one of them, and she made her opinion known, very loudly, in the middle of the street the next day. The gossip was all over Westgarden in a matter of hours. I was mocked in the streets."

Anger flared through Natalie's body. "That hag!"

A sudden smile brightened Brandon's face. He silenced her seething with a kiss, grinning against her lips. "I just want you to know, there are no fond feelings with her. I could have happily lived my life never seeing her again."

"I hope *I* see her again," Natalie grumbled.

A smile broke through her scowl as his arm snaked around her waist and pulled her closer. The sensation of her bare, smooth skin pressed against the mass of his hairy battle-hewn frame thrilled her. Her worries seemed insignificant, held in his embrace.

"No one has ever meant as much to me as you do, Nat."

"I love you." The words slipped from her lips, as easy as breath.

They seemed to hit him with all the force of a hurricane, stealing the air from his lungs. His eyes glazed as his lips parted.

Natalie's mind raced; it was too soon, too much. For weeks, they had come close, admitting to loving pieces of each other, but they had never spoken those words. She braced herself for rejection.

"Goddess... I...people have said that to me so many times over the years." His voice was hoarse as his eyes scanned her face. "But you mean it, don't you? You truly mean it."

"I do." She reached out and brushed his silver temples with her fingertips, cradling his cheek with the palm of her hand.

Closing his eyes, he leaned into her touch. "Nat, this is... it's all new to me. I know my reputation, I know people think of me as experienced... worldly, but I've never been in love before. I've never been someone's... suitor? Their sweetheart?" He gave a slight laugh, as though his own words took him by surprise. "All I know is, I loved you from the moment I walked into that cottage and saw you swinging the blade around, declaring yourself to be the Lioness of Blackmere." He gave a soft chuckle and raised his hand, curling his fingers around hers.

Her cheeks reddened. "Oh no. Please don't let that be the moment you fell for me."

"It was, and I'll remember it always." His hand lowered, grazing along the curve of her hip. "By the Goddess, I want to climb on the roof of the inn and shout it to the world. I love you, my Lioness of Blackmere."

"Stop! Someone will hear you." Natalie laughed and buried her face in the softness of his chest. "Besides, I'll never be a champion. I'm about ten years too old to debut, and far too squat."

He reeled back; his brow creased in indignation. "*Squat?*"

She knew what was coming. Before she could curl up and hide her body, he took both of her wrists in his hand and pinned them over her head. "How dare you, that's my love you're talking about."

"Brandon!" She laughed as he lowered his head and kissed her stomach.

Unlike the women who made their living as champions, Natalie's life had been comfortable, and she had wanted for nothing. Her stomach was soft and her breasts, hips and thighs full and thick. She had never felt self-conscious about her figure until she met lean, muscular champions like Genevieve and Sara.

With her wrists pinned above her head, and her feet wedged between his thighs, there was nothing for her to do but squirm and hold in her squeals as Brandon trailed kisses across her stomach, edging down towards her hips.

"You're beautiful," he whispered, tickling her skin with

the gentle flutter of his lips. "And the entire time I was out today I fantasized about every part of you."

"You did?" She sank her teeth into her lower lip as he worked his way back up towards her breasts.

"Aye. Some parts more than others, I'll admit."

Her back arched as his tongue traced the sensitive underside of her breast. He stopped just short of her nipple. She arched her back, desperate for more.

"Being with you at the Guild is going to kill me." His fingertips glided along the center of her torso, trailing from her breasts down to her navel. Desire pulsed between her thighs. "Intimacy between champions and squires is forbidden. If we get caught…"

"I know." Natalie shivered beneath his touch. The clatter of hooves rattled on the road below, echoing the frantic rhythm of her pulse. "So, we should make the most of our privacy tonight."

"I intend to." he whispered as he brushed his fingers in languid strokes around the curve of her hips and along her thighs. She yearned to part her legs and invite his touch, but he had her knees firmly pinned together.

"Are you going to tease me all night?"

"I'm going to do whatever my lady wants me to do." He released his hold on her wrists and rocked up onto his knees pushing apart her thighs and positioning himself between them. His lips curled into a grin as he looked down on her naked body. "You're the most beautiful woman in all the world, Nat."

She felt her cheeks tighten and turn red, as her breath grew light. His hard cock curved upwards above her thighs, and his soft, hairy stomach tensed beneath her gaze. She longed to touch him, to pleasure him, but they had all night, and he was always eager to please her first.

She held her breath as distant footsteps pounded on the wooden stairs. A whimper pressed against the barrier of her lips as he kissed her tender inner thighs.

The frantic knock at the door struck panic into her heart and chilled the air in the room.

Brandon leapt from the bed, snatching his breeches from the floor. He turned to the door. "What do you want?"

"*Brandon?*" The voice from the corridor was whispered, but harsh. "*An urgent message for Brandon of the Champion's Guild.*"

He made a growling sound of displeasure at the back of his throat. "Aye, give me a moment."

Natalie clutched the bedsheets to her chest. She stared wide-eyed around the bare room, looking for a place to hide. "Where should I go?"

"Under the bed!" Brandon hissed as he threw on his tunic.

She darted out of the bed and lowered herself onto the floor, wrapping the sheets around herself to protect her skin from splinters. Scrambling across the dusty floorboards, into the safety of the shadows her heart pounded in her ears, and the rush of blood around her body left her lightheaded.

She pressed her body to the floor and peered out as Brandon smoothed his hand over his hair. Taking a deep breath, he approached the door.

CHAPTER

FOUR

The dusty air tickled her throat. Tears stung her eyes as she choked in silence, biting into the back of her arm to stop herself from coughing.

The messenger stepped into the room bowing his head as he wiped his forehead on his sleeve. "I bring a summons from the Guild Master. He says you are to head to the Guild tonight, without hesitation. The feud has gone on long enough."

"We're leaving tomorrow. Tell him we'll be there the day after." Brandon was stoic, a mountain weathering the seasons without so much as a flinch.

"He wants you there by sundown tomorrow, he says."

A frustrated breath. "Very well."

"I'll ride ahead and tell him you're on your way."

Their words grew muffled as they stepped out into the hallway. When the door finally clicked shut, and the messenger's footsteps faded, Brandon turned to the bed and lowered his head. "You can come out."

She heaved herself into the open, clutching the sheets to her chest. Brandon's eyes were dark and heavy, his brows separated by a deep crease. She crossed the room, reaching out to comfort him. "Do we have to go?"

"Aye. We have to leave, tonight." His voice was just a whisper, sharpened by resentment. "I've been summoned back to the Guild. I can't refuse. I'm sorry."

"Has something happened?"

He bent over and collected the neat pile of her clothes from the foot of the bed. "They want the feud between Henry and I resolved." A bitter chuckle shook his shoulders. "He'll stand trial before the other champions and the Guild Master will decide his fate."

Natalie took her clothes and began to dress. "Isn't this what you want?"

"It would be, if I wasn't already certain of the outcome." The color drained from Brandon's cheeks as he strode towards the door. "Meet me in the stables when you've dressed. I'll leave word for Darius to bring our belongings with him tomorrow."

Her throat closed. "Brandon?"

"I have to go." He disappeared into the dark corridor.

Natalie hurried through dressing, her heart racing. Her fate would be decided the next day. Her guilt would be decided.

She hurried out of Brandon's room and into her own. There was little for her to bring along, save for a small bag containing spare clothes. She fished through her belongings, until she found a letter from her mother, addressed to the Guild Master.

With the letter secured in her jacket, she tiptoed down the stairs into the bar, and out through the door into the stables. Brandon was running back and forth, frantically tending to each of the horses. The stable hands stood with their backs pressed against the wall, keeping clear of the charging bull.

Brandon's mount, the enormous grey stallion aptly named Big Lad, watched his master with soulful brown eyes as he slowly munched his oats.

"Your horse is ready," Brandon huffed as he hauled Big Lad's saddle onto his back.

Natalie turned to her own black mare, who she had taken to calling Fliss. The mare was saddled and bridled and watching the proceedings, pinning her ears back against her handsome head.

Natalie turned towards the wide-eyed stable hands. "We can handle it from here. Thank you."

They bowed and scurried away, relieved to have been dismissed.

"Brandon." She spoke firmly as she stepped towards him. "Slow down and speak to me."

"We can't waste any time, Nat. The longer this takes, the more likely it is that my heart just gives out altogether." He raised his eyes as she blocked his path and released a shuddering breath. "Oh, Goddess, Nat, what do you suppose he's told them? Do they know about us?"

"If they do, we'll deny it. He can't prove anything."

"Henry's the favorite, Nat. If I'm thrown out of the Guild, I'll lose my income. Without prize money I make just enough each year to pay my mother's bills. If I can't send money, my mother can't afford the healer, or food, rent, taxes..."

She staggered beneath his weight as he crumpled into her embrace. His size and strength crushed her. Still, she held him, showering his shoulders in kisses, and hoping that somehow, she could give him courage. "How much is it? I can help—"

He took a deep, shuddering breath. "You can't. Neither I nor my mother would lay that burden at your feet. I scrape together ten gold coins each year and it's barely enough."

Natalie felt herself pale. It was almost her entire yearly allowance. "I'm sorry." She would have given anything to steal him away, to take him back up to the sanctuary of his bedroom and hold him until morning. Her eyes stung from exhaustion, and the honeyed wine still fogged her thoughts. "Whatever happens at the Guild, Genevieve and I will back you up. My mother and I will attest to your bravery and her gratitude for your services. You've done nothing wrong."

She held him, stroking the back of his neck with her fingertips.

He straightened his back and looked around the stable, as though embarrassed as his show of vulnerability. "Thank you, my lady. Henry has to pay for what he did."

"He will," Genevieve's voice came from the doorway. She strode into the stable, already dressed. "I heard the commotion. I've left word for the others that we're heading to the Guild."

Brandon turned to her, relief smoothing the creases above his eyes. "The Guild has summoned me. I have to head out now."

"Whatever happens, you have Nat. You have my support, and the love of the champions."

Brandon nodded slowly. He took a deep breath. Natalie felt her body uncoil as he smiled. "Thank you."

"It's been a difficult time for all of us." Genevieve strode into her mount's stall and heaved the saddle onto her chestnut's back. "Once we're at the Guild, we can work towards restoring life to how it should be."

Natalie reached out and squeezed Brandon's hand. "You don't have to face this alone."

"Thank you, both of you. I don't know what I would do if you weren't here."

"You don't ever have to worry about that," Natalie assured him. "You are loved."

He lowered his head and sighed. "Well, then. Let's go home."

CHAPTER

FIVE

As a girl, Natalie had dreamed of running from her home in Caer Austwick and riding out to the Champion's Guild. She had imagined brightly colored banners fluttering on the ocean breeze, and the sun gleaming on tranquil topaz waves. It was a place of magic and majesty, where any person who stepped beneath the ivory gates was welcomed and given an equal chance to prove their mettle.

The reality, she found, was much more terrifying.

Rain drizzled down her back, and the grey sea swelled below. Her knuckles paled as she gripped the reins and kept as much distance as possible between her horse and the yawning edge of the cliff. She prayed the path would not crumble beneath Fliss' hooves, her breath quickening with every slow step. Being so elevated had never affected her before. She could stand on ramparts and climb the spiraling stairs to the tallest castle towers without a second thought, but with the sea swelling beneath her, crashing against the ragged rocks, every fiber in her body wanted to flee.

"Are you alright, love?" Brandon called behind her.

She dared not open her mouth to speak as her stomach lunged towards her throat.

"Nat?"

In the corner of her eye Big Lad's grey coat blocked the crashing waves. She flinched as Brandon reached over and placed his hand on her shoulder.

"It's alright," he called to her above the roar of the waves. "Nothing's going to hurt you."

She allowed herself to look at him. His drenched hair hung dripping around his face, and his beard was dusted silver with droplets. The light was beginning to fade, and the toll of riding for an entire day and most of the previous night was apparent in the shadows beneath his eyes. He blinked the rain from his lashes and tilted his head towards the sea. "It's just a bit choppy out today."

"Come away from the edge!" She called out, heart leaping as he rode casually beside her. Her voice was flint sharp as she reached out to grip his sleeve. It was a futile gesture; she was too weak to hold on to him if he fell.

"Nat, we've space to ride five abreast. I've ridden this track a thousand times. It's safe."

Heat crawled across her chest as she forced herself to turn and focus on the path. Genevieve rode in the distance ahead, following the road, which snaked along the cliffs and towards the Guild headquarters.

"We're almost there," Brandon assured her. "I'll ride with you the entire way."

"You're certain it's safe?"

"I wouldn't bring you here if it wasn't."

"You must think me so foolish."

"Not at all." His kind, warm smile gave her a little more courage as they progressed down the road. "Have you ever been this far south?"

"Never." She sniffed and wiped the raindrops from her nose onto her sleeve. "I haven't seen the ocean since I was a young girl. I was expecting it to be blue."

Brandon swept his bedraggled hair back from his eyes and chuckled. "Well, I'll have to give you a proper introduction on a nicer day."

As they made their way past the cliffs, Natalie found she could breathe a little easier. They edged their way down a winding path, surrounded by lichen-spotted grey boulders, crowned with brown bushes of frost-withered heather and yellow gorse flowers. The roar of the ocean faded behind hills of coarse grass, which rustled in the wind.

"My lady," Brandon pulled back on Big Lad's reins and brought the horse to a halt.

Natalie followed his lead. With a smile, she noticed he had decorated Big Lad's mane with intricate braids. It was a habit he employed when he was feeling nervous.

Brandon leaned forward and cupped her cheek in his hand. His thumb brushed along her cheekbone and sent her pulse fluttering. "I still wish I'd taken the time to lay with you last night." There was a sadness in his eyes, sorrow and regret. "These may be the last moments we have any privacy, for a while."

She melted beneath his touch as his thumb skimmed

lower, until he reached the curve of her lips. He traced their shape, his own lips parted in desperate longing. Their secret burned in her chest like a ball of molten iron. She was in love with Brandon, and the thought of having to keep her distance from him, when all she wanted to do was hold him, was harrowing.

"These are difficult times, my love. For all of us, but more so for you." She leaned towards him and wrapped her hands around the back of his head, pulling him towards her lips.

His lips curved upwards against her kiss as she all but fell from the saddle. Her heart ached with need for him.

When their kiss broke, he looked down, and swallowed hard, the weight of the world a yoke on his shoulders. "When we're in the Guild, I won't be able to tell you that I love you as often as I want to. I won't be able to kiss you, to touch you... I've been trying to think of something we can do, some secret code that only you and I know, so I can tell you how I feel without saying it."

Natalie pressed her lips together as her heart swelled. Her hands drifted up towards the ram's head brooch on her collar, but that was too obvious. Everyone knew the Blackmere sigil.

She reached into her pocket and found a smooth copper coin. "Here."

He took it and clenched it in his gloved fist. "Thank you. When you see me with it, you'll know that my heart belongs to you."

She smiled, pressing her teeth into her lower lip. "And how do I let you know?"

He raised an eyebrow as he peered around them. Without a word he climbed down from the saddle and crouched down among the gorse bushes. When he returned, he held a small black feather, no longer than Natalie's index finger.

"May I?" He gestured towards the brooch on her collar.

Natalie leaned down towards him, letting the tip of her nose graze against his cheek as he fastened the feather behind the pin. She scattered kisses along his cheek.

"There," he said, his voice low. He turned his face slightly, so near their lips almost touched. "Now we can let each other know."

Natalie's heart bolted at the sound of hooves on the road ahead. She sat upright as Brandon stepped back from her. Genevieve trotted around the corner, windswept and soaked through. "I was beginning to think you fell into the sea."

Natalie straightened her back. "We're coming."

Genevieve turned her mount and jutted her chin ahead. "There's a welcome party at the gate. Henry's with them."

The sea air seemed to blow colder. Natalie's nerves prickled along her spine, as her pulse quickened. After almost a month of searching, seeking revenge, they had finally found him.

Brandon turned on his heel. He placed one foot in a stirrup and bounced back into the saddle, flicking the coin up into the air with his thumb, and catching it in his fist. "Let's get this over with."

CHAPTER

SIX

I am just as guilty as he is. I might well have put the bolt in the back of Robert's head myself.

Natalie did not notice the towers of the gatehouse until they were almost on top of her. The enormous castle was perched on the highest point of the cliffs, surrounded by a white stone wall.

The voice in the back of her mind taunted her as she, Brandon and Genevieve approached the latticed iron gates. It grew silent in the presence of the man staring at her.

Henry Percille, the man known in the arena as The Dragon, waited for them. The corner of his lips curled into a smile as they approached. Beside him stood a handsome older man, whose age was only apparent by his mane of white hair and the silver of his carefully groomed beard. He held himself with the strength and poise of a young man in his prime, and his warm, tan skin creased as he smiled.

"Brandon, Viv," the older man greeted the champions with a bow. "I appreciate you coming here so quickly."

"Guild Master," Brandon's voice rumbled in his chest. He brought Big Lad to a halt and glared down at Henry. Natalie's body tensed in anticipation of an outburst, but the champions remained still, silently glowering at each other.

"I see we have a guest?" The Guild Master's question snapped Natalie to attention.

She reached inside the breast of her jacket and pulled out a letter, fastened with a white rose seal. She caught the faint scent of her mother among the pages, dried flowers and sharp, sweet mint. "I'm Lady Natalie Blackmere, sir."

"Well met, my lady," the Guild Master took the letter and bowed, but his voice betrayed his weariness. He took a deep breath and braced himself, as though another stone had been added to the burden he already carried. "We should get out of this weather. But first I want to make it absolutely clear, there is to be no fighting inside the Guild. We'll settle this dispute like civilized people. Like a family."

"You needn't worry." Henry's bright blue eyes flickered towards Natalie and narrowed as he smiled. "I'm just happy to see my dear friends alive and well."

Natalie's back bristled as Brandon tensed at her side. Her calves twitched with the desire to leap from her horse, seize Henry and demand he confess.

Henry Percille, the man who had arranged the attack on Blackmere, who was more concerned with his reward for saving the castle than with the lives of others, grinned at her. The last time she had spoken to him, she had rejected his offer of marriage in exchange for the salvation of her people. Long had she harbored the suspicion that the reason he had wanted to marry her was so he could hide his guilt behind a noble name.

How she longed to see him pay.

At the Guild Master's command, the gates were opened, and they rode into the fortress.

The sight before her was enough to distract Natalie's attention from the vengeful storm gathering in her mind. They travelled through a courtyard, lined on one side with training rings, and on the other with a list, a long fence in stretch of sand, where the champions could practice the joust. At the top of the courtyard was the keep, gleaming white against the dull steel sky and sea. The grey slates of the conical tower roofs were obscured by wisps of low hanging cloud.

Despite the rain and the tension between the champions, the sight stole her breath. She was in Brandon's world, the place where he had grown from a Marshdown boy into a legendary fighter. It was the place where he had celebrated victories and mourned defeats, where he had become the man she loved. She watched his back and saw some of the tension drop from his shoulders. He was home.

A pressure against her ankle drew her attention downwards. Henry walked beside her, gripping her foot in the stirrup. She recoiled, her instinct telling her to kick out at him, but the urgent look in his eyes commanded her to be silent.

"Just remember... I know about you." His face hardened as she looked down on him. He glanced towards Brandon. "I know."

Natalie's throat closed as he strode ahead to walk beside the Guild Master.

They handed the weary horses to a group of squires in the stables and made their way on foot to the fortress's keep.

The Guild Master pulled the enormous wooden doors open and led them inside. After the day spent in cold rain, the heat from the keep added to her fatigue. Natalie's eyes were raw, aching from lack of sleep, but she forced them to stay open as they made their way through candlelit corridors, past shining suits of ancient armor, kept polished in pristine condition.

She walked beside Brandon, grazing her knuckles against his and hoping her presence gave him some comfort. She could hear the tremble in his breath, see the color drain from his cheeks.

"I'm here."

He brushed his hand against hers and offered her a fleeting smile.

They reached a second pair of wooden doors. The Guild Master heaved the doors open to reveal a round chamber. Dozens of men and women stood around the room, every one of them dressed in tunics embroidered with the sword sigil of the Champion's Guild.

Brandon's shoulders slumped as he stepped into the room. He released a weary sigh. "Is all this necessary?"

"This matter will be settled before the Guild. We're family, and this dispute pains us all." The Guild Master turned to Brandon and Henry. Genevieve's gentle sigh drew his attention. "Are you willing to speak on the matter, Genevieve, if we need you?"

She folded her arms across her chest. "Yes."

He nodded, before lowering his head towards Natalie. "And you, Lady Blackmere? Since you are the injured party, I feel it only fitting that you are present."

Natalie's throat clamped shut. She looked to Brandon for guidance. The muscle in his cheek leapt, as though he fought to keep his words contained. A gleam of bright copper, barely visible through the cracks between his clenched fingers steeled her heart.

"Thank you," Natalie said, irritated by the tremor in her voice. She had addressed crowded rooms before, and she had crumbled beneath the pressure. Her mother and father had insisted she learn how to wear a bold façade in public. As a child, she would be made to give speeches and recite poetry before her family's esteemed guests.

One such incident haunted her as she followed the champions into the center of the circle. It was during a mid-winter party, when her cackling uncle demanded that she entertain his guests by reciting all forty verses of The Ballad of Barthalow by heart. The slightest hesitation or stutter meant she had to begin again. She did not make it past the second verse before she burst into tears and had to be escorted from the hall.

A shudder travelled down her spine as the eyes of the champions fell on her.

The Guild Master turned to Natalie. "Now, Lady Blackmere, before I try to untangle the mess brought to me by Brandon and Henry, might I ask if there is another reason why you have graced us with your presence."

Natalie's ears burned as she cleared her throat. "I'm

here to squire, sir. My mother, Lady Austwick requested I work here for a year, to repay Sir Brandon and Genevieve for what they did at Blackmere."

"A squire?" The Guild Master smiled and shrugged a shoulder. "Have you done anything like that before? What do you know of horses?"

"A little," Natalie lowered her head. "Not much. I can clean stables and feed them. But I've been learning how to help someone dress in armor—" Her ears burned as she stood beneath the scrutiny of the people she respected. "All the details are in the letter I gave you."

The Guild Master smiled. "So, you know the difference between a gauntlet and a gorget?"

"Yes sir. A gauntlet is a glove." She raised her fingers to her collar and brushed them against the black feather. "A gorget protects the throat."

In the corner of her eye, a smile flickered across Brandon's face. During their studies, he had cemented her knowledge of the gorget by trailing kisses along her throat. The memory of his lips stole her breath and sent warmth to her cheeks.

The Guild Master nodded his approval. "Very good. Well, you'll still have to prove your usefulness, noble or no. I can't let just anyone join the Guild, otherwise every person in Aldland would be barging our doors down."

"Thank you, sir. I won't disappoint you." Natalie stepped back and tried to quieten her heart. She would prove herself, no matter what they asked of her.

"I'll meet you in the courtyard tomorrow after breakfast

and put you through your paces." The older man took a deep breath and shook his head slowly. "Now, onto a far graver matter. I'm sure by now, we're all aware that we lost a good number of our best fighters in Blackmere. Henry brought us news of this terrible tragedy. Though he believed Brandon, Genevieve and Lady Blackmere to be among the list of the dead."

"I have never been happier to be mistaken," Henry chimed in, his handsome face split into two by a broad, well-practiced grin. "Nothing has made my heart soar higher in recent times, than seeing my dear friends return to the Guild—"

"However," the Guild Master held up his hand to silence Henry. "The day after your arrival, we received word from Brandon, stating that the attack on Blackmere, was actually arranged by you, Henry."

Natalie's stomach tensed as Henry turned to Brandon. His blue eyes widened in shock, the picture of innocence. "By me?"

"Aye." Brandon's expression was hard and level, but above the collar of his tunic, a tendon in his neck throbbed, and redness crept up his throat, disappearing beneath the dark shadow of his beard. "The leader of the bandits confessed to me that he was hired by a champion to stage an attack. I believe that champion to be Henry."

"Based on what?" The Guild Master arched his eyebrow and folded his arms across his chest. "Did he give Henry's name?"

"He did not." Brandon lowered his head. "But I trust

my gut. Henry's attitude towards the whole attack was one of... opportunity."

"It wasn't I who came out of Blackmere having seized an opportunity." Henry's face reddened, and his mouth contorted in outrage. The threat was clear. Brandon's lips closed. Henry nodded and gave a bitter laugh. "And is this bandit with you? Did you bring him here to testify?"

"He's dead," Brandon muttered.

Henry scoffed. "After everything we've been through, Brandon. You come here throwing around baseless accusations."

"Robert died," Brandon snapped. "He died right in front of me."

"And you think I killed him?"

"No, not directly, but—"

Henry's breath heaved as his pale blue eyes glistened. "The Guild is my family. Rob was like a brother to me, Brandon. And you... you're like my own father. I would never endanger your life. Think about what you are throwing away."

Brandon's lips snapped closed.

Henry raised his eyes towards Genevieve. "And what say you? Hm? I rode with you to Stoneclough, to try to find help. We rode through torrential rain to try to bring an end to the madness."

Natalie's heart clenched. Henry's eyes clawed at her, carving away her confidence piece by piece. His lips parted, as though to speak again, before he turned away in disgust. Brandon's eyes were distant, glazed over and his lips pressed together in a thin line.

The Guild Master rubbed his thumb and forefinger across his forehead. "Is this true?"

Genevieve lowered her head. "We did. Henry did try to convince Lord Stoneclough to lend aid to Blackmere, but the request was denied."

"So, it seems Henry went out of his way to try to help." The older man released a labored breath and shook his head. "And Lady Blackmere, do you have anything, even a shred of evidence that it was Henry who arranged it?"

Tears pricked in her eyes, heated and spurred by frustration. "The bandit leader, Walden Fray said—"

"The dead one?" Henry snapped.

"Yes. Before he died—"

The Guild Master held up his hand to silence her. "Brandon, Lady Blackmere, if the only evidence you bring of Henry's guilt is the vague testimony of a dead bandit, then there's little I can do for you. I won't destroy a young man's career on the back of hearsay."

Brandon gave a bitter laugh and shook his head. They were defeated, and Henry stood triumphant besides them.

The Guild Master continued, "Henry and Brandon will both remain members of the Champion's Guild. Henry, you may continue to participate in the Midsummer Melee in Westgarden, if you wish to, but I expect you to act appropriately, and to be a paragon of sportsmanship."

"Thank you, Guild Master," Henry bowed.

The air in the room brightened and hushed chatter trickled through the surrounding crowd of champions.

"I'm not done." Brandon announced.

The Guild Master sighed and turned to him. "My decision on the matter between you and Henry is—"

"It's not about that. I'm not done competing." Brandon's lips pressed into a hard line as the room fell silent. "I'm fighting in the Midsummer Melee too."

"You intend to participate?" The Guild Master's eyes narrowed. "We heard your melee performance at Blackmere was over before it began."

The red glow on Brandon's neck broke free of the shadow of his beard, erupting over his cheeks. "This year will be different."

"Goddess have mercy. Don't injure yourself. You're not a young man anymore, and you've nothing to prove. No one would blame you if you wanted to retire."

"I want to fight."

"Very well. Pending the outcome of Lady Blackmere's assessment, you'll have a squire this year too. Perhaps this will be the Bear's final roar." The Guild Master's face lightened, satisfied by his decisions. "As always, participants and their squires are not permitted to leave the Guild until you set out for the melee. You are dismissed."

Natalie frowned at the Guild Master's declaration. "We can't leave?"

"To prevent outside influences, bribes, access to substances which may enhance the performance of our champions..." The Guild Master dismissed the unpleasant topic with a swipe of his hand. "Not that I for one moment suspect any of our champions of such dishonorable tactics, but...we must follow the rules."

Taking a deep breath Natalie nodded in understanding.

She would be bound to the Guild until midsummer, but at least she would be with Brandon.

"Thank you, Guild Master, for dealing with this matter fairly." Henry sighed. His sincere gaze fell to Natalie. "My dear Lady Blackmere, I'm sorry for what happened to your castle. I hope we can move on from this unpleasantness."

CHAPTER
SEVEN

"The slimy, good for nothing bastard!" Brandon growled as he stormed around the corner. "I knew, I *knew* the Guild Master wouldn't punish him. Goddess forbid there's any rupture in the Guild's family."

Natalie hurried along the corridor after him, her legs trembling with nerves and exhaustion. "Where are we going?"

"My room. I need you with me. I need you."

Her heartbeat thundered in her ears. "Brandon if we get caught—"

"I don't care, Nat. I don't care. Let them kick me out." He stopped, and his broad shoulders slumped. His breath was heavy and ragged, his eyes clouded. "I don't mean that."

Natalie stood beside him, reaching out to touch his arm, to offer him comfort and tenderness. The realization of where they were stayed her hand. Her fingers recoiled midair, curling into a loose fist and dropping to her side.

He shook his head slowly. "I knew they wouldn't believe me."

Natalie stood, frozen and helpless. She longed to hold him. "But we know the truth."

"Aye, and what good is it?" He staggered back against a wall, pressing the back of his head against the stones. "I wish we didn't have to come back here. I wish we could just go, run away together and have a real life without hiding."

Natalie turned to check the corridor was clear. The only sound was that of the rain pattering against the leaded windows, the wind howling against the stones. The distance between them was unbearable.

He needed her. She needed him.

Brandon's breath snagged in surprise as she crushed herself against him, wrapping her arms around his waist and resting her head on his chest. He was soaked through from the rain, and the cloying scent of horse and wet wool tickled her nose. The thunder of his heart steadied against the rhythm of her own. She closed her eyes and savored the sensation of his arms winding around her, shielding her, enveloping her in his embrace.

"Forgive me," he whispered against her hair. "There are a lot of memories here. Good memories."

"That doesn't make it any easier Sometimes the good memories hurt most of all."

"Aye."

"I'm here." She lifted her head to look into his eyes. "Whatever you need me to do, I'll do it. If you want to talk, I'll listen. If you need to run, I'll hold onto your hand and follow you no matter where."

His smile broke her heart. Those eyes, so full of kindness and sorrow, love and mourning. "Will you come with me to my room? I can't face it alone."

"Anything."

They walked together in silence. Her fingers flexed at her sides, yearning to feel his touch, but as they approached the champion's living quarters, it became apparent just how little privacy they would be afforded if she had a mind to sneak to his bed.

The doors of each room had been removed, leaving nothing but an open, gaping arch in the stones, leading into their bedchambers. Men and women walked through the hallways, some in their tunics or armor, others in various stages of undress. They were like living statues, their muscular physiques carved from different shades of marble. They greeted Brandon with wide, perfect smiles, some of them clapping him on the back and emphasizing his new knighthood. "Welcome back *Sir* Brandon."

They were just them as intimidating in person as they were in the arena. Their daunting strength, beauty and confidence clenched Natalie's stomach muscles as she passed, hoping none of them paid her any attention.

Her cheeks were blazing scarlet by the time Brandon stopped just before a doorway at the end of the hall.

She waited beside him, pressing her hand against the small of his back to comfort him. "I'm here."

His breath shook as he lowered his head. "Thank you."

The cause of his sadness became apparent as they stepped through the arch of the doorway and into the chamber. The room contained two beds, facing each other, and above each of them was a shield. One of the shields was painted blue, with a ferocious brown bear snarling at the center. The other was black.

As Natalie approached it, she could make out the faint silver shimmer of the paint in the layer beneath the black, the ghost of claw marks. Ironclaw.

Her throat tightened. They had painted over his sigil, erased him. "Brandon…"

"They paint over the shields if someone leaves, to make way for new champions." Brandon's voice wavered behind her. "I suppose they did it after they found out he was gone. I didn't think it would be so soon."

Natalie turned, tears stinging her eyes. Brandon was sat on the end of his bed with his hands clasped together in front of him, his forearms braced on his knees. A muscle in his cheek twitched as he bit down his sorrow. "I think some part of me still expected him to be here, with that ridiculous grin spread across his face. He was my best friend." His voice was barely audible. "I miss him."

Brandon shattered, burying his face in his hands.

She hurried towards him, caring nothing for the Guild's rules, or the champions out in the hallway. In an instant she was before him, wrapping her arms around his shoulders, pulling his head against her breast as the first of his tears began to fall.

He shuddered against her as she ran her fingers through the silken brown of his hair, huddling over him, shielding him from the empty bed and blackened crest. Her balance faltered as he wrapped an arm around her thighs, and the other around her waist, pinning her to him, as though at any moment she might drift away from him.

She had done this. It was her failure which rendered Brandon so broken.

As she held him close, his tears soaking into the wet padded fabric of her gambeson, Natalie became aware of a figure standing in the doorway.

Genevieve stood staring at the black crest. Her throat bobbed, and she bowed her head before stepping into the room.

The warrior sat on the bed beside Brandon and lay her arm across his back. "I'm sorry, Bear."

"He's gone," Brandon whispered.

The doorway darkened again, filled with solemn champions. One by one they crossed over the threshold into the room and gathered around Brandon. Some reached out to place a hand on him, others simply standing beside him, a show of solidarity, camaraderie, and love.

The room was filled with champions as Brandon raised his head and released Natalie from his embrace. He raised a shaking hand to wipe the tears from his cheeks, looked around at the surrounding crowd, and bowed his head.

"Thank you." His voice was rough, as if the broken pieces of himself were only just coming back together. "I'm... I'm glad to be home. I suppose it just takes time."

"We're here." Genevieve nudged his side with her elbow and smiled. "All of us. We're family."

Natalie stepped back to allow the champions closer to Brandon. They hugged him, clapped him on the shoulder, ruffled their hands in his hair and drew fragments of smiles from his lips.

Only one figure remained on the outside, glaring through the doorway.

Natalie's chest hollowed as Henry's usually cold eyes fixed on her in a burning stare.

CHAPTER

EIGHT

That night, Natalie awoke drenched in sweat. The image of Robert slumped at the tavern table lingered long after her nightmare ended.

She lay alone, trembling in a bare room. As a squire, she was not permitted to sleep in the same wing of the keep as the champions, and being considerably older than the other squires, she slept separate from them too. Having brought no possessions, the room was pitifully empty. Candlelight danced across the rough grey stone walls, and the wooden bedframe creaked beneath her as she turned and tried to shake the image of Robert Trevaryn's lifeless face.

The ocean whispered in the dark outside her bedroom window, and the unfamiliar groans and creaks of the castle tormented her. Still, she considered herself fortunate not to have to share her room with a stranger. But after just a couple of weeks of falling to sleep in Brandon's embrace, sleeping alone was as comfortable as sleeping in a patch of thorns.

Knowing Brandon was near, that he was so close, yet untouchable, was torture. She longed to hold him, to comfort him as he tried to sleep in the same room as Robert's empty bed. The temptation to sneak from her room, tiptoe through the corridors and climb into his bed plagued her. She so desperately needed to be held, but to do so would take everything from him. He was so loved by the champions, and she had already taken so much from him.

The agony grew more intense as the night dragged on. There would be hundreds of nights spent in similar distress throughout the year. Hundreds of nights she would be forbidden from being near him.

She gave up on sleep and lay twirling the black feather between her fingers, wishing with all her heart she could be with him.

When at last the sun rose, she was raw-eyed and ill-tempered. Her mood grew darker still when she remembered her mettle would be tested by the Guild Master that morning. If she failed, she would be sent away, and she could not see Brandon at all until at least the summer.

That, and the fear of disappointing her mother, drove her from the bed.

A scuffed wooden armoire stood in the corner of the room. The hinges squealed as Natalie opened the doors to look inside. A selection of simple clothing had been left for her, tabards embroidered with the champion's guild sigil, woolen breeches, padded jackets and plain dresses.

Selecting a pale blue dress, she ran her hand across the thick texture of the wool. It was nothing like the soft fibers of the Blackmere flocks, but still, it reminded her of home.

She hurried through dressing and wandered through the keep, following the savory scent of breakfast and the sounds of chatter and clinking cutlery, until at last she found the banquet hall.

The hall was divided into two sides, with squires sitting on benches at long wooden tables which filled half the room. The champions occupied a smaller table at the other side.

Her heart lifted as she saw Brandon. He was sitting at the head of the champion's table, his smile brightening his face as he sat in animated conversation with his friends. Her breath caught in her throat as his eyes turned to her. The creases beneath them deepened as his grin widened.

Heat blossomed across Natalie's face as she returned his smile. Her exhaustion was forgotten, melted away by the warmth of his eyes.

She tucked the black feather beneath the pin of her brooch as she wandered towards an empty spot at the end of the squires' table.

The breakfast tables were filled with food, roasted chickens, boiled eggs, fruits, porridge, and jars of golden honey. There was enough food to feed an army on the squires' table alone. The Guild wanted the youngest members to grow up strong, to become champions themselves. It warmed Natalie's heart to see them treated so well.

She filled a bowl with porridge and honey, and ate silently, sat apart from the others, as she took in the grandeur of the dining hall. Her eyes drifted up to the enormous chandelier made of antlers, which hung above them in the center of the ceiling.

Each wall was decorated with bronze plaques, engraved with the names of victors of various tournaments. She delighted in finding Brandon's name on many of them, especially the list of the victors of the Grand Tourney which occupied a place of honor at the head of the hall. The Grand Tourney and the Midsummer Melee were the most esteemed contests, where only the most elite and beloved champions battled. There were smaller, less renowned competitions, which were fought by those less experienced. Her eyes drifted down the names. There were many she recognized:

Oliver Tilman- The Viper

Millicent- The Seraph

Ulric Wykhelm- The Fanged Beast.

She grimaced as she reached the most recent entry, *Henry Percille- The Dragon.*

His name soured the porridge on her tongue.

"Impressive isn't it?" The crooning voice raised the hairs on the back of her neck and sent a shiver down her spine.

Turning around in her seat, she was faced with cold blue eyes as Henry crouched behind her. She recoiled at the sight of him, as though confronted with a venomous snake preparing to strike.

"I can't tell you how satisfying it is to see my name on there." He rubbed his palm across the smooth, square line of his jaw. "People like you will never know the thrill of seeing hard work and dedication pay off."

Natalie shook her head and lowered her spoon, resting it in her half-emptied bowl. Though her heart was racing, she tried to keep her voice steady. "And yet you risked being banished from the Guild and caused the deaths of your brethren, all for a run-down castle like Blackmere."

"I'd watch my mouth if I were you. Anyone can throw around accusations." He chuckled and raised himself towards her, leaning in close so that his breath slithered across the bare skin of her neck. "Our families were once not so different, long ago. My family were nobles, warlords, respected and feared, living among untold riches in Percille Castle. But our birthright was taken from us." His eyes raised towards the intricate chandelier. "I'm the first of my family to come home."

"Percille Castle?"

He darted out his arm and snatched the feather from her pin.

Her body tensed, preparing to spring after it. "Give that back."

"Now, now." He smiled and stood, holding the feather across his palm. With a smirk, he curled his fingers into a fist. "It only takes a moment to lose everything, and it may never be recovered. You'd do well to remember that."

Her heart broke as he let the crumpled feather fall to the table. It landed in the middle of her bowl, crooked and ruined.

He gripped her forearm, his strong, unyielding fingers pressing against her bone. Crushing pain radiated from wrist to elbow. "If the Guild Master receives one more accusation from you or that oaf, I'll ensure neither of you are safe to travel to within one hundred miles of my home. Understood?"

The hum of excited conversation carried on around

them, oblivious to Natalie's distress. She had sat so far from the squires they did not notice Henry's grip on her arm, and the champions' view was obscured by the food-laden table.

With her eyes fixed on Henry, she commanded herself not to give him the satisfaction of knowing he was hurting her. Gritting her teeth against the pain, she nodded.

"Behave yourself." He grinned and released her arm. Casually, he strode out of the dining hall, leaving her to attempt to rescue the feather.

"Prick." She rubbed her arm grimacing at the bright pink blotches where his fingers had held her. The feather was crooked and coated in the goop of oats, but she picked it out and attempted to fix it.

Sudden movement distracted her. In the corner of her eye, Brandon barreled out the door, chasing down Henry in determined strides.

Natalie leapt to her feet and followed, the rush of adrenaline spiking her veins as she ran out into the corridor. She turned the corner as Brandon pinned Henry to the wall by his shoulders.

She froze. Liquid fire raged through her veins at the sight of the confrontation. The two men snarled, faces reddening as they glared at each other.

"Don't think I didn't see that," Brandon growled. His face was inches from Henry's. "You're nothing but a sniveling little coward."

"Unhand me," Henry spat.

Brandon's eyes flickered towards Natalie, then fixed onto Henry like a predator sizing up his prey. "Apologize to her."

"For what? A damned feather?"

"You know what you did. Apologize, before I make you."

"You'll *make* me? Really now, you'll risk your old heart giving out over something so silly." Henry's grin split his face in two. "What is she to you? I mean, it's obvious you're swiving her, but is it something more, I wonder?"

Natalie held her breath as Brandon's grip on Henry's shoulders loosened.

The younger man chuckled and brushed his shoulders with the back of his hand. "Do you love her? Because correct me if I'm wrong, but love is forbidden for us champions, is it not?" He cocked his head to the side, reveling in the clenching of Brandon's jaw. "It would be a shame to tarnish such an illustrious reputation with gossip, wouldn't it? Imagine losing all those titles. How many is it? Five?"

"Six," Natalie glowered. Brandon's eyes flickered towards her, as though a longer glance would be an admission of guilt. She clamped her lips shut.

A slow smile crept across Henry's face. "Six. That's an awful lot to lose."

"Aye," Brandon said, jutting his chin upward. "More than you'll ever know."

"How's your mother doing, Brandon? It was so kind of you to pay for such skilled healers, but it would be an awful shame if those funds were to just... stop. I wouldn't do anything to jeopardize my career if I were you." Henry's grin widened as he stoked the fire in Brandon's blood. "So, you intend to compete in the Midsummer Melee then?"

"I intend to win," Brandon growled, raising his head and standing at his full height.

A thrill coursed through Natalie's body. Brandon's gaze did not falter as Henry snickered in his face. He was immovable, steady, like a mountain looming above a barking dog.

Henry drew back, but the smug smile never left his lips. "You'd better be on your best behavior then, hadn't you?"

The air cleared as he turned his back, skulking away from Natalie and Brandon towards his chamber. Her heart crashed against her ribs.

"I'll find you another feather." Brandon took a deep breath and flexed his fingers, as though attempting to rid himself of the sensation of touching Henry. "Did he hurt you?"

"Oh, no." She flexed her arm, smiling to hide the slight ache which still lingered. "Thank you."

"For?"

"Standing up to him."

"I had to." The corner of his lip quirked as his eyes raked across her. "You're blushing."

She shrugged a shoulder and tucked the bedraggled feather beneath her pin. When it was secure, she allowed herself the indulgence of looking at him fully. His dark blue woolen tunic was tight against his frame, accentuating the size of his biceps, the curve of his stomach. She longed to peel it off him, to feel the softness and strength of his body against hers.

"Nat?"

"I need you." The whispered words left her lips before she could stop them.

His face reddened as he lowered his head. She heard his breath catch in his throat, and the shudder of longing when it finally emerged. "My lady... Nat... I..."

She took a step towards him, heart fluttering as she caught the scent of him, both comforting and exciting. If he asked it, she would bend over right there, bracing herself against the windowsill, or pull him into some dark, secluded room and ride him until he shattered. Goddess, she would take him in the middle of the breakfast table, with all the other champions watching.

His throat leapt as the tips of his ears glowed red. "My lady... I... we can't. I want to, so badly. I've thought of nothing else all morning."

She reassured him with a smile. "Perhaps we'll find somewhere secret where we won't be troubled?"

"I'll look." He shifted his weight, tucking his hands beneath the belt at his hips, as though he did not trust them not to reach out for her. "I'll find something." He closed the gap between them, stooping to whisper in her ear. "When I do, I'm yours, and I'll see to it my lady is satisfied, as many times as she wishes."

His lips were so close the velvet softness of them fluttered against her ear. Her body tingled, filled with desperate need. Releasing a trembling breath, she tilted her face towards him. His eyes widened as he straightened his back and raised his eyebrows. She followed his gaze. The Guild Master ambled down the corridor, a group of champions flanking him. Sara and Darius were among them.

"There he is!" Darius cried, a wide smile spreading across his face. "It's so like you to run away in the middle of the night. I searched the whole tavern for you in the morning, calling out your name like some jilted, lovesick barmaid. And I hear your quarrel with Henry is resolved, and we can return to being a big happy family."

Brandon frowned and shook his head, but a fleeting smile betrayed his cold demeanor. "You followed me? I was hoping I'd lost you."

Darius laughed and gripped Brandon's forearms. "You will never lose me, Sweet Bear. True love always triumphs." The men embraced each other, Darius resting his head on Brandon's broad shoulder. "Ah, it's good to have you back home. No one in the Guild hugs as well as you."

The Guild Master sighed. "Goddess give me strength. You two carry on like that and I'll have no choice but to have you banished." He turned towards Natalie and bowed. "Lady Blackmere, I'll be with you in the courtyard shortly. I trust you have found the Guild to your liking so far?"

"Yes, sir." She smiled, hoping the blush on her cheeks was not too obvious. "But please, call me Natalie. My mother is the current Lady of Blackmere."

"Ah, yes your mother. I believe I met her once in the Tourney at Caer Austwick... goodness... near forty years ago."

Natalie's brightened. "You did?"

"Aye. 'Course, she was just a girl then, and you wouldn't have even been born. It was back before I was the Guild Master, when I was just Oliver Tilman."

"You were more than *just* Oliver Tilman," Brandon

chuckled. He shook his head and turned to Natalie. "He's the Viper."

The wind was knocked from her lungs. "Surely you can't be serious," Natalie gasped. "You're *the* Viper?"

Darius rolled his eyes. "Wonderful, now he and Brandon are going to start comparing titles again."

Natalie bit down her excitement. "Forgive me. It's an honor to meet you, sir." She bowed to the Guild Master, heat washing over her. "And Darius, Sara, it's good to see you again."

"Lady Blackmere." Her name sounded bitter on Sara's tongue. The champion bowed her head and turned to Brandon, a fond, teasing smile playing across her lips. "So, Old Man, we hear you're planning to compete in the Midsummer Melee. Are you sure you're up to it?"

"At present, probably not." Brandon straightened his back and hooked his thumbs beneath his belt. "By midsummer, I'll be back to my peak."

Darius laughed and placed his hand on the curve of Brandon's stomach. He flexed his fingers, pinching the soft flesh beneath his tunic. "We'd better get training then. Less ale for you, more eggs. More steps." His smile broadened. "Many more steps. We'll get you back to fighting shape."

"Come now," The Guild Master sighed. "Breakfast is almost finished, and we need to get today's training under-way. Lady Blackmere, I'll be with you shortly."

Natalie held back a grin as the Guild Master ushered the champions away to the dining hall, leaving only her and Brandon.

"Well." Brandon raised his eyebrows and widened his

eyes. "You see how fast word spreads here. Everyone already knows I'm competing."

Natalie gave him a half smile. If word of something like that had spread around the Guild so fast, rumors of their relationship would infest the keep in moments. As much as it pained her, they would have to maintain their discretion.

A bell clanged in one of the towers above, followed by the scraping of chairs and the clatter of crockery in the dining hall. Footsteps pattered down the stone hallway as a stampede of young squires headed towards them.

"What does the bell mean?" Natalie asked.

Brandon pulled her aside to let the procession of youths pass. "It means it's time to start practice."

CHAPTER

NINE

When they reached the courtyard, Brandon was swept away by a swarm of excited champions. Natalie hung back, still unfamiliar with her surroundings. In stark contrast to the previous miserable day, the sky was clear and blue, freshened by a sharp sea breeze. She closed her eyes and listened to the cackling sea birds soaring on the wind, feeling as though she could happily lie on the floor and nap.

"The Guild Master told me to show you around." Sara's sharp voice sent a jolt through Natalie's chest. The pale woman chewed as she spoke, wiping her mouth on the back of her hand. "Let's just get this over with."

Natalie followed as Sara led her around the courtyard. The Snow Fox pointed out the various areas set out for training, hurrying through each description as though she would rather be doing anything else. Along the cliffside wall were pulleys loaded with netted rocks, huge boulders to be lifted and carried, weighted sleds, and thick tree trunks, all intended to test and develop the champions' strength and physiques. There were combat rings for melee and unarmed fights, the list for jousting, target ranges for axe throwing and archery. The tour concluded at the top of a winding stair which led down to the beach. The steps were carved into the grey stone cliffs.

"One of the Guild Master's favorite drills is to have us run up and down the stairs as many times as we can. There are over a thousand steps." Sara grimaced.

Just the thought of climbing them once made Natalie's legs ache. She stood on the top step, peering down the seemingly endless stairway, her heart kicking against her ribs. Her legs trembled. "It's a long way down."

Sara smirked. "It's a much longer way up, I assure you." Just as quickly as it had appeared, her smile evaporated, leaving her features hard and cold. "The Guild must look like a hovel compared to your castle."

Natalie gave a chuff of laughter. "This is far more impressive than Blackmere, I assure you."

"Ah but what of your other castle?" Sara's eyes grew distant. "The one you grew up in."

Natalie's stomach dropped at Sara's biting tone. Few buildings in Aldland—save for the royal palace in their country's capital—were as grand or as beautiful as her childhood home. "Caer Austwick is... beautiful. I consider myself exceptionally fortunate."

"Fortune has little to do with it. You nobles live on the backs of your subjects, profiting from the hard work of others. You don't care who gets crushed beneath your jeweled slippers," Sara gave a bitter chuckle and shook her head. "But, perhaps here you can find out what honest work looks like?" The Snow Fox took a step towards her. "Here, you live by our rules, understand? Just because you were born on silks, doesn't mean you're anything special."

Natalie's heart pounded, and her ears rang as Sara walked away, heading towards one of the melee rings, where Brandon and Darius were practicing. The woman glanced over her shoulder and signaled for Natalie to follow.

Trailing after her, Natalie could not argue with Sara. She had little love for the nobility herself, though she had always lived a comfortable life, supported by the very system she held in such low regard. Most of the other nobles she had ever meant were consumed by their own importance. Their people went to bed with empty bellies whilst their lords and ladies feasted.

"Lady Blackmere." The Guild Master's voice roused her from her thoughts as she reached the edge of the sparring circle.

The Guild Master stood at the side of the sandy circle, with his arms folded across his chest. In the center of the ring, Brandon and Darius faced each other on either side of a crimson ribbon which lay across the sand. Both fighters were bare from the waist up.

Natalie told herself not to look at Brandon's body and stir the need inside her, but the more she resisted, the harder it was to look anywhere else. Heat crawled up her body. He towered above Darius, standing half a head taller and twice as broad. His lips slanted in a cocky grin as he looked down at his opponent.

Darius returned his leer, his toned body tensed. "Are you sure you're up to this, Sweet Bear. I'm not going to go easy on you."

Brandon snickered. He crouched down, and held his hands at chest height, tensing his fingers like claws towards Darius. "I'm sure."

"Kick his arse, Brandon," Sara goaded.

A deep, disapproving growl sounded in the Guild Master's throat. "First man on his arse loses." He held up an arm and brought it sharply down in front of him. "Fight."

Darius ducked beneath Brandon's arm, and kicked the larger man's legs out from under him with a graceful swipe. Brandon fell hard, the air rushing from his lungs in a ragged grunt as he hit the ground.

Natalie's heart lurched against her ribs. She wanted to bolt to Brandon's aid as he lay groaning in the sand, but she forced herself to remain still.

The Guild Master inhaled slowly through his nose.

Darius's broad smile spread across his face. "Big boys fall hard, don't they?"

Red-faced, Brandon rolled onto his front and climbed onto his knees. "As long as we get back up, it doesn't matter."

"You want to go again?"

Natalie pressed her lips together to disguise her smile as Brandon stood and dusted off his hands. He gave the other men a sharp, determined nod. "Aye."

Her heart leapt as he cast a glance at her, barely long enough for anyone else to notice. The spark in his eyes assured her he was unhurt, that he would keep trying until he won, that he was in his element. Pride tied a knot in her throat as he prepared himself for another bout.

Once again, the Guild Master commanded the two men to fight. Brandon lunged, gripping Darius by the shoulders as the younger man tried to hook his ankle around the back of Brandon's knee. They grappled together, teeth bared, and knuckles pale as they locked onto each other. Brandon's strength and size matched Darius' skill and energy, the equilibrium sending both men crumpling to the ground.

"We'll call that a tie." The Guild Master announced. "Do you need a moment, Brandon?"

Brandon's chest heaved as he stood and fought for breath. He held up a hand, dismissing the Guild Master's concerns.

The Guild Master shrugged. "Very well. Again."

The men continued to wrestle. Every bout ended, with Darius emerging the victor, or the match being too close to call. The flush of color across Brandon's chest darkened as he fought again and again. The muscles in his cheeks leapt between matches as he bit down his frustration, but otherwise he remained calm and determined.

Natalie's desire stirred as she watched him. Even in defeat he was strong and powerful, and he was hers. Her desire for him was whetted by his straining muscles, glistening skin, the quiver and undulation of the softer parts of him. She longed to touch him.

Sinking her teeth into her lips she released a long sigh. She froze as the Guild Master turned to her.

"I was very sorry to hear about what happened at Blackmere."

Blackmere. It would haunt her forever. The death, the panic, her guilt. She lowered her eyes and fought back the nausea rising from her gut. "It was terrible. So much was lost by so many, not least the Guild."

"Aye, we'll be feeling the sorrows of those dark days for years to come." He raised his arm to command Brandon and Darius to fight again. "I must say, I was surprised to learn you fought by Brandon's side. I wouldn't have expected it."

"Blackmere is my home, sir. My people's lives were in danger, and..." Her voice faltered, stifled by the shortness of her breath. "If not for my failings..."

"You mustn't think that." The Guild Master offered her a smile. "I've made enough mistakes in my life to know you can't focus on what might have been."

"I'm so sorry about Robert and the others."

His throat bobbed as he watched the men sparring. "As am I."

Natalie kept her eyes on Brandon as he fought. It seemed for a moment that he would win. "You weren't at the Tourney."

The Guild Master chuckled. "Me? No, I haven't left the Guild's walls for... thirty years, at least. My duty is here, training the recruits, organizing the contests and ensuring our champions have a good life. Once I took up the position of Guild Master, I surrendered my freedoms. At least, until I retire."

Brandon slammed into the earth, groaning as Darius sat astride his chest.

The Guild Master let out a disappointed sigh. His eyes widened. "I'm terribly sorry, Lady Blackmere. This was supposed to be your assessment, and I think we rather got carried away." His attention snapped back to the fighters, as Brandon released a pained cry from the ground. Darius leapt to his feet, triumphant.

The Guild Master lifted his chin towards the two men. "Brandon, you're needed."

Her breath caught in her throat as Brandon approached. Eyes downcast, he stood before her, his chest flushed pink and heaving, his breath as hard as it was when they lay together. Wet sand clung to his skin.

"Yes sir?" Brandon's voice was thick and husky from the effort.

"Clean yourself up, and then come with us." The Guild Master gestured towards her. "Lady Blackmere—"

"Natalie, please." She bowed to the Guild Master.

He smiled. "Natalie, you'll dress him in full armor, as part of your assessment. If you do well, I'd be happy for you to act as Brandon's squire for the year, if Brandon agrees."

"I agree." Brandon's answer leapt from his throat.

Natalie bit the inside of her cheek to keep from smiling as the Guild Master rubbed his eyebrow.

"We work well together," Brandon added, color rising in his cheeks. "We've fought side-by-side, and she risked her life to save me. There's no one I'd work better with."

Natalie's smile broke free, despite her efforts to restrain it. Pride swelled in her chest, and she wanted nothing more than to kiss him.

The Guild Master cleared his throat, "Well, then I'm sure the assessment will go well. Let's make our way to the armory."

They paused to let Brandon draw water from the well. He filled the wooden bucket, then tipped the water over himself. Natalie tried to block out his sharp gasps and growls as he bathed in the cold water.

When he had washed away the sand they set off towards the keep. They crossed the courtyard, caressed by the fresh sea breeze. Even in the cool air, Brandon's body emitted waves of warmth.

As they drew closer Natalie's heartbeat quickened. She had dressed Brandon in his armor plenty of times, but now that she would be tested, her mind blanked. They entered the keep and walked through the silent corridors towards the armory.

The Guild Master cleared his throat. "I hear you're a fan of the Grand Tourney."

"Yes, sir." Her voice trembled as she spoke. "Being here is an honor."

"We got your letters every year. I do apologize that it took so long for us to get round to you, but there are many things we need to take into consideration, not least the size of the prize, and the facilities each noble can provide for our champions to use during the Tourney. Blackmere was, unfortunately, relatively low on our list."

Natalie smiled with practiced grace and tried not to feel insulted. "It's understandable. Blackmere isn't the wealthiest of lands."

"Might I be frank with you?" The Guild Master halted. "Brandon, go on ahead and ensure we have everything ready for the assessment."

"Yes sir." Brandon cast an apologetic look towards Natalie and continued on his way to the armory.

She looked after him, wishing with all her heart she could follow.

"I will admit," the Guild Master began as Brandon disappeared into the distance. "I have some concerns about you working with Brandon. I know you are only here for a relatively short time, but I also know from your letters that you were an admirer of his. I need your word, that absolutely nothing untoward will happen between you or any of the champions, and I will be having this conversation with Brandon too. Champions are unlike any others in Aldland, we sacrifice the chance to find true love, in exchange for the love of thousands. There's nothing more important to me, than keeping this little family together. A broken-hearted champion is a dangerous one. Promise me you will abide by our rules."

The air in the keep was stifling. Natalie forced a swallow. "You have my word."

Liar.

The Guild Master's eyes brightened. "I know this is an uncomfortable conversation, but romantic relationships and fornications are forbidden here at the Guild."

"I understand sir."

Yes, I understand, and I'm lying through my teeth.

"Thank you, my lady, and I apologize if I've made you uncomfortable. If I'm honest, had you come here ten years ago when Brandon was in his prime, I would not have allowed it. He... well, not to besmirch the man's character, but he was rather fond of casual relations when let out from the Guild." He chuckled. "He'd ride out to every minor contest, roaming the streets like a tom cat afterwards. I'm sure you've heard the songs. But he's calmed down, and though he is past those glory days, he still has a lot to lose. I'm sure your own reputation is just as important to you."

She gave him a half smile and a single nod. Her heart beat so loud she was certain he could hear it.

As they resumed their journey down the corridor, Natalie wondered if Henry had already laid the foundations of doubt at the Guild Master's feet. Her letters must have only been one of hundreds which arrived each year, and she knew for a fact that Brandon had kept them after the Guild Master was finished with them. There was little chance he remembered hers.

She was a nervous wreck by the time they reached the armory. Her head spun with questions and suspicions, and the voice at the back of her mind, was a constant reminder of her treachery.

"Here we are," the Guild Master beamed.

Natalie's nerves were forgotten as she stood in awe. Candlelight glimmered from hundreds of pieces of polished armor and weapons. The armory was as grand as any palace or shrine. Each set of armor was laid out in its own blue-velvet-lined booth, and above them hung decorated crests, the same as the ones above the champions' beds.

"Most of our champions and their squires don't know how to read or write," the Guild Master said. "Using their sigils makes it easier to find their belongings."

"They don't get lessons?"

"No. A lot of them come from poor families, Lady—Natalie. They get by though, with the sigils."

"But what about letters. What if they wish to write to their families?"

"They do occasionally receive letters, mostly the squires or, as you know, letters from admirers of the champions. We have a messenger who comes once a month. Sometimes they'll find someone to read it for them, but more often than not... It matters not. We are their family now." He smiled. "Now, let's get to it, shall we?"

She found Brandon's bear crest and stepped into his booth. There were two full suits of armor, one practical and plain, the other more ornate. The shelves at the back of the booth were adorned with helmets, and in the center one of them, shaped like a bear's head, snarled at her.

Her vision blurred as she inspected the array of shining steel. There were so many parts, so many buckles and straps, it seemed like piecing together a shattered vase.

Forcing out a breath, she assured herself she knew what to do. They had practiced so many times.

The air at her back warmed as Brandon stepped up behind her, his breath blowing faintly across the back of her neck. "You can do this."

The Guild Master's words echoed in the back of her mind. She had promised him, a man she respected, a man who was like a father to Brandon, that she would maintain a professional relationship with the champions. But she was a liar, and no matter how many promises she made, how many oaths she swore, she could not stop the skipping of her treacherous heart.

She screwed her eyes closed and tried to shake away her desire.

Focus.

Brandon chuckled, plucking the bear's head helmet from the shelf. He turned to the Guild Master. "New helmets?"

The Guild Master returned his amusement. "I thought they would add a little more flair to the contests. Lady Luray paid handsomely for the Midsummer Melee this year and she does so love her theatrics. If you had decided not to compete it would've been your retirement gift."

Brandon chuckled and placed it back on the shelf. "I'll wear it with pride, Sir, in the arena at Westgarden."

The Guild Master pulled a large hourglass down from a shelf and set it atop a barrel. His eyes settled on Natalie. "Are you ready?"

"I am." She clenched her fists to stop her fingers from trembling.

The Guild Master nodded. "I would expect a seasoned squire to be able to arm a champion for the joust in twenty minutes. You have half an hour."

Without another word, he turned the hourglass, unleashing a cascade of white sand flowing from top to bottom.

Natalie's heart leapt as she focused on her task.

She snatched a thick, brown canvas jacket from Brandon's booth and helped him dress in it. The jacket was covered in knotted laces, which ran across his shoulders, down his back and chest. As Brandon fastened the jacket over himself, Natalie crouched to attach the greaves around his calves. Her pulse pounded in her throat as she worked.

Next came the cuisse to protect the top of his legs. She attached the left side first, tying it to one of the laces at the hem of the jacket. Her throat closed and her ears grew hot as she reached between Brandon's thighs to buckle the top strap.

Her fingers fumbled the buckles as her hand brushed against the hard heat of his cock. The twitch in Brandon's thighs at her touch was barely perceptible, but it sent a flood of wildfire through her body. Kneeling before him, her hands between his thighs, her cheeks reddened. Above her, his throat bobbed, the pink flush spreading above the neckline of his jacket. It was torture for them both.

At last, she pulled the buckles tight, and sat back on her heels. His lower legs, and the top, back and outside of his thigh were encased in steel.

"And what about the inside of his thighs?" The Guild Master asked. His arms were folded across his chest.

Natalie froze, doubting herself. "He... doesn't wear any there. He'll be riding a horse."

A flicker of a smirk passed over the Guild Master's lips. "Good."

She huffed the air from her nose and got back to work on attaching the other side. If the Guild Master was going to try to trip her up like that, then she would have to trust her knowledge.

She hung a chainmail skirt around Brandon's waist and fastened it to the laces at his back and stomach.

With a groan she stood on shaking legs. His bottom half was done. She cast a glance over her shoulder at the small pile of sand at the foot of the hourglass. She was making good time.

"Breastplate," she whispered. She found a stool and set it behind him, before heaving the steel breastplate over Brandon's head. She stepped down and pulled the straps at his sides until it sat flush against his chest. "Too tight?"

"A little... there. Perfect," Brandon whispered as she loosened the plate.

She risked a glance at his face. The creases at the corners of his eyes deepened as he gave her a reassuring smile. Pink bloomed on the apples of his cheeks, and his eyes were dark with desire.

Natalie lowered her head and told herself to concentrate. When the breastplate was secured, she found the plackart to protect his abdomen and tasset to shield his groin. The silver barrel of the plackart fit snugly over his stomach and flared out at the bottom into a jointed skirt, like the scales of an enormous silver serpent.

When the buckles and laces were secure Natalie stepped back and smiled. Only his arms, head and throat remained exposed.

She examined the vambraces, which were set on a bench at the back of Brandon's booth. At the elbow of each was a metal plate, to protect the wearer from the blow of a lance. One side was larger than the other. She selected the smaller of the two and hung it from his right shoulder.

"Are you certain?" The Guild Master's voice sent a chill down her back.

Natalie nodded as she buckled vambraces on his arms, securing them with straps at his forearms and inside of his elbow. "He's right-handed, so blows will be coming to his left side. He needs more protection there. The smaller cowter goes on his lance arm, so the lance doesn't jar."

The Guild Master chuckled. "Good. You know your stuff."

"I've dreamed of this for a long time," Natalie smiled as

she finished tying the top of the vambrace to the lace at his shoulder.

With a smile, she lifted Brandon's steel-clad left arm and let him rest it on her shoulder. The weight of his muscular arm, along with the steel, almost buckled her knees as she attached a pauldron to his shoulder. As with the cowters, the pauldron on his left was larger than his right.

She switched sides, facing towards the Guild Master as Brandon leaned his right arm on her shoulder. There was still plenty of white sand in the top of the hourglass, and the Guild Master's brows were raised in pleasant surprise.

As she tied off the second pauldron, Brandon's fingers brushed against the nape of her neck. Her body tensed at the tender caress, and the thrill of his touch spread like lightning throughout her body. She tore herself away to attach the hooked lance rest onto the right side of the breast plate.

Fetching the small stool once more, she stood on top of it to attach the gorget around his throat. They stood face to face as Natalie pressed her lips together. It was a rare thing to stand the same height as Brandon the Bear.

His lips parted. She longed to kiss him, to press through his soft, dark beard and find his warm, eager lips. As she buckled the gorget she feasted on the sight of him; his long, dark lashes framing his rich brown eyes, the silver at his temples, the faint creases carved from decades of laughter and life. She fought back a sigh. He was beautiful, and he was hers.

She snapped herself from her daydreams and stepped

down to fetch Brandon's gauntlets. She held them steady so that he could push his hands inside. As he held out his right hand and uncurled his fingers, the copper coin sat in the center of his palm. She smiled as she took it and slipped on his gauntlet, holding the coin tight for safekeeping.

There was only the helmet left.

"Closed face for jousting," she declared, before the Guild Master could quiz her.

She pushed the helmet down over Brandon's head and turned, triumphant, towards the hourglass. Her insides twisted as Henry sneered at the Guild Master's side.

Henry smirked and raised his eyebrows. "Excellent work, Lady Blackmere. Goodness. It's almost as if she knows your body inch by inch, Brandon."

Brandon turned behind her, his armor clanking with every movement. His breath was amplified in the helmet, and the nervous tremble sent Natalie's own pulse racing.

"Thank you," Natalie raised her chin and folded her arms over her chest. She held the copper coin tightly. "I've worked hard to become adept at this."

"Clearly," the Guild Master smiled. "Well, Brandon, I'll leave it to you how you spend your afternoon, though after today's bout with Darius, I'd suggest you work on your stamina. Registration for the Midsummer Melee will take place next week."

"Sir," Brandon's voice echoed inside his helmet.

"And set your squire to work. See that she keeps busy."

Natalie pressed her teeth into her lower lip as she grinned. "Thank you, Guild Master."

Her heart cartwheeled with excitement. After years of

wishing and fantasies, she was a squire of the Champion's Guild. She could barely suppress the squeal swelling in her throat as the Guild Master strode out of the armory.

"Congratulations." Henry cast a glance towards the ragged black feather pinned on her breast and smirked. "I feel as though things are going to get very interesting around here."

As he strode down the row of booths towards his own armor, Natalie's excitement turned to boldness. "Henry?"

"Squire?"

"I know you think you've gotten away with it, with what you did at Blackmere, but it'll follow you for the rest of your life." She relished the anger flashing across his face, but she paid for the satisfaction as her words seeped into her own heart. "Even if no-one believes us, even if we never speak a word of it again, we know what you did, and so do you."

The muscle in his cheek leapt as he clamped his jaw shut and about-turned towards his armor.

Natalie smiled and hoped that he did not see the quake in her legs as she set about untying the laces on Brandon's vambraces.

CHAPTER

ELEVEN

Putting on Brandon's armor had stirred Natalie's desire. Being so close to him, touching him, even through layers of canvas and steel, filled her with need and longing. Fighting the urge to act on her desires had been difficult.

Undressing him was torture.

They were no longer the only champion and squire in the armory. Clanking metal, hissed curses, and the grunts of encumbered warriors filled the room. Further down in his own booth, Henry stood, his jaw tight and his fists clenched, while his young squire dressed him in armor.

Natalie's breaths were fast and light, fanning the flames in her parched throat as she worked loose Brandon's buckles, peeling away his armor, piece by piece, to reveal the man she loved— and the body she craved.

As she reached her arms around his torso to unbuckle his breastplate, Brandon bowed his head towards her. "Nat..."

She looked into his eyes, not daring to speak.

His voice was a hoarse whisper, barely audible above the thunder of her pulse. "I can't stand this." He growled in frustration. "I want you."

The steel breastplate came loose, leaving him in his canvas jacket and breeches. He stood back but kept his eyes on her as he unfastened the jacket, inching it open to reveal the thatch of dark hair on his chest and stomach. He pulled the jacket from his arms, the muscles of his shoulders flexing as he freed himself of its confines.

Natalie's lips parted to make way for her stilted breaths. The rush of blood to her core left her lightheaded.

His lips quirked beneath the dark shadow of his mustache. "You're blushing again."

She pressed her lips together. "Can you blame me?"

"Not really." His eyebrow arched as he suppressed his smile.

The heat in her cheeks intensified at his playful cockiness. It was a side of him he rarely revealed, a remnant of the young man he once was, a man who enjoyed all of life's pleasures and knew they were bountiful. She lowered her eyes and buried her grin.

She longed for his lips, for the lingering kisses he liked to trail across her shoulders. The memories of their last nights together haunted her. She could still feel the crush of him on top of her, still feel the gentle friction of his beard against the tender skin between her thighs.

He took a step towards her, and she chanced a fleeting glance up at him, before lowering her eyes once more. If she stared any longer, she would lose all sense.

"Nat?"

She could barely manage a breathy "Hm?"

"Did I overstep?"

"No. Of course not." Her answer burst from her lips, louder than intended, and rang around the armory, drawing sideways glances from the nearby champions and squires. Henry's arched eyebrow sent blood rushing to her face, consuming her features in a backdraft of heat.

She inclined her head towards the door and made her way out into the hallway. Brandon followed. When they were safely out of earshot, Natalie stopped. She took a deep breath and turned to him. "Goddess, this is agony."

"Aye, it's only been one day. We still have nearly a year of this."

"The Guild Master made me promise him that our relationship was purely professional."

Brandon frowned, his lips quirking in amusement. "He did?"

"Aye. And yet again I'm lying to the people I respect the most." Natalie's vision blurred as she gave a bitter chuff of laughter. "I don't want to endanger your livelihood, I don't want to jeopardize your mother's health, but Goddess, being so close to you and not being able to act on my desires... I feel like I'm burning up."

He smiled and gestured for her to walk beside him down the hallway. "I'm still looking for somewhere they won't find us," he said, his voice a low growl which vibrated throughout her body. "But it feels as though Henry's constantly there, watching. He's just waiting for his chance to go running to the Guild Master."

"I probably shouldn't have provoked him."

Brandon shrugged and let his hands fall to his sides. "Sod him. The worse day he has, the better I feel."

Natalie stifled a chuckle as he heaved open the door to the keep. They stepped outside into the dazzling midday sun and were met with the chaos of battle.

At least, it appeared that way to Natalie.

Swords clashed, horses charged, and battle cries tore the air as hails of arrows thundered into targets. The champions were training, every one of them perfecting their disciplines in hopes of achieving greatness. The air seemed to crackle with excitement and energy.

Exhilaration swelled in her chest, erupting from her in a burst of laughter. This was the world of the champions, Brandon's world, and now hers.

"Are you ready?" Brandon smiled at her.

"For what?"

The blood drained from Natalie's face as Brandon held out his hand, gesturing towards the endless stairs leading down the cliffside.

"I told you I'd take you to the sea."

CHAPTER

TWELVE

Every muscle in Natalie's body clenched. Her toes curled inside her boots, gripping the earth, as though the sea would swell to the top of the stairway and suck her down into the inky depths. Her chest was tight, her throat closed against the scream building in her chest.

Brandon looked back at her from the stairway, his eyes scouring her features, searching for the cause of her distress. "Nat?"

"I can't." Her voice was fraught, pitiful to her own ears. "I can't."

"I promise it's safe. I would never let anything happen to you."

Tears stung her eyes. A voice in the back of her mind told her she was being irrational; for centuries, champions and their squires had climbed up and down the stairs carved into the cliffs, but her legs were iron rods, set deep into the stones of the courtyard.

"Please..." The rest of her words were lost to the trembling of her body.

Brandon climbed one step back towards her and brushed his hand against her upper arm attempting to soothe her fear. "Even if you did fall you wouldn't go far. It turns back on itself every thirty or so steps."

She turned to him, incredulous. "Thirty steps is still a bloody long way to fall."

"Less than a thousand though."

Her fear waned a little at the sight of his slanted grin, but her body refused to move. "I... can't. Not today."

Brandon bowed his head. "I'll never make you do something you don't want to, but I know you can do it."

She stepped back away from the staircase, feeling more at ease. "Thank you." She sniffed as the cool sea air whipped around her. "I promise I'll do it one day."

Brandon smiled and shielded his eyes against the sunlight. "Whenever you're ready." He scuffed the toe of his boot against the top step and chuckled. "I'll be honest, it's not much fun, but if I'm to compete at Midsummer, I need to be fit."

Natalie gave a broken sigh as he turned to descend the stairs. The wind ruffled the brown and silver strands of his hair as he turned back to her, and her fingers flexed with the urge to run her fingers through it. "What should I do while you're gone?" She checked to make sure they were not at risk of being overheard and added. "Besides pine away after you, obviously."

His smile widened. "Whatever you like. This is your home now, for the year, anyway."

She gave him a half smile and pushed the strands of hair back from her face. "But I'm your squire, Sir Brandon. I'm yours to do your bidding, to serve your every whim, to fulfill your every desire."

His teeth flashed amidst the dark brush of his beard. "Stop, or it'll be my turn to blush."

She chuckled as he turned and began his descent. The urge to follow him overwhelmed her fear for a moment, before realizing how close she was to the precipice. She watched Brandon until he disappeared behind a turn and brushed her fingertips against the black feather.

Taking a deep breath, she turned from the ledge and took stock of the bustling courtyard. It did not take long for her to find a familiar face amongst the sea of strangers.

Genevieve practiced in one of the axe-throwing pens. She was dressed in a loose cream-colored shirt, tucked into fitted tan breeches, the defined muscles of her thighs and calves straining against the linen. A cry burst from between her clenched teeth as she hurled her axe into the bullseye of a wooden target board.

"Impressive." Natalie said as she approached.

Genevieve stormed towards the target and wrenched the axe from its resting place. "I'm pretending it's Henry's head."

"Understandable."

"It's doing wonders for my aim."

Natalie chuckled and watched as Genevieve threw the axe again. It flew through the air, pounding against the center of the target and lodging itself deep within the red circle. "How are you doing?"

"My friends are dead, the man who killed them saunters around like he owns the Guild, and my mind is over a hundred miles away, dreaming about a woman who may have already forgotten I exist." Genevieve yanked the axe from the target and stormed back to take another shot. "I'm fine."

Natalie flinched as the axe thundered into the board, just left of center. "It can't be easy."

"It isn't." Genevieve wiped her forehead on the back of her arm and took a drink from a cup made from a grey and black mottled bull's horn. "How was your assessment? Are you staying?"

"Yes." Natalie stood a little taller as her pride swelled. "I'm officially a squire."

"Good. Your absence would be noticed if you were sent home."

Natalie fought back a laugh. "You're too sweet."

Genevieve smiled momentarily before setting her cup back down and preparing to throw again. "How are you finding the Guild?"

"It's..." Natalie scrunched her nose. "I feel like I'm in the way. I thought everything would be more regimented."

"It's up to us to decide how to train. Some champions run their squires ragged with drills and practice. Others, like the Bear, they're probably a little too soft." She snickered. "I mean that in every conceivable way, of course."

Natalie gave her a half smile. "Where's your squire?"

"I don't know." Genevieve raised her arm in preparation to throw. "I don't really need one for this. He's probably off practicing for his own event."

Natalie's heart leapt. "We can do that? We can compete too?"

"There's a squire melee contest in the intermission between rounds. If your champion is already competing, and they're happy for you to take part you can, though I suspect yours will let you do whatever you like." She arched an eyebrow. "I thought you knew everything about the champions?"

Natalie felt herself redden. "I know everything about the Grand Tourney, not about every event."

She stood and watched Genevieve throw, alternating between single and double handed throws.

The idea of competing, even in a squire's contest sent a shiver of excitement through Natalie's spine. She had always dreamed of becoming a champion and competing in the same arena as a squire was closer to her fantasies than she had ever hoped for.

As she imagined the roar of the crowd, and the thrill of victory. Their cheers were silenced as reality crashed down around her. She was twice, even thrice the age of some of the other squires, yet their training far surpassed hers. It was a pointless endeavor, and the only certainty was humiliation.

Frustrated, her eyes wandered towards the top of the stone staircase. She wondered how far Brandon had gotten, whether he was still running down the stairs, or if he had begun the long climb back to the top.

She gave a start, realizing that Genevieve was looking at her.

"Do you think your love can survive this?"

"Why wouldn't it?"

Genevieve shrugged. "It isn't easy to hide love. You, especially, wear it all across your face when you're near him, and when he's out of your sight. And the Bear is different than how he was before he met you. He smiles to himself sometimes, and I know he's thinking of you." She glanced towards the stairs and sighed. "But this year will take a toll on you. It has to. Being so far from Jenny is hard, but if she was here... I don't think I could stand it."

Natalie found herself struggling to swallow before she spoke. The idea of keeping their burning secret for months to come was agonizing, but the alternative, the suffering it could cause to those closest to Brandon, would be far worse. "It has to work."

Genevieve flung her axe with her left hand, barely striking the outskirts of the target. She clenched her jaw in frustration and turned to Nat. "I hope so. Seeing your love... it gives me hope, and at present that's all I have."

Natalie leaned against the fence and watched Genevieve throw axes. Her eyes would turn towards the stairway often, and each time she looked she was disappointed. Champions and their squires took off down the stairs, some dressed comfortably, others in armor, and some wearing weighted packs to increase the difficulty of their task. Brandon did not return.

It did not take long for the younger, fitter champions to make their way back up the staircase, their chiseled physiques gleaming from their exertion. Natalie took comfort in the fact that none of them seemed concerned about Brandon's safety, and none of them reported he had met with a grisly fate on the cliffside.

At last Brandon appeared, his head coming in to view first as he lumbered up the final flight of steps. His cheeks shone pink above the dark brush of his beard, and his forehead was slick with sweat.

Swooping joy filled her at the sight of his smile.

He panted, leaning forward to rest his hands on his thighs. He laughed between gasps of air. "Oh, by the Goddess. I hated every second of that. I need to sleep."

"I'm proud of you," Natalie grinned as she approached him and gently rubbed his back. His clothing was soaked beneath her palm.

Genevieve spun the axe around in her hand and shook her head. "Oh Bear..."

"Oh Bear indeed."

Natalie's blood cooled at the sound of Henry's voice. He stood behind Genevieve, dressed in a gleaming suit of armor. His squire stood two paces behind him. The lad was perhaps sixteen, tall and slim, with blonde, straw-like hair which flopped over his eyes as he stared down at his boots.

Henry smirked and walked towards Brandon. Agitation bristled down Natalie's back, as her fingers curled into fists.

"Forgive me for interrupting, but I'm really trying to wrap my head around this," Henry cocked his head to the side. A faint crease appeared between his eyebrows. "You were once the paragon of the Champion's Guild. No one could even compare to Brandon the Bear. I've told you, haven't I, that you were the reason I worked so hard as a squire? I wanted to be just like you."

Brandon stood straight, digging his fists into his hips as he battled to rein in his breaths. "Aye."

Henry crumpled, hanging his head low in mock shame. "But how did it come to this? How is it that a man, once so great, could become..." He gestured towards Brandon, his hand sweeping from the level of his head to his feet. A grimace warped his features. "This?"

Brandon's voice remained firm and level, even in the face of insult. "Wait a few years, I'm sure you'll find out. You can't stay on top forever."

Henry's eyes settled on Natalie, and his lip curled in revulsion. "Perhaps not, but I'll never allow myself to fall *this* far."

Blood boiling, Natalie took a step forward, but was stayed by Brandon's gentle grip on her shoulder. She forced the air from her nose as her desire to go after Henry burned at the nape of her neck.

The Dragon smirked. "That's right, keep your dog leashed. I hear the flocks of Blackmere are plagued by rabid bitches, I would hate to suffer the same."

Brandon reeled towards him. "That's it—"

Henry stepped back, snickering as he raised his palms to halt Brandon's advance. "Now, now, old man. Defending your lady's honor doesn't go over well here." Satisfied that his insults had cut deep enough, he chuckled and turned on his heel.

A whimper sounded in the back of Henry's throat as he blundered directly into Genevieve's chest. She peered down at him, as though she was debating whether to squash a particularly bothersome insect. The wind howled around the courtyard, like a goading crowd.

"Step aside, big girl," Henry growled. "I have no quarrel with you."

"Of course." Genevieve smiled sweetly and raised her voice a little. "Little boy."

Henry's squire pressed his lips together, hiding a smile as his champion's face reddened and turned on his heel. With a bow, the lad followed after the Dragon as he headed towards the cliff steps.

"I'll see you in the ring," Brandon called after Henry. He nodded his thanks to Genevieve and turned to Natalie, his expression both thunderous and apologetic. "I'm sorry. I should've—"

"No, you shouldn't do anything. You can't rise to his insults, the moment you do, it puts us in danger."

Brandon lowered his eyes and nodded his head. "You're right."

"There's nothing you can do, and he knows it. Besides, I'd rather be the rabid bitch of Blackmere than some stuck up prissy little prick like him."

Genevieve chuckled, drawing a grin from Brandon. "I like her."

"Me too," he grinned.

Natalie's heart fluttered as he flipped the copper coin on his thumb. She turned towards the keep and gestured for him to follow. "I'm hungry."

"Aye." Brandon wiped his damp forehead on his arm. "Let's eat."

THIRTEEN

Days blurred into weeks. Natalie would awaken, eat, and help Brandon dress in his armor. He would spar, then with her aid, change into more comfortable attire, and begin his routine of climbing the endless stairs. Her longing for him only grew as the days went by, and the need for him became a constant source of torture from which there was no release.

Between dressing Brandon in the morning and stripping his armor in the evening, there was little for her to do but wait. Wherever she went she was in somebody's way. It became her routine to watch Genevieve throw axes whilst the warrior woman grilled Natalie on every small detail of Jenny's personality.

"Does she have a favorite flower?" Genevieve released a strained cry as she flung her axe at the target with both hands.

Natalie frowned and tried to suppress her amusement with a cough. "I honestly don't know."

"I thought you were friends."

"We are but, unbelievable as it may be, we've never spoken at length about flowers."

The champion grunted in frustration. "Well if you had to guess which she likes best?"

"Maybe she doesn't like them? Perhaps that's why she never speaks of them."

"Everyone likes flowers. Don't be ridiculous."

With a grin, Natalie leaned against the fence of the axe-throwing pen. "The only time she ever mentioned a flower was when she was talking about how she longed to meet The Thorn of the Rose."

Genevieve's cheeks darkened. She scratched her eyebrow and took aim at the target once more.

A sigh escaped Natalie's lips as she turned her attention to the sea. The sun glittered on the surface of the water, beautiful but dazzling, as white gulls soared above. It was a stark contrast to the still, dark waters of Blackmere.

She was yet to summon the courage to descend the steps to the beach, and though her desire to see the ocean up close called to her, her fear outweighed her curiosity.

"So... roses then?" Genevieve cleared her throat. "And if you had to guess which color roses she might like best—?"

"Viv, I'm sure she'd like anything you sent her." Natalie stood upright and brushed off her hands. "I want to train for the squires' melee contest."

Genevieve shot her a look and blinked. "You?"

Natalie tried not to feel offended by Genevieve's surprise. "Yes, me."

"And what if you get hurt? I've met your mother,

remember? If we send you back to Blackmere scarred and broken, I've no doubt she'll bring her army here and kick down our gates next."

Natalie chuckled. "She'd call it character building. Don't worry. Is there a spare blade I can use?"

Genevieve scuffed her boot across the courtyard stones and chewed her lip as she thought on it. At last she shrugged. "Check the armory."

CHAPTER

FOURTEEN

Pale sunlight gleamed on polished steel as Natalie made her way past the unoccupied, silent booths. She shuddered, imagining the lifeless helmets watching, turning towards her as she crept through the stalls. The urge to check over her shoulder every few steps plagued her.

At the back of the room was a small door, leading to a store of spare armor and weapons. Natalie's body bristled as she placed her hand on the cool wooden door.

"It's fine," she whispered to herself. "There's nothing to be afraid of."

She held her breath and pushed. A scream surged in her chest, and her heart thundered as she was met with two wide eyes.

A male voice hissed at her. "What are you—?"

"By the Goddess!" She gasped, clutching her chest.

The boy in the armory mirrored her gesture, grasping at

his own chest and pushing the wheat blonde hair back from his forehead. "You scared the life out of me."

Natalie rolled her eyes and took a soothing breath. She recognized the young man as Henry's squire. "Aye, likewise."

"What are you doing sneaking around in here? This stuff is for squires."

"I am a squire." Natalie frowned at the rows of dusty armor and weapons which had long lost their shine. "Besides, even if I wasn't, I thought it was for everyone to use?"

"It's for those who can't afford their own yet." The boy turned his back on her and lowered himself to sit cross-legged on a pile of sandbags. "You're a noble lady, aren't you? You can afford your own equipment."

Natalie bit back her retort as she found a tangle of blades stuck inside an old wooden bucket. Some were rusted brown, others had good steel, but their leather grips were worn and tattered. She sorted through them, inspecting each one, until she found a blade tucked inside a battered leather scabbard. She pulled the blade from its sheath, inspecting the dull steel. What it lacked in elegance it made up for in sturdiness. It would do.

As she strapped the blade to her hip, the rustle of paper caught her attention.

The lad frowned as his eyes scanned a creased piece of parchment and his throat bobbed as he swallowed.

"Is everything well?" Natalie asked.

"Don't know." He shrugged and refolded the paper, tossing it to the ground. "I can't read it."

"Would you like me to read it for you?"

The young lad glanced at her from the corner of his eye and shifted on his seat. He gave a one shouldered shrug. "If you want to."

Natalie crouched to pick up the discarded letter.

She was fortunate to have been taught to read and write. The skill was common enough among the highborn nobles of Aldland. It helped them manage the lands and accounts, allowed them to communicate between neighboring lands, but it was a luxury few others were afforded.

The year she became the Lady of Blackmere, Natalie had found one of her duties involved dealing with written correspondence for her people. They depended on her.

Finding herself running the castle and its lands alone, her days were quickly filled by other duties. Rather than allow the task of letters to slip, she acquired the services of an apple-cheeked lady by the name of Matty who offered literacy tuition to anyone who asked. Matty also penned letters for people and read their correspondence for them if they could not do it themselves. The bills for the services were sent directly to Natalie.

She pressed her lips together and hoped her mother had still found money to pay Matty while taking care of Blackmere's accounts.

The letter in her hand was penned by shaking, uncertain fingers and stamped with the little bird seal of Finchburrow. She read the top line and raised her eyes towards the lad. "Your name's Tommy?"

He nodded and leaned towards her, peering at the top of the paper. "Is it from my mum?"

Natalie cleared her throat. "My Dearest Tommy. I am proud of you and miss you every day. You are an uncle now. Your nephew's name is Caleb. With love, mum."

She looked up from the page. His eyes glistened like the sunlight on the sea, and his chin quivered as he held back his tears. "She said that?"

"Aye. It's all here."

His throat twitched as he crawled across the floor towards her. "Read it again. Please."

She did so, following each word with her finger as she read. "My Dearest Tommy. I am proud of you and miss you every day. You are an uncle now. Your nephew's name is Caleb. With love, mum."

He nodded slowly and wiped the tip of his nose on the end of his sleeve. "Thanks."

"My pleasure." She handed the note back to him, which he quickly folded and shoved inside his jacket. "And congratulations."

"Don't tell Henry I'm in here." He stood and brushed off the seat of his trousers. "He thinks I'm running the steps."

"I won't." She smiled as she raised herself from the floor. "Don't worry."

The boy darted from the room without a second glance.

The rapid tap of his footsteps faded as he left the armory. She wondered how many letters had gone unread in the Guild, how much news and good tidings, how many people were unaware of births and the deaths of loved ones.

She resolved to pay attention when the messenger

arrived at the end of the month, to see how many letters were delivered. Perhaps, she could help.

Placing her hand on the hilt of the sword at her hip she smiled to herself, and left the silent armory, the empty eyes of the helmets staring after her.

CHAPTER

FIFTEEN

"Do you have a favorite flower?" Natalie swung her blade towards the straw dummy, striking the center of its chest. The weather was warm for the time of year, and most of the champions had taken their meals outside, basking in the courtyard like silver-scaled lizards.

Brandon leaned against the wall beside her, grimacing at a plate of hard-boiled eggs. "A flower?"

"Viv said everyone does."

Brandon took a deep breath and pursed his lips as he forced the air out. "I'd never really thought about it. Do you?"

She turned to him and smiled. Clad in his armor he was absurdly large and bright, a beacon shining against the wall. "Sunflowers."

Brandon's smile was broken by the sharp clank of armor coming towards them. The atmosphere in the sunny court-

111

yard seemed to darken as Henry, Darius and Sara approached.

"Sweet Bear," Darius greeted, tipping his head towards Brandon. His eyes passed over Natalie as though she had no significance at all.

"Yes, love?" Brandon replied, drawing a broad smile from Darius's lips. "How can I be of service."

"You're such a charmer," Darius chuckled, reaching out and placing his hand over Brandon's heart. "But we come bearing unpleasant news."

Natalie frowned and put her blade back into its sheath as Brandon pushed back from the wall and stood upright.

Henry's jaw leapt as he looked towards the sea. "Your squire was caught stealing supplies."

"What?" The word sprang from Natalie as her heart kicked against her ribs. "I haven't stolen anything."

Sara's lip curled. "You were seen leaving the armory with Guild supplies. The weapons in there are not for you."

"This?" Natalie placed her hand on the grip of the sword at her hip.

"They're for everyone to use," Brandon's voice was low and level, but the intensity of his glare was scorching. "I'm sure that blade has passed through the hands of every one of us."

"*She* is not one of us," Sara snapped. Natalie's pulse raced as the pale woman's eyes raked across her. "She's a noble. She shouldn't even be here."

Natalie stepped away from the training dummy and stood beside Brandon. She looked to Darius and Sara. "Have I done something to offend you?"

"Besides stealing?" Henry frowned. As Darius and Sara's eyes bore into her, the faintest hint of a grin danced across Henry's face as he touched the tip of his tongue to his teeth.

Brandon held out his arm, creating a barrier between Natalie and the champions. "Stop. Just stop this." His command was loud and clear, drawing the attention of the other champions around the courtyard.

Natalie's breath shuddered from her lips. She was torn between the instinct to defend herself, and the desire to run. The champion's eyes burned into her, and in turn, she glared at Henry.

"Nat isn't a noble here," Brandon took a step towards Darius. "She's a squire. She doesn't get any more respect than any other squire, and she definitely doesn't get any less. Understand?"

Darius lowered his head and nodded. "If you say there was no ill intent, then I trust your judgement."

"Thank you," Brandon reached out and squeezed Darius's shoulder.

Sara pressed her lips together and exhaled through her nose. Her eyes flickered between Brandon and Natalie as her face hardened. "Just make sure you put it back where you found it."

Natalie frowned. "I will. After I've finished using it."

"Watch yourself," Henry sneered as the champions turned their back on her.

Her muscles unfurled as they walked away. "Henry's determined to make our lives miserable, isn't he?"

"Aye," Brandon sighed, his eyes following the retreating champions every movement.

Over by the stables, Henry's squire, Tommy, pushed a wheelbarrow of manure. His cheeks blazing scarlet. He kept his eyes low as he walked, not daring to look her way. Frustration brewed in Natalie's heart. She had helped Tommy, and he had betrayed her anyway.

She clenched her jaw and turned back to the dummy. Her heart rate slowed with the dissipation of the conflict.

"I'm sorry," Brandon said. He sighed and looked out to the sea. "I knew they'd be wary of you at first, but I thought they'd accept you eventually."

"Whatever I've done to offend them, it was not intentional."

"You haven't done anything. It's who you are, not what you've done." He released a breath and ran his ungloved hand through his hair. "Darius's family lives under a noble-woman who keeps the taxes so high that every penny he earns he sends back to his mother. They can still barely put one meal a day on the table."

"That's awful."

"And Sara's father is noble. Her mother was his scullery maid. Once he found out she was carrying his child he threw her out. She was destitute. Sara was born in a back alley and spent the first years of her life on the streets. Her mother sent her alone to the Guild when she was six years old, and we had no choice but to take her in."

Natalie's heart hung heavy. She lowered her blade as the weight of the revelation draped across her shoulders.

The champions' animosity towards her made sense. She was an outlet for their frustrations and sense of injustice.

Brandon placed his hand on top of hers. "I'll speak to them and tell them you aren't that kind of noble."

"You don't need to." Natalie offered him a comforting smile. "I'd rather show them with my actions than force them with the words of the man they admire."

His eyes lingered on hers and his lips parted a little. "As you wish, my lady."

The look sent pulsing heat coursing through her body and her throat became parched. She wondered if he hungered for her as much as she craved him. It had been weeks without so much as a friendly embrace.

"My champion." She turned and drew her blade, thrusting it towards the dummy's chest. "Well, now there's so much fuss over the sword, I suppose I'd better keep up with my training."

"Viv tells me you're planning to compete in the squire games?"

"I was. That is, if it's acceptable to my champion?"

"I wouldn't even consider stopping you." He took her sword hand and adjusted the placement of her fingers on the grip, his touch sending sparks through her nerves. "And if you like, I'd be happy to find time to train you."

"I'd like that." Her breath failed her as he grazed his lower lip with his teeth.

His eyes were dark and his breaths shallow. "My lady, it's been too long since I held you."

She sighed as he traced the peaks of her knuckles with

his fingertips. "Oh, Brandon, I can't stand this. There has to be somewhere we can go."

"There is." His voice was hoarse as he glanced towards the stairs. "But it isn't easy to get to."

Icy fear dripped down her spine as she understood the meaning of his words. "The beach?"

"Aye, and only for a few moments. It's the best I can do. The keep is crawling with people, the stables are constantly watched. There are rocks down there we can hide behind when no one is near, but it means climbing down." He grimaced. "And of course, back up."

Natalie swallowed hard. The thought of climbing down the stairs, or more specifically, plummeting down them, made her nauseous. Her eyes trailed across his features, the soft pink of his lips beneath the thick dark thatch of his beard, the deep warm brown of his eyes, and the creases worn around them. Her breath hitched at the thought of kissing him.

"Let's go." She could hardly speak through her nerves.

His eyes widened a little. "Now?"

"Aye." She stood, legs shaking beneath her. "Do you want to change out of your armor first?"

He glanced down his chest and shook his head. "No. I'll try to do it with the armor today."

Natalie released a shaking breath and set her jaw. Her head grew light as they made their way towards the top of the staircase. The endless abyss stretched out beneath her as she peered over the cliff's edge. Her hand darted towards the wall, fingertips digging into the cracks between the stones.

"My Lady, are you certain?" Brandon's voice was low, and his eyes pleading. "I don't want you to feel like you have to do this."

She released a long breath and nodded. "I can do it." Summoning all her courage she lifted a foot and lowered it onto the first step. The stone was worn smooth, curved downwards in the center by centuries of wear.

"You're braver than anyone I've ever met," Brandon said as he stepped down beside her.

"If I were brave, this wouldn't be so difficult." She took another step, moistening her arid lips with the tip of her tongue.

Brandon's smile made her heart swell. "Well, then you'd just be unafraid, not brave."

They reached the bottom of the first flight, where the staircase turned at a right angle to run parallel with the cliff. The sea-chilled wind whipped through Natalie's hair, stealing the air from her lungs as it pushed her towards the cliffside.

"Pardon me," a young champion called as he raced down the steps in full armor, sending a spike of panic through Natalie's heart.

"Easy," Brandon soothed, offering his arm. "I won't let anything happen to you."

Her body revolted against her mind, tensing, screaming at her to retreat to the safety of the courtyard. She closed her eyes and thought of Brandon, of the softness of his lips and her desire to be alone with him, even for a moment.

Opening her eyes, Natalie linked his arm and together they continued the journey down, zig-zagging down the cliff face. The sea breeze battered them, pebbling Natalie's skin with goosebumps. A dense mass of billowing clouds hung low over the ocean.

"You run up these every day?" She called out above the roar of the wind and waves.

Brandon grimaced and chuckled to himself. "Run is a strong word. I stagger most of the way."

A laugh burst from her, easing some of her tension. His closeness spread warmth across her body.

They stepped aside to allow a champion to charge past them on his climb back up the steps. "I used to be able to run all the way down and all the way up, back when I was younger and fitter."

"And you will again."

He raised his eyebrows and glanced out towards the incoming clouds. "If I'm honest, more often than not, when I'm climbing back up, the doubt starts to creep in. Part of me knows I'm a fool for believing I can do this. Perhaps I should give up."

"No." Natalie reached out and brushed her fingertips against the cold steel of his arm. She darted her hand back as though the metal was scalding, checking over her shoulder in case anyone had seen. "You can't give up."

Brandon followed her gaze towards the empty stairs behind them. "Henry's a little more than half my age, and he's by no means the only competition. I can't underestimate Darius, and I just know that one day Viv's going to snap and put all of us on our arses."

Natalie paused on the steps, allowing her aching muscles a brief respite from the relentless climb down. "I know you can do this. You're Brandon the Bear. People sing songs about your strength and courage."

"I'm not the man I was."

"I believe in the man you are now."

Brandon smiled, though his brow still hung heavy. "Sometimes the only thing which gets me to the top of the steps is knowing that you'll be up there waiting for me."

"Well today I'm beside you." She reached out and pressed a hand to his forearm "And I will be every day onward if you need me to be."

"You aren't afraid anymore?"

She gave a chuff of laughter. "I am, a little. But this is the most privacy we've had in weeks, and it's more than worth it."

His eyes creased and brightened. "Well then, I'd be honored if you came with me."

"Then I'll do it. And if you need further encouragement, I'll sing all the songs I know about you as we climb, loudly and enthusiastically." Natalie grinned as she set off back down the stairs.

His lips quirked as she passed by him. "That's not necessary."

As they continued their journey, they were overtaken by champions every few minutes, some charging downwards, others slogging back up, their breaths strained and heavy.

"We won't have much time," Brandon reiterated as they neared the end of the stairs. "Those clouds look like trouble."

"I just need to be alone with you, even if for a moment."

By the time they reached the bottom of the stairs, Natalie's back and thighs were throbbing from the effort, but her pain was forgotten as she stepped onto the pale brown cushion of sand. Her eyes widened as she took in the sight.

The tang of the sea filled her lungs as she pulled in a deep breath, tucking her hair behind her ears as it whipped around her. The waves roared as they lapped the shore, tumbling over each other to coat the sand in foam. Further along the coast the waves beat against the cliffs breaking against the rocks in cascades of white spray.

"It's incredible," Natalie called above the roar. She grinned, pulling an errant strand of hair from her face.

Turning towards Brandon, she was greeted by his gentle smile. Droplets of water spotted his armor.

He squinted and looked up at the sky. The clouds were gathered, and hung over them like a watchful, bitter deity. "Here comes the rain. We'd better hurry. The steps get blocked off in bad weather."

Natalie's heart sank a little with the knowledge that their stolen minutes had already dwindled to seconds.

A clatter sounded above them on the stairs as a champion and her squire jogged down. When they reached the bottom, they greeted Brandon with a nod and began the long climb back up.

Brandon watched them closely, ensuring they were out of sight. Satisfied by their momentary solitude, he took Natalie's hand and led her under the slant of the stairs, to a cluster of grey boulders spotted with white limpets. Natalie barely had time to catch her breath when he turned to face her.

He wrapped his arms around her, holding her tight against the ironclad expanse of his chest, as though at any moment she would be swept away from him.

She stood on her tiptoes, pressing her face to his neck, breathing in the soft, warm scent of his body. His breath shuddered as he pressed his lips to the top of her head.

"I love you," she whispered against the throbbing pulse in his throat.

"And I love you, with my every breath."

Natalie's heart swelled with joy as he covered her head in kisses. She tilted her head towards him and looked into his eyes. "My champion." Reaching up she brushed the hair back from his forehead, letting her fingers trace the arc of his brow. "You're the most handsome man in all of Aldland."

The corner of his lip curved upwards. "You flatter me, my lady."

"I only say what I see." She reached up to caress his cheek, so hot beneath her palm. "And I know you can do this. I know you can win. You're stronger than anyone I've ever known."

"Until I lay my eyes on you and I become the weakest man who ever lived."

She smiled. "Then I'm weak too. Not a moment has passed where I didn't want to kiss you."

He lowered his head towards hers, his lips slightly parted. "Well who am I to deny my lady her desires?"

At the touch of their lips, Natalie's heart roared with the ocean, drowning the rest of the world. He brought his hands to the sides of her face, holding her gently, shielding her from the wind which danced around them. A moan escaped her lips as yearning coursed through her body, sending pulses of heat and excitement through her. When they broke apart, she was breathless, clinging to him as her legs trembled beneath her. The world spun around them.

"You're perfect," he breathed, brushing his nose against hers.

They held each other a moment longer, until he glanced up at the sky, concern etched on his brow. "I'm sorry we can't spend longer here. The steps can be dangerous when they get wet."

His breath blew hot against her knuckles as he kissed the back of her hand, fanning the flames scorching her cheeks.

"We'll come back tomorrow, and the next day, and the next." She kissed him again, sealing her promise.

They followed their footprints back towards the steps and begrudgingly began their ascent.

The pleasant ache of their kisses soured as they began the climb. It did not take long for Natalie's legs to begin throbbing, for talons of sharp pain to grip the muscles in her thighs and calves. The rain came down harder the higher they climbed, and it felt to Natalie as though hours passed before they reached the top.

The few moments they had stolen were worth every step.

As they climbed the final stretch and found themselves back in the courtyard Natalie raised her face to the raindrops. They were cool and refreshing on her burning skin. Her ribs ached from her raw and ragged breaths.

The Guild Master approached. "Are you the last? You saw no one else?"

"No," Brandon nodded, still fighting to catch his breath. "Just us."

The Guild Master gave Brandon a concerned look, before he took a key from his belt and swung a wooden gate across the gap to block off the staircase. "By the Goddess, Brandon. You need to slow down. You're not a young man anymore."

"Aye, and glad of it." Brandon chuckled. Though Natalie's breath steadied, her chest grew tight as he brushed his hand against the back of hers and flashed her a victorious smile. "Come on, let's get out of the rain."

CHAPTER

SIXTEEN

The next morning, blue sky glistened in pools of water on the courtyard stones as Natalie and Brandon emerged from the keep. A bubble of nervous excitement swelled in her chest as she gripped the hilt of the blade at her hip.

"I can't believe I'm training with the legendary Brandon the Bear at the Champion's Guild," she gushed as they headed towards one of the melee rings. "What will we work on today?"

"We'll see how much you remember from our last training sessions." Brandon smiled beside her. Like her, he wore a steel breastplate and a helmet, enough protection to train, but not as cumbersome as full armor. He unlatched the gate of the training ring and stepped aside to let Natalie through.

"Thank you, Sir Brandon."

As she passed him, he sighed, leaned towards her and whispered, "You're even more lovely when you're excited."

Heat crashed over her as she stepped into the soggy sand. It sloshed beneath her steps, clinging to her boots as she turned to face him.

"Now," he began, striding towards her with his sword in his hand. "In a melee contest, your goal is to strike your opponent's breastplate with your blade, without letting them touch yours." He tapped his ironclad chest with the tip of his blade. "Once a breastplate is struck, the fight is over."

Natalie gave him a nod. Excitement swelled in her chest pressing against the confines of her throat.

Brandon took a step back, standing in a wide fighting stance. "Very good. Now, strike my breastplate."

His confidence and authoritative tone stoked her desire for him. His eyes darkened as he looked at her, and in that moment, she was no longer his love, or even his ally. They were opponents, rivals. His stern demeanor excited her.

Natalie forced out a breath and raised her blade. "I think I'll rather like having you as a teacher." She struck out towards his chest. Her breath was snatched from her as he swatted her aside, and the tip of his sword tapped the metal on her chest.

"You can do better," he growled.

Heat fanned across her cheeks as she struck and was blocked again. She bit down her frustration and struck from a lower angle and was defeated just as easily.

"Come on, Nat. I've seen you fight for your life before. Hit me."

"I'm trying." She lunged for him.

As easy as taking breath, Brandon halted her attack,

swiping her blade from her hand and tapped her breastplate. Her sword landed in the wet sand.

Natalie cast him a thunderous look as she crouched to pick up the blade.

He laughed. "You'd be just as annoyed if I went easy on you."

"I'm more annoyed at myself than anything." She wiped the sand from the hilt onto her trouser leg. "I feel like I've never held a blade before."

A warm hand gripped her shoulder, and his eyes sought the light in hers. She wanted so badly to kiss him, to tear away the steel and leather, and press her body to his.

"You'll get better," he said. Her chest tightened as he leaned closer, until his lips were level with her ear. "And I'll reward each of your victories with my tongue."

She bit down her grin as desire pooled between her thighs. "I knew you would be an excellent teacher."

He stood back and beckoned her towards him. "And now you have something to fight for. Hit me."

She fought back her smile, took a deep breath and fixed her eyes on his. Anticipating his defense, she struck out. Her arm ached as she attacked again and again, the force of his block sending pulses of pain through her shoulders. He swept his blade around, under her arm, and tapped her breastplate.

Natalie threw up her arms in defeat. "I can't beat you."

"You've beaten me before."

"Well that was different. That was... you were distracted."

He chuckled. "I'm distracted every time I'm near you."

Natalie fought back a smile and pushed out a breath. "Fine."

"Don't try to plan your attacks ahead of time, just react. Look for opportunities, gaps in my defense."

She nodded and prepared to strike. Brandon raised his guard.

Their blades clashed. She struck again and again, testing his reactions. Within moments sweat poured beneath her armor, but she kept up her attack, drawing every ounce of energy she had as she advanced on him. She drove him backwards towards the edge of the ring. When his back touched the fence, she feigned an attack low to the left, then struck him from the right. The clang of her blade against his breastplate was the sweetest music she had ever heard.

A broad smile spread across his face. "Good. Excellent."

She fought to catch her breath, digging the knuckles of her fist into her waist as a cramp seized her muscles. "Goddess, this is harder than it looks."

"But you did it."

The warmth in his eyes sent her heart fluttering. She wiped her brow on her sleeve. "You went easy on me."

"Not at all, even if I benefit just as much from your prize as you do."

"I doubt that."

That cocky grin, and the darkness in his eyes, would be her downfall. How she longed to pounce on him.

"You have your breath back?" he grinned.

"Almost."

"Good, now try to hit me again."

CHAPTER

SEVENTEEN

Natalie's soaring elation crashed to the earth as night drew in. No matter how much time they spent together during the day, after supper the squires and champions would be sent to opposite wings of the keep, and the ache of being apart would begin anew.

She lay on her bed each night, staring up at the dark brown boards on the ceiling, longing for his touch, counting down the moments until they were together again. It was unlike Natalie to awaken early, but each morning her fluttering stomach drove her from her room.

Brandon would silently greet her in the banquet hall, his broad smile bright in the midst of his dark beard. Their eyes met frequently as she ate her breakfast. She kept to herself, sitting on the end of the bench, away from the younger squires, who acknowledged her only with disinterested glances.

It was during one such morning, when the castle was already warm from the late spring sun, that Natalie's breakfast was disrupted by a presence at her side. She gave a start as Henry's young squire, Tommy, squeezed onto the bench beside her.

"Good morning, Lady Blackmere," he whispered. He cast a sideways look towards his peers and turned, angling his back towards them

Natalie's face flushed. "Have you come to accuse me of stealing again?"

"No!" His eyes widened. "Oh Goddess, I was hoping you'd forgotten that."

"How could I forget?"

He lowered his voice. "Listen, Henry caught me leaving the keep that day, and he demanded that I told him what I was doing."

"So why didn't you tell him the truth?"

Tommy sniffed and lowered his head. "He would've smacked me if I told him I was hiding from him. I panicked and said I was following you. I knew they wouldn't punish you the same. I didn't know what else to do."

Natalie paused. "What do you want?"

He glanced towards the champions' table. Henry's eyes narrowed as he glanced towards them. "Meet me in the courtyard when the bell tolls. It won't take long."

Natalie frowned and shook her head in an attempt to clear her confusion. "What's going on?"

He reached out and placed his hand on her wrist. "Please, Lady Blackmere. I need your help."

The desperation and sincerity of his plea removed her doubt. She gave him a single nod and returned to her breakfast.

Tommy stood, bowing slightly. "Thank you, my lady." He joined the rest of the squires, fending off their whispered questions with stoic silence as he ate his breakfast.

When the bell tolled, Natalie made her way out of the banquet hall, following the stream of squires out to the courtyard. A warm breeze fluttered the loose, olive green linen of her shirt. Summer was still weeks away, yet the southern sun had already darkened the freckles on her arms and cheeks. It had been years since she had seen them.

Shielding her eyes from the piercing light, she searched the courtyard. Tommy stood by the stables, gesturing for her to follow him.

"This is absurd," she grumbled to herself as she made her way across the bustling courtyard. Squires were running around, preparing each training area for use, straightening targets, cleaning manure from the list and raking the sand.

When she reached the stables, Tommy ducked behind a wall without a word.

She frowned. "Are you planning to bludgeon my brains out if I follow you?"

"No, I need your brains," he chuckled. As she turned the corner, she checked behind her, ensuring they had not been followed. "I need help."

"So you said."

"My mum's letter." He pressed his lips together. "Henry found it last week. He ripped it up and burned the pieces to punish me for being late for practice."

"I'm sorry."

"*My Dearest Tommy. I am proud of you and miss you every day. You have a nephew called Caleb. With love, mum.*" He tapped his temple and grinned. "I remember it though, thanks to you, and I want to write back to her. I want to tell her I'm safe and happy and doing her proud."

Natalie felt herself soften. "Do you want me to teach you how to write it for yourself?"

He shook his head. "That's very kind of you, but there's no time. The messenger comes here to deliver letters on the last day of the month."

"That's tomorrow."

"Yes, my lady," he lowered his eyes and shoved his hands in his pockets. "So, I was wondering if you could write down what I say and we could ask the messenger to take my letter to Finchburrow? I have a little money to pay him."

Movement in the corner of her eye caught her attention. Brandon waved to her in the melee fighting ring, his breastplate hanging loose around his tunic, the unbuckled leather straps hanging down to his hips. She waved back to assure him she was well.

"Would you do it?" Tommy pressed her, his eyes wide and pleading. "I promise it'll just be this one time."

"Of course." She gestured for him to follow her as she made her way over to Brandon. "I'll write as many times as you need me to, don't worry. Fetch parchment, a quill and ink to my room this evening. We'll work on it after supper."

"You have my gratitude, Lady Blackmere. Please don't let anyone know, especially not Henry, or the Guild Master." He bowed as they approached Brandon. "Good morning, Sir Brandon. I'm sorry to have kept your squire."

"It's no trouble at all." Brandon pulled a blunt blade

from a rack of swords and thrust it through the air. "I think I'll train without full armor today anyway."

A pang of guilt struck Natalie. "Are you certain? It won't take long to dress you properly."

"Aye, I'd rather just get started. If nothing else, fighting unarmored will encourage me not to get hit."

Tommy chuckled. His eyes were filled with longing as he watched Brandon prepare for his drills. "I'll spar with you a bit, if you like, Sir?"

Brandon's eyes creased as he smiled. "Well I don't know if I'm quite skilled enough to fight you, but I'll give it a go."

Tommy laughed and picked a blade from the rack. His cheeks flushed red as he stood opposite Brandon, his stance just as formidable, but for the slight tremble in his sword arm.

Natalie stood back, leaning against the fence as Brandon and Tommy fought. Climbing the steps every day had revived some of Brandon's former strength. His breath came easier, his body did not fatigue so easily.

Though Brandon was close to three times Tommy's age, he moved with unexpected swiftness, deftly blocking each blow. Their smiles broadened with every clash of their blades. Brandon's excitement and pride were contagious.

The squire called for a break as he fought to catch his breath, rubbing an ache from his shoulder. "You've gotten a lot better."

"Aye?" Brandon grinned a little as he took a sip from a wooden cup. "You think so?"

Natalie's smile faded as a figure skulked towards them.

Henry stormed across the courtyard, his face bloodless and his lip curled.

Tommy paled at the sight of his champion. The tip of his blade sunk towards the sand as he stepped back, putting Brandon between him and Henry.

"Do you think I'm ready to take him on?" Brandon said quietly.

Tommy nodded. "I'd bet my life on it."

Brandon chuckled as he set down his cup. He wiped his moustache on the back of his sleeve and sighed. "I hope so."

Tension coiled in Natalie's body. The sun shone in the clear blue sky, but the air in the courtyard was heavy, thick, as though a storm brewed around them. "Please be careful."

Henry's features were twisted in outrage as he approached the circle. "What in the Goddess's name is going on here?"

"I'm sorry." Tommy's back was rigid. "I was helping Sir Brandon train."

"Are you his squire?"

Tommy's voice weakened as his eyes darted towards Brandon, to Natalie, and back to Henry. "No."

"So whose squire are you?"

The air in the circle was cloying. Natalie's heart pounded in her throat. "Stop this."

Tommy closed his eyes and answered Henry, his voice trembling. "Yours."

Henry ran his tongue across the top row of his teeth and tilted his chin towards Tommy. "Get out of the circle, squire. Come here."

Natalie breathed in slowly, reminding herself to remain

civil. It would be easy, so easy, for Henry to have her banished from the Guild, and the lives of Brandon's family endangered. Her body tensed as both Henry and Tommy approached her.

A sharp crack rang through the air as Henry back-handed Tommy's cheek. "If you ever leave me waiting in the armory again, I'll have you thrown off the cliff edge, do I make myself clear?"

Natalie whirled around, putting her shoulder between Henry and his squire.

The lad trembled at her back, clutching his cheek. "Yes sir."

"You even try it, and I'll launch you into the sea before you can lay a hand on him." Brandon growled from the center of the circle. His expression was dark, his eyes, normally so kind and gentle, were black abysses.

Natalie's heart lunged against her ribs as the storm between them surged.

"I'm sorry. Are you really threatening me?" Henry snickered, shoving Natalie and Tommy to the side.

Her vision tunneled. The Guild, the courtyard, and even the ocean disappeared, until the world consisted of nothing but Brandon and Henry, and the trembling boy at her back.

Brandon's mouth curled into a smile. "Not at all. I'm just warning you of the consequences of your actions." He prowled towards Henry with his sword arm relaxed. The younger man recoiled as he approached. "Now take up your sword and try hitting someone bigger than you for once."

CHAPTER

EIGHTEEN

"Brandon, are you sure?" Natalie's fingers shook as she tightened the straps of his breastplate. "Let me dress you properly, please."

On the other side of the circle, Henry and his squire prepared for the impending fight. The younger champion's eyes were murderous, burning into them. Natalie could easily imagine him living up to his nickname, The Dragon, smoke curling from his flaring nostrils, fingers curled into savage talons, fire burning in his veins.

"I don't need it," Brandon's voice was low and distant, as though only a fraction of him remained in the courtyard. "I need to be fast to beat him. The armor will slow me down."

"I'd rather you lose than get hurt."

He reached his arm around his chest to pin her hand to his side and tightened his fingers around hers. "I'll be fine. It's just practice, and if I can't face him here, what hope do I have two months from now when I face him in the Melee?"

There was desperate longing in his eyes, desperation, a

135

maelstrom to quench Henry's fire. There was no use in trying to persuade him to back out from the fight. All she could do was lend him some of the strength he needed to win.

"Then fight well, my champion." She stepped back, giving him a clear path towards the ring.

His face hardened at her words and he gave a single, determined nod. As he stepped into the circle, her heart began to pound. The air bristled with anticipation of the bout. Across the ring, Tommy finished buckling Henry's breastplate, darting back from the champion as though he had just untethered a ravenous beast.

A battle brewed in Natalie's heart. Some part of her, the part which adored the tourneys and longed to see the legendary fighters in action, could not bear to turn away. But her love for Brandon, her desire to see him safe, chipped away at her courage as the two men assumed their fighting stances. Her vision blurred as the blood drained from her face.

"Tourney rules," Brandon announced. "Only strikes to the breastplate count. Strikes to the face result in immediate disqualification."

Henry snickered. "It doesn't surprise me you'd be afraid of a real fight."

A flash of wildfire tore down Natalie's throat. Whether Henry had led the bandits to Blackmere or not, the fact remained that he had run from them whilst Brandon had returned to face forty bandits alone. She bit her tongue and forced the air from her nose.

Brandon did not rise to the taunt. He raised his sword,

and prepared to fight. Henry's laughter died down as he widened his stance, and met his opponent's eyes.

The first clash of steel sent piercing pain through Natalie's jaw. She was back in Blackmere, fearing for Brandon's life as he dueled the bandit leader. The blades were blunted, but when wielded with such force, could still cause lethal damage. The muscles in her legs tightened and trembled.

Brandon's breath was heavy, but his movements were drawn from a seemingly bottomless pool of strength. He blocked each of Henry's strikes, his eyes following every movement of his opponent. The clatter of metal drew the attention of the champions and squires practicing in the courtyard, and a crowd gathered around the ring.

Genevieve pushed her way through the spectators, her eyes wide. "The Bear and The Dragon?"

Natalie could only nod as she reminded herself to keep breathing. The galloping rhythm of her pulse did not slow as Genevieve's fingers cupped her shoulders.

The woman's breath fluttered against her ear. "He's doing well."

It was true.

Henry's face blazed scarlet, as rivulets of sweat poured from his forehead. The Dragon was fast, skilled, determined. Brandon was stronger. Against the sheer brute force of a man so large, Henry crumpled as though he was made of straw.

He staggered back, legs folding beneath him as he stumbled in the sand.

Natalie's heart emptied as Brandon's blade clanged

against Henry's breastplate. The gathered champions roared in celebration.

"Not bad," Brandon gasped, his broad smile creasing his eyes. "But you're going to have to do better than that."

Elation swooped through Natalie's chest as he reached down to help Henry to his feet.

Brandon the Bear was back.

But the world stopped turning as Henry thrust his blade upwards, and Brandon's blood spattered the courtyard.

NINETEEN

"Let me go!"

Genevieve's grasp faltered, and Natalie charged into the ring. Her feet sunk into the sand as though she was in a dream, and no matter how hard she ran, she could get no closer. Dropping to her hands and knees, she crawled across the ground. When she was close, she reached out, gripping Brandon's arm as he clutched at his eye.

"Brandon!" She gasped as blood pooled between his fingers, spattering his breastplate, a steady crimson drip on the shining steel. "Brandon?"

Henry still lay panting on the ground, his wide eyes darting between Brandon and the other champions. He pleaded to the crowd. "I thought he was thrusting towards me with his sword arm. I thought he was going to hit me."

She barely heard him over the pounding thunderous drums in her ears. "Brandon, please. Say something. Can you see?"

Brandon's lips pressed together in a thin line as he breathed slowly, in through his nose and out through his mouth. His cheeks paled as his balance wavered. "Healer," his voice was faint, little more than a shuddering whisper. "I need to... take me to the healer."

Tears burned Natalie's eyes as she helped him to his feet and walked with him back towards the keep. It was impossible to see the extent of the damage beneath so much blood. The murmurs of the crowd faded behind them. She glanced behind them, at the trail of blood droplets spotting the stones in their wake, at the concerned faces of the people who followed. Genevieve was not far behind them, flanked by Darius and Sara.

"Bear?" Genevieve called out as she jogged to his side. "Say the word, and I'll cut down him for you, Guild be damned."

"No."

Darius drew closer, his fingers curling around Brandon's bicep. "How bad is it?"

Natalie's chest tightened as they awaited his response.

"I don't know." Brandon's staggering breath brought fresh tears to her eyes. He was afraid. "I can't see."

She held his hand as they entered the keep, guiding him through the gloomy corridors, past the banquet hall, to a part of the castle Natalie had never visited. There were no decorations on the walls, no proud suits of shining armor, just bare stone walls and brilliant sunlight pouring through leaded windows.

"Almost there," Sara assured Brandon. She darted

ahead to push open the wooden door at the end of the corridor.

Natalie was pushed aside as the champions piled into the room. She craned her neck to try to see over their tall, broad bodies, but to no avail.

"Get the Guild Master," Sara instructed bluntly, as she pulled the door closed. "You don't need to be in here."

Natalie stared at the wooden door, her heart shattering as their chatter continued behind it. There was nothing more she could do to help, other than to deliver news. To them, she was a squire, and her relationship with Brandon was simply professional.

As she walked down the corridors, searching for the Guild Master, she cursed herself for not intervening. If Brandon had lost his sight, his position in the Champion's Guild was uncertain, and his income even more so. He could no longer compete. Fear snaked through her guts, and wound around her lungs, as she approached the chamber where Henry and Brandon's hearing had been held several months ago.

The Guild Master stood at a desk in the center of the chamber, bracing his weight on his hands as he peered down at a pile of parchments. His face was creased in concentration and his broad shoulders were buckled beneath the weight of his task.

"Yes?" He growled without ever looking up. He slammed a drawer shut, and secured it with a key, which he slipped into his pocket. "What is it?"

Natalie steadied her breath. Heat flashed across her face and her vision blurred.

He looked up. "My apologies, Lady Blackmere. How may I be of service?" His eyes dropped to her hands, to the blood staining them. Brandon's blood.

"What happened?" He stepped back from the desk, striding across the room towards her. "Who is it?"

"Brandon. He's—"

The Guild Master stormed past her, taking off down the corridor towards the infirmary.

Natalie could neither move nor speak. She stared down at her trembling hands, at the black crescents of blood beneath her fingernails, and silently, she wept.

CHAPTER

TWENTY

Natalie stared out towards the ocean. The sun dipped into the water, brilliance fading to ember red as evening drew in. There had been no word from the infirmary, and she had seen nothing of Henry since the incident.

Her body shook, her energy whittled down to shreds.

The sea breeze tightened the skin beneath the tracks of dried tears on her cheeks. A chill bristled across her spine as footsteps drew near. She dared not hope as she turned around.

"The Bear lives," Genevieve announced, raising her palms to the sky. She joined Natalie at her side and braced her hands on the top of the wall separating the courtyard from the precipice.

Natalie turned to face Genevieve. "And his sight?"

"The blade missed his eye," She drew a line down one eyebrow with her fingernail. "Once he was cleaned up, his sight returned."

Relief crashed over Natalie, and for the first time since that morning, she felt her shoulders relax. "Thank the Goddess."

"There was a lot of blood, but he'll be fine by tomorrow. Don't worry."

"I just want to see him, even just for a moment."

Genevieve placed her arm around Natalie's shoulders and pulled her close. The warmth of her body was soothing. "He knows you didn't leave by choice. You'll see him tomorrow and see that all is well. He's just lying in his bed, feeling sorry for himself."

Natalie rested her head on the woman's shoulder. "I don't know if I can sleep tonight. I just... I wish there were something I could do."

Genevieve checked over her shoulder. Though a few champions remained in the courtyard, they were distracted by their training. She sighed and tightened her grip around Natalie, speaking low beside her ear. "Before we came to Blackmere, The Bear was not doing well. He was losing badly in the tourneys, but he was also losing himself. He was sad, all the time."

Natalie looked down over the wall, at a sliver of sand barely visible between the sea and the cliffs. The first time she saw Brandon, he was sitting alone at the back of the tavern, staring into a cup of warm ale. For years she had dreamed of meeting the legendary Brandon the Bear, the warrior, proud and arrogant. A man who knew he could have any woman he fancied, a champion unlike any other. She had expected unmatched greatness, unrivaled strength, a man so handsome, so self-assured, she would be powerless to resist his charms.

But Brandon had not met her expectations. In fact, he had shattered through them, surpassing them in every way.

Genevieve gave a chuff of laughter. "I knew he liked you, the moment I saw you both together in the tavern."

"You did?"

"There was light in his eyes again, and a smile I hadn't seen for a long time."

Despite her anguish, Natalie felt herself melt and a smile broke through her concern and sadness. She brushed the hair back from her eyes as it whipped around, carried by the breeze.

She swallowed hard. "Many years ago, I had a husband." The words hung in the air before her. It was strange to say them aloud. "He died, not long after we married, but we'd been friends for many years. I mourned my friend, for a long time. Today, I felt that same grief clawing at me again. When I saw Henry thrust his blade, I was afraid I'd lost the person I love more than any other. I should have brought his helmet."

"Did he ask for it?"

Natalie shrugged a little under the weight of Genevieve's arm. "No, but—"

"Then he wouldn't have worn it. I've known the Bear for many years. He's a stubborn ass when he wants to be." Genevieve grinned. "He's reckless and foolish, but you know that. I love the man dearly, but he was not blessed with subtlety or self-preservation. He's the type of man who'll run into a bandit infested castle alone to prove his love. And he's the type of man who'll show a bandit his middle finger, and have it severed for his trouble."

A soft laugh erupted from Natalie's lips. "You have a point."

"But he's a good man, and I'm glad he's happy. And I'm glad you're happy too." Genevieve stepped back, leaving Natalie to her thoughts.

"I am." Natalie nodded and watched the sun sink into the water. The sky and sea bruised pink and purple.

The gentle whoosh of fire igniting caught Natalie's attention. Genevieve lit torches around the melee ring. The orange glow cast long, black shadows across the courtyard.

"Come on then." Genevieve smiled as she unsheathed her blade. "If you've no intention of sleeping, then you can help me train."

TWENTY-ONE

Natalie's shoulders throbbed as she tiptoed through the torchlit corridor towards her room. Training with Genevieve had kept her distracted, even if just for a few minutes at a time. The Thorn of the Rose was a stricter teacher than Brandon, drilling Natalie until she barely had the strength to stand. Yet as she drew closer to her room, pride swelled in her chest. Whilst she was nowhere near the standard of the champions, she was not half as bad of a swordswoman as she had feared. She had come close, agonizingly close, to beating Genevieve in one round.

She brushed her fingertips against the pommel of the blade at her hip, grinning at the aftershock of the elation. For a moment she allowed herself to believe she could hold her own in the arena, hear the cheers of the crowd, and feel even a glimmer of what it meant to be a champion.

As she turned a corner, a figure sat huddled against the door of her room. Tommy snored softly, clutching a sheet of parchment to his chest. By his side was a raggedy speckled quill and a small, brown glass pot of ink.

Guilt struck Natalie's heart as she crouched beside him. She reached out and squeezed his shoulder. "Tommy?"

He stirred, blinking his bleary eyes and wiping his lips on his sleeve. "Lady Blackmere." He straightened his back and checked around him to ensure his precious writing equipment was still nearby. "I'm sorry. I fell asleep."

She helped him to his feet and pushed open the door. "No, I'm the one who should be sorry. I'd completely forgotten."

Shadows flickered and stretched against the walls as she lit a candle.

Tommy hovered outside the door, as she tossed the blade onto the bed and pulled a spare chair over to her desk. She sat on a small wooden stool and patted the seat beside her.

"Are you sure?" The parchment crunched against his chest and he held it tight. "I can come back next month if it's a bother?"

"I'm sure."

He perched on the stool by her side and set the parchment on the desk. "How is he?"

"Viv tells me he's well. The blade didn't touch his eye." She dipped the tip of the quill into the pot, scraping it along the bottom to find enough ink. Her eyes fell to the dark patch of crimson on Tommy's cheekbone. "Does it hurt?"

"I'm fine." He sniffed and scratched the end of his nose with a trembling finger. "So, I've already practiced what I'm going to say."

He stared at the paper, lacing his fingers together on his lap. He did not want to talk about it. Natalie released a breath and prepared to write.

The letter did not take long. She addressed it to the lady of Finchburrow, with a note requesting that she read it to Tommy's mother at the address he gave her. The lad watched the tip of the quill intently, his brows creased as she wrote.

When she was finished and the ink dried, she read it back to him, following each word with the tip of her finger. "Dear mum. I am well and hope you are too. I am happy at the Guild, training hard to become a champion. I am squire to Henry Percille. In two months' time, I will be in Westgarden for the Midsummer Melee and will compete in the squires' contest. I will make you proud. With love, your Tommy."

"It's good." He smiled. "Thank you."

Her eyes were raw as she smiled back at him. "It was my pleasure, and if you ever need another let me know."

"You're too kind, Lady Blackmere."

He stood and bowed, taking the letter from her with a grateful smile.

"And Tommy, if you need anything else you can come to me, or Brandon or Viv."

She hoped he understood, but he left the room without further comment.

Natalie crawled into bed, falling asleep the moment her head touched the pillow. That night in her dreams it was Brandon, not Robert who was skewered by the bandit's crossbow bolt. The tip pierced his eye as Henry roared from the balcony above, fire curling around them, consuming the tavern.

She awoke drenched, the linen of her shirt dark and wet, and, to her horror she realized, still spattered with Brandon's blood. Panting as the dream subsided, she realized it was morning. Her limbs still ached as she rolled from her bed, washed in a basin, dressed and tore from her room still chewing a root to clean her teeth. The banquet hall was already full, but the banter at the champions' table was unusually quiet, and Brandon was not there. Neither was Genevieve.

Natalie's stomach flopped uneasily as she sat at her usual seat at the end of the squires' table. Fears that Brandon's injury had somehow worsened in the night plagued her. Despite the growling of her stomach, she could barely eat her breakfast as she waited for the toll of the bell.

Her heart darted as someone spoke at her side. "Excuse me?" A girl, no more than fifteen years of age, stood close to her seat, clutching a scroll in her hands. It was tied with a frayed length of twine. "You read letters?"

At the far end of the table, Tommy's cheeks blazed scarlet. Whatever was on his plate was surely of great interest, as he refused to look up from it.

Natalie smiled. "I can."

The girl gingerly handed her the scroll. "I got it last year, in the winter. I tried asking some of the champions, but they told me to clear off."

As she unfurled the letter, Natalie frowned. "Who'd you ask?"

The girl's eyes flickered towards the champions' table,

to where Henry sat alone. The very sight of him roiled Natalie. She read through the letter quickly to put the girl out of her misery. Her heart sunk as she read the ill tidings. "You're Jocelyn?"

The girl nodded. "Joss."

"I'm so sorry, Joss. Your aunt passed a year ago."

The girl nodded slowly. Her dark brown eyes shone with silvery light. "At least she's not hurting anymore. Thank you."

Natalie returned the letter and watched as the girl sat back among her friends. The bell tolled, its dour clang cutting through the gentle hum of conversation and sending a jolt of panic through Natalie's chest. Brandon had not come to breakfast.

She stood and made her way to the courtyard alone, trying to ignore the sideways glances and whispers from the other squires.

TWENTY-TWO

Finding a familiar face, even one who looked at her with disinterest, gave some comfort. Natalie welcomed the sight of Darius training over by the wall.

He was shirtless, his muscles straining as he heaved on a rope connected to a pulley, hauling a net of heavy stones up the sheer cliff face. The long cords of his hair swung behind his back as he worked. She approached him slowly.

"Yes?" He panted, keeping his eyes ahead. "I'm in the middle of something."

"How is he?"

"Who?"

Natalie took a deep breath. She was used to the aloof coldness of the other champions by now, but she had little energy to entertain it. "Brandon."

The muscles in his shoulders slumped as he sighed. Darius secured the pulley and turned to take a drink of water. His chest rose and fell as he waited for his breathing to return to normal and stared at Natalie in stoic silence.

"Very well." Natalie nodded slowly and turned away from him. "I'm sorry to have bothered you."

"He's on the steps, training with Viv."

His answer settled against her back like a comforting blanket. If Brandon was training, then he was well. She turned back to Darius and bowed. "Thank you."

He gestured to the unoccupied pulley beside his. "You need to work on your strength if you want to wield a sword well."

"You want me to train with you?"

He shrugged a muscular shoulder. "Brandon and Viv seem to like you. I trust their judgement."

She walked to the unused pulley, took the rope in her hands and tugged, one arm, then the other, over and over. Within moments sweat prickled on her forehead. Her palms burned with every hard-fought pull.

"Keep it up," Darius grinned. He resumed his training, working a little faster than Natalie. "My squire, Joss, tells me you read her letter this morning."

Memories of delivering the bad tidings clawed at her chest as she fought for her breath. She should have taken more time, delivered the contents of the letter a little more delicately. "I didn't realize she was your squire. I'm sorry it wasn't better news."

"The nature of the message can't be helped. But I know she appreciated receiving it." A faint smile danced across his lips and faded just as quickly, replaced by a strained grunt as he yanked the pulley.

Natalie's muscles burned as she forced out her words between gasps. "I'm... happy to help. The Guild Master... said that... few here ...know... how... to read...or write."

"Well we didn't all grow up with servants and tutors." Darius smirked scornfully. He grimaced and cast a dour look towards the keep. His expression hardened. "Some champions were taught, the ones from better families. Henry can read his own letters well enough, but forgets his teaching when asked to help others."

She pressed her lips together, then moistened them with her tongue, reminding herself that as far as she could tell, Darius was at least companionable with Henry. She would have to tread carefully. "That... hardly... surprises... me."

The champion wiped his gleaming brow on his forearm and nodded towards her pulley. "Just keep at it. Talking makes it harder."

As they worked, synchronized and silent, Natalie bared her teeth against the deep ache in her arms. When she could bear it no longer, she tied off the pulley and shook out the pain, stretching her arms out in front of her.

Darius chuckled. "I'm impressed you lasted that long."

"That was dreadful."

"If you do this every day, you'll have the strength to wield a blade in no time." Something to his side caught his attention. "Ah! There's my Sweet Cycloptic Bear!"

Natalie's heart leapt as she turned. Brandon stood at the top of the steps beside Genevieve. The sleeves of his tunic were cut short, and the muscles in his arms were burnished from his exercise, glistening with perspiration. It was as though every day he added stones to the mountain of his strength. She held herself in check as she walked towards him, even as a voice at the back of her mind screamed at her to run into his arms.

Fighting the urge with every step, she approached slowly, holding back a smile.

"My lady," Brandon greeted her, his gaze raking across her. His left eyebrow was split into two by an angry red gash, and the skin around the wound was bruised dark purple. He raised his hand and gestured to it, giving a one-shouldered shrug. "I've been in worse states."

"Once a reckless fool, always a reckless fool," Genevieve muttered.

Natalie blinked back stinging tears. "I was so afraid." She took a deep breath to calm the trembling of her lips. "I thought I'd lost you."

He lowered his head and took a step towards her. "Never."

The moment dissipated as Genevieve cleared her throat and said loudly, "Good morning Guild Master."

Natalie's back stiffened as their leader approached from the keep. His face was etched with concern, his mouth downturned as he drew close to Brandon and inspected the wound above his eye. "You're a bloody halfwit. You were so close to losing it."

"Aye." Brandon's lips quirked at his own pun.

The Guild Master did not share his amusement. "If you practice armed combat without a helmet again, you're out of the Melee, understand? I'm not having my champions blinded because of some cock-waving contest."

The smile slid from Brandon's lips. "Yes sir."

"Good." The Guild Master cast him a last disapproving glance. "Now, I've spoken with Henry at length about what happened between you two, and he insists it was an accident."

Natalie scoffed.

"An accident?" Genevieve snapped. She took a moment to compose herself. "The fight had ended, and Henry stabbed Brandon in the eye. How is that an accident?"

The Guild Master exhaled through his nose and tightened his jaw. He looked so weary, like a parent exhausted from his children's squabbles.

Beside her, Brandon shook his head. "Aye. It was an accident. Heat of the moment."

The Guild Master nodded, relief slackening his stance. "From what I hear, you bested Henry. Was it a decent bout?" He looked to Genevieve for her opinion.

"I could barely contain myself," Genevieve said flatly.

Brandon stifled a grin.

The Guild Master nodded. "Well, I don't know what's given you this second wind, or whether it'll last." He took a step towards Brandon and lowered his voice. "The crowds love an underdog but remember what we talked about last night. The alternative would be an incredible opportunity for you." He stared into Brandon's eyes for a moment. "I want it to be you."

Brandon nodded and bowed his head. "I'll consider it."

Satisfied, the Guild Master brought his hands together in a single, sharp clap. "Less than two months to go until you ride out for Westgarden, we'll see how this plays out."

"Aye sir," Brandon bowed his head.

"And Lady Blackmere," The Guild Master turned to her and gripped her shoulder. "Make sure he has his helmet, next time."

"Yes sir." She bowed.

"Very good. Back to training."

"Sir?" Natalie's heart began to race as a question burned on the tip of her tongue. The Guild Master looked at her expectantly. "I've been thinking about what you told me, about the squires and champions being unable to read letters."

The Guild Master's lips thinned. He glanced towards Brandon and Genevieve. "Yes?"

"I'd like to do it for them, with your blessing. When the messenger comes at the end of the month, I can read their letters to them and help them reply."

A muscle in the Guild Master's cheek leapt as he looked at her. His hesitancy heightened her suspicions. The less communication the champions had with their loved ones, the more they would cling to the Guild, and the fiercer their loyalty.

He raised his chin and his nostrils flared. "I doubt it's a service many will want to use, but if you do this on your own time, then who am I to deny the Lady of Blackmere?"

Relief crashed around her. "Thank you, sir." She released a heavy breath as he left. When she was certain the Guild Master was gone, she turned to Brandon.

He was smiling, the corners of his eyes creased. Slowly, he raised a hand, as though he wanted to reach out towards her, to touch her. He thought better of it, curling his fingers and dropping it to his side. "I'm sure many will appreciate it."

"It's the least I can do." She released a nervous breath. "What did he mean when he said he spoke to you? About the opportunity."

Genevieve shifted her weight between her feet and raised her eyebrows. Brandon kept his eyes on the ground. At last he answered, "He was just suggesting I retire from fighting, after the accident."

Natalie frowned. "You truly believe it was an accident?"

"No," he said. "But I doubt the Guild Master will banish one of his highest earners, even if he believed it. He'd find some reason to forgive Henry."

Genevieve rolled her eyes. "You're right. I hate it, but you are."

"So, what are you going to do?" Natalie asked.

"I'm going to face Henry in Westgarden." Brandon's voice was low and deep, like rolling thunder on the horizon. "There's a reason he hasn't told the Guild about Nat and I. He's letting me get my hopes up, and he's certain he can humiliate me in Westgarden. I'll fight him, and I'll fight harder than I've ever fought before. I want to beat him fairly, and publicly. Losing to me will wound him far deeper than anything."

Natalie's heart beat faster. "But you beat him yesterday and look what happened. What's to stop him from hurting you again?"

"In public? I don't think he'd tarnish his reputation. He believes he could easily win the Grand Tourney this year and I doubt he'd risk losing the chance."

"Did you think he'd have our friends murdered too, Bear? I don't know that I would put anything past him." Genevieve shrugged her reluctant agreement. "But you lost more than any of us at Blackmere. However you see fit to defeat Henry, I'll support it."

Natalie's heart thundered as he turned to her. She nodded. "If you think this is the right thing to do."

"Aye. I do. The fall will be much harder the higher he thinks he's climbed. And between now and Midsummer, I plan to train hard, Guild Master's opportunities be damned." Brandon pressed his lips together and drew a shaking breath.

A sense of unease crept up on Natalie, but she assured herself that Brandon knew what he was doing. He was more experienced with fighting and competitions than anyone else, save for the Guild Master himself.

"I'm with you," she said, forcing a smile. "No matter what."

"Thank you." He gestured towards the stairs. "My lady, would you care to walk with me?"

"Again? You just got back?" Even as she spoke, she began walking towards the stair. She needed to be alone with him, if only for a minute. "If you keep running up and down these steps, you'll be willow-thin by Midsummer."

The bark of his laughter sounded at her back. "It'll take more than a few steps, I assure you."

CHAPTER

TWENTY-THREE

Their feet skipped on the steps as they hurried down. Months of practice had lessened the challenge, and eroded Natalie's fears. It did not, however, dampen their passion as Brandon lifted her from the bottom step and carried her across the sand to their hiding place.

"Only one set of footprints," he grinned in answer to Natalie's questioning look.

"You continue to surprise me, Sir Brandon."

They ducked behind the limpet covered rocks, their frantic hands grasping at each other as their lips met.

Tears pricked Natalie's eyes as she touched her fingers to the swollen bruise above his eye. "I was so afraid."

"I scared myself," he whispered against her mouth. "I thought for a moment I'd never see your face again." He pushed her hair back, raking his fingers through the silken strands of copper and sucking her lower lip between his.

He stifled her moan with a kiss and pressed his body

against hers. The weight of him against her ignited the heat at the junction of her thighs. His kisses left her breathless, and always desperate for more. She wrapped her fingers around the back of his head, holding him to her, tugging his lips with her teeth.

He trailed kisses down her neck, sending sparks of pleasure through her body. They had never pushed their luck further than frantic kisses, always fearful of being followed. She pressed her lips to his ear. "I want you. I can't stand it anymore."

A growl vibrated from his chest to hers as he pushed her harder against the rocks. His hands stroked her waist, curving up and around to caress her breasts through the wool of her tunic.

Her body shivered at the thrill of his touch, the intensity of his hold. She needed him, needed his skin against hers, the heat of his strong and beautiful body. Raking her nails across the mass of his biceps, she trailed kisses along his neck.

His erection pressed hard against her belly. "I want you too."

A deeper, more desperate growl rolled through his chest as his hands dropped to the lace of his breeches. He pulled them down enough to allow his cock to bounce free.

She quivered with excitement as she tugged down her own trousers and stepped out of one of the legs. Her heart pounded in her throat as he craned his neck around the boulder to ensure they had time. She ran her fingers along the length of his thigh as his muscles twitched beneath her touch.

Satisfied they were alone he hooked his hands beneath the cheeks of her backside and pressed her up against the rocks. His bicep strained as he lifted her left leg to his hip and, with his other hand, ran his fingers through her folds, sinking his teeth into his lower lip, his broken breaths sighing his approval.

"Brandon..." she gasped. "Do we have time? For me..."

"If there's time for me, there's time for you." His breath blew hot against her ear. "I'll never leave you unsatisfied."

Natalie arched her back, aching for him. For a man capable of such blunt, brutal force, he was careful with her, firm yet tender, and always attentive. Her pleasure was paramount to him.

When her need for him grew too strong, she reached out and gripped the firm, round cheeks of his backside and pulled him towards her. The pressure of him against her opening almost drew a cry from her. She stifled her whimpers against his shoulder as his fingers circled her clitoris.

"Are you near?" He whispered.

She could only nod as she sank her teeth into his shoulder to stifle a cry.

His breath hitched as he entered her, and for a moment he paused, shuddering, his eyes closed, and lips parted as he bathed in the sensation of her.

Natalie gasped as he rolled his hips, long, languid strokes, as though they had all the time in the world. The motion sent a shiver through her body, tightening her nipples beneath the layer of wool. "Hurry," she gasped.

He leaned forward, tightening his hold on her thigh as he began to thrust. He pumped his hips in short, sharp movements as his fingers continued to coax pleasure from her.

Her climax built quickly against the relentless bounce of his hips. She grasped at his biceps, feeling the thick ropes of his muscles strain as he held her.

"I love you," he gasped before pressing his lips together to stifle a growl. The tendons in his neck strained as his blush crept across his throat and his cheeks flushed pink. "I won't let anything take you from me."

Natalie's muscles clenched, tensing around his length as she climaxed. Her mouth hung open in a silent cry as waves of pleasure broke across her. He was only a few thrusts behind, coming undone with his face buried against her neck as he moaned. His knees buckled, and he slid from her, spilling onto the sand.

She stood on her tiptoes and kissed the creases between his eyebrows. "I love you too."

They held each other, breathing together as their pleasure ebbed, and the reality of the pressing danger dawned on them.

The soft patter of leather-clad footsteps froze the blood in her veins. Brandon tucked his cock back into his breeches and peered around the boulder as Natalie dressed. Without a word he slipped around the rocks and took a few bounding strides towards the steps.

"My Sweet Bear!" Darius's voice cried from beyond the boulders, sending a jolt of fear through Natalie's heart. "By the Goddess, I thought you were in trouble."

"Just taking a breather before climbing back up."

Brandon chuckled, his voice fading as he led the other man away from their hiding spot.

Natalie waited, her back pinned against the stone. She held her breath as the men talked, their conversation muffled by the roar of the ocean. They had been mere seconds from discovery. The fear coiled in her belly, but it excited her just as much.

The men's voices faded.

Natalie remained on the beach, ensuring there was enough distance between them before she followed their footsteps back towards the steps, and began her lonely climb.

She could smell him in the fibers of her tunic, still feel the pinch of his fingers against the soft flesh of her thigh. Pressing her teeth into her lower lip, she climbed on shaking legs, back to the courtyard, basking in the glow of their secret passion.

CHAPTER

TWENTY-FOUR

Genevieve's blade tapped Natalie's breastplate, sending a spike of disappointment through her heart. It was the latest defeat in a long run of humiliating losses. Natalie cursed at the sky, gasping for air and shaking out her aching limbs. Her body ached from weeks of strength training with Darius, sparring with Genevieve, and climbing the steps with Brandon.

"You're too tense." Genevieve circled her, balancing the pommel of her blade on the palm of her hand and balancing the sword upright. "Perhaps some ale would help?"

"How can I not be tense?" Natalie sighed. She pulled off her helmet and wiped her brow on her sleeve. "The contest is in two weeks, and I'm terrible."

"You're not terrible," Genevieve dismissed her by bouncing the blade into the air and snatching it mid-fall.

Brandon chuckled from the side of the ring. He leaned forward, bracing his weight on the fence. Natalie's chest hollowed at the sight of him. It was difficult to remain focused when he watched, especially when the sleeves of his tunic were rolled up to his elbows, displaying the corded muscles of his forearms. The wound across his eyebrow had mostly healed, leaving a faded cerise scar. If anything, it made him even more handsome.

Natalie worked her dry throat and tried to focus. She pushed her helmet back on her head. It had been over a week since they had been able to spend any time together, and even then, they had only managed a few stolen kisses on the beach before they heard the clatter of armored foot-steps on the stairs. The intensity of the champions' training had more than doubled as the Midsummer Melee loomed before them. She fancied the intensity of her desire had more than tripled and her confidence in her ability to wield a blade had shrunk tenfold.

Taking a deep breath, she shifted her feet into her fighting stance and awaited Genevieve's blow.

"Are you sure? You don't want to rest first?"

Natalie shook her head. "I'll rest after midsummer."

She kept her eyes ahead, refusing to look at Brandon, at his strong arms, the patch of hair just barely visible at the top of the collar of his tunic.

Her blade clashed with Genevieve's, once, twice, before the tap on her breastplate brought an end to the bout. Natalie's loud curse echoed around the courtyard. She placed her hands on her hips and sighed. "I can't do this."

"Take a break," Brandon suggested. "You never perform well when you're frustrated."

"The Bear's right," Genevieve shrugged. "You're sloppy. You're thinking more about past defeats than what's happening now. Rest up." She took a step towards Natalie and lowered her head. "And your thoughts are over there, with him anyway."

Defeated, Natalie nodded. She sheathed her sword and left the ring. Before she had even passed through the gate, Genevieve began slashing at a straw dummy, striking with the elegance and power of a viper.

She let her shoulder press against his arm as she watched Genevieve. The desire to be near him, to touch him, was constant.

"I'll never be that good," she said softly.

"She's a champion, and she's trained for years." Brandon looked down at her and smiled. "Besides, you're not competing against Viv. As long as you relax, I think you have a good chance against the other squires."

"You truly think so?"

"Aye, you've seen real combat. You've fought without armor against people who weren't just scoring points. Not many here can say that."

She smiled at his reassurance and felt the heat creep across her chest. "Well perhaps before the contest we can sneak away, and you can help relieve my tension?"

He inhaled sharply, looking out towards the horizon as his cheeks flushed. "If you think it'll help..."

Natalie bit down a grin. Copper gleamed in the sun as he rubbed the coin between his thumb and forefinger.

A commotion by the gate caught their attention. Squires and champions gathered, some of them jeering, but others stood in solemn silence. In the center of them, the Guild Master stood, speaking to a pair of squires in the center.

Natalie held her hair to the top of her head, cooling the back of her neck as she squinted across the courtyard. "What's happening?"

Brandon cleared his throat and sighed deeply. "There were two squires, caught in the back room of the armory."

"Caught?" The meaning of his words settled on her as she watched. "Oh."

The Guild Master turned the squires away, ignoring their pleas as he ushered them from the gate. The other squires herded behind him.

A disapproving growl sounded at the back of Brandon's throat. "Poor sods."

"What'll happen to them?"

"They're banished from the Guild." Brandon sighed. "If they're lucky, they might go back to their families, but not many have that option."

Guilt clawed at Natalie. She and Brandon risked the same punishment, every time they snuck down to the beach. If they were discovered, they would be banished and disgraced, and Brandon would lose everything.

"I won't let anything happen to us," Brandon whispered. His eyes raked across her face, down to the brooch on her chest. A gentle smile broke through her fear. "You've worn your feather every day since we arrived."

"I have." She looked down at it. Though she had tried many times to straighten it out after Henry had crumpled it, it was still bedraggled.

"I never did find you a new one, did I?"

"I'm rather fond of this one. Besides, if the feather can

survive being crumpled and dropped into porridge, then we can survive this year."

"And every year after," he said softly. "No matter what stands between us."

His words hung in the air between them. In six months, Natalie would have to return to Blackmere and resume her responsibilities as a noble. They had not discussed what would happen then. It was a quandary without an ideal solution.

Many times, as she lay in bed alone, she rehearsed asking Brandon if he would consider becoming the Lord of Blackmere, but the Guild was his life. His love for the other champions, the young squires who looked up to him, the rush of adrenaline which came from competing, left the question locked inside her. To ask him to abandon everything he had worked so hard for in favor of a life he knew nothing of, after only knowing her for a few months, seemed absurd.

Brandon had not mentioned anything more about the possibility of retirement, and she had not pressed the issue. His renewed strength made it seem unlikely. People dear to him depended on his salary, after all, and winning competitions would only ease their financial issues. Still, every month she hoped that he would receive a letter, telling him his mother was well, and had no more need for healers or medicine.

She leaned closer to him, hoping he took as much comfort from her closeness as she did from his. "We'll weather the storm."

Genevieve thrust her blade into the dummy's chest. "At least you're together now."

"You'll see Jenny again," Brandon said.

The champion scoffed as she pulled out her blade and prepared for another strike. "It's a lost cause. How long was it before we came to Blackmere? How many other towns will host the Tourney before we return?"

Natalie smiled. "And I'll ensure she's able to go to them."

Genevieve paused, staring at the ground. "You will?"

Natalie nodded. "I swear it."

A clatter of hooves interrupted Genevieve's grateful smile. A messenger, clad in crimson, rode through the gate towards the keep, as the Guild Master walked by his side. Most of the champions in the courtyard remained engrossed in their training, but a small crowd of hopeful squires and champions followed.

They gathered on the steps to the keep, eagerly waiting as the Guild Master called out their names. The squires grasped their letters and huddled together. They cast glances towards Natalie, whispering among themselves.

"I think your services are needed, my lady." Brandon nudged her with his shoulder.

"Aye," she sighed with a smile. "I'll see you later."

Wrenching herself from his side, she approached the gathering. Their excitement was palpable. A month ago, only a handful of squires had approached her with the request for letters, but now their number had swelled. From the looks of things, she was in for a long night of cramping hands and ink-stained fingers. She bit back a smile.

Tommy was among the squires, beaming at a letter fastened with the Finchburrow seal. His cheeks dimpled with joy. "I think she wrote back."

"That's wonderful," Natalie beamed as the squires gathered around her, jostling to have their letters read first.

"Genevieve?" The Guild Master called, holding the corner of a letter between his thumb and forefinger.

Natalie stepped back to allow Genevieve through the crowd. She took the letter and glanced towards Natalie, her eyes wide and searching for answers. The letter was sealed with a ram's head.

"News from Blackmere?" The Guild Master cocked an eyebrow.

"Must be." Genevieve did not blink as she walked away, tucking the letter beneath her jacket with a steady hand.

The Guild Master turned to the messenger and clapped him on the shoulder. "Will you stay the night?"

The messenger's shoulders relaxed as he patted his horse's neck. "Aye, it would be a welcome rest sir."

"Very good. In that case, squires and champions, you have until morning if there is anything you wish to send out." The Guild Master cast a sideways glance at Natalie. "Carry on."

Inside the castle, Natalie navigated the keep's corridors back to her room, a line of chattering squires and champions following her. Her cheeks ached from the size of her grin.

"Read mine first," Genevieve insisted as she followed at Natalie's heels. "Months with no word, and now this. Perhaps something's wrong? It could include news from your mother. Perhaps—"

"Stop worrying." Natalie chuckled as she opened the door to her room. She jerked her head towards the desk, which now had two chairs permanently set before it. A pile of parchment, and a full pot of ink awaited her. "Take a seat."

Genevieve strode inside and perched nervously on one of the chairs.

Turning her back to hide her amusement, Natalie inched the door closed behind them. "Form a line," she instructed the people waiting anxiously outside as she unbuckled the straps on the side of her breastplate. "I'll call you in one by one."

She closed the door, and turned towards Genevieve, barely able to contain her smile.

TWENTY-FIVE

Natalie pressed her fingers against her lips as she peered down at the letter on her desk. Her parted lips formed silent words as she read the sentences over again. Seeing Jenny's handwriting, stamped with Blackmere's sigil, brought a sense of longing. Her mind tangled the apprehension of returning to her duties, with the dull ache of homesickness.

Genevieve paced back and forth across the room, her fingers laced together on the top of her head. "Do you think she means it?"

"I think so. Why would she write if she didn't?"

"Read it again."

Natalie moistened her lips and read. "*Viv, I've thought about you every day since you left. Though I know it is only a distant dream, I find myself hoping that you will return to Blackmere one day. Back to me. You are in my dreams, always. Jenny.*"

"Do you think it's code? Maybe something's wrong."

A chuff of laughter burst from Natalie. "Code for what?"

Genevieve buried her face in her hands and sighed.

"You're blushing." Natalie bit her lip. Sympathetic butterflies cavorted in her own stomach as she awaited Genevieve's verdict. "What are you going to do?"

"I've been asking myself the same thing for almost six months. Do I leave my life as a champion behind on the off chance that this is love? We were only together for a short time, and even then... we took things slowly, one day at a time."

Natalie stood and took Genevieve's hands in her own. The warrior's palms were rough and calloused beneath her soft fingertips. "Do you want to reply to her?"

Genevieve blinked slowly and took a deep breath. "Not yet. I need time to think about what I should say. Perhaps next month."

"Just let me know. I'm more than willing to help."

Genevieve bowed her head in thanks. When she spoke next, it was barely louder than a whisper. "If I followed my heart, I would run from the Guild now, but this is my home, my life. These people are my family." She dropped her hands to her sides and gathered the letter from the desk. "You and Brandon give me hope... that your love is worth his sacrifices." She reached the door, brushing her fingertips against the handle. The muscles in her back tensed and relaxed as she drew a breath. "At least, I hope it is."

Natalie's breath caught in her throat as the warrior left the room, leaving her to her thoughts. Genevieve's words lingered in her mind for the rest of the evening. The question of the nature of Brandon's sacrifice hovered above her as she worked her way through the letters.

She found comfort in the smiles and excitement of the squires and champions as they heard their loved ones' voices again. Some of the champions' letters made her blush; expressions of desire from lords and ladies who craved the opportunity to share their beds with Aldland's elite warriors.

By nightfall, Natalie's hands were cramped from hours of writing, and her ink-stained fingers bore the indent of the quill. As light failed entirely, and the last of the squires left, she glanced at the stack of letters on the corner of her desk and smiled, exhausted and satisfied that she had given them even a shred of comfort.

She slumped against the backrest of her chair and tried to flex the life back into her fingers. Her stomach growled, but dinnertime had long since passed.

A gentle knock at the door, brought a weary smile to her lips. Word of her services was still spreading around the keep, and many of the letters she had been brought were months old. Reading and replying to them all was turning out to be a monumental, if rewarding task.

"One moment please," she called, taking a moment to rest her eyes. She could manage one more, if she could only stay awake.

"My lady?" The voice on the other side of the door sent her pulse racing.

Weariness forgotten, she leapt to her feet, bolted across the room and pulled open her door. Brandon stood, leaning against the stone wall. His eyes raked across her figure, stealing her breath. For six months she had dreamed of him coming to her room. Her stomach fluttered in anticipation.

"I have special permission from the Guild Master to come here." The corner of his mouth lifted into a smile. "He wants to speak with me afterwards, so I can't stay long. I came to ask, if you have time...would you please write me a letter?"

"Of course." She smiled and stepped aside to allow him to pass.

"Thank you, my lady." He stooped below the doorway, his eyes scanning the bare walls, the blade proudly displayed on the window ledge, boots caked in dried, flaking sand.

Natalie sat down at the desk and offered him the second chair. "Who are you writing to?"

The chair creaked beneath him as he sat. He took her hand in his, stroking her knuckles with his thumb. "My parents."

"Oh?" She smiled basking in his gentle touch.

His eyes lingered on hers, near black in the candlelight, before drifting down to her mouth. Her breath snagged in her chest as he leaned forward. The air thickened as he inched towards her, until his beard tickled her cheeks, and at last his lips met hers.

She was lost in the sensation of him as he wrapped his arms around her, pulling her against his chest. His kiss made her dizzy, sending fire flowing through her veins. She craved the body beneath her fingertips, the softness and strength of him. When he broke away, her eyes remained closed, as she sat enjoying the aftershocks of pleasure.

"I've wanted to do that all day." His voice was low and thick with desire.

"Then you must be able to read my mind," she grinned. "Because I wanted it too."

He chuckled and straightened in his seat. "I wish we had longer."

"As do I." She took the quill from the ink and scraped the nib across the lip of the pot, draining the excess. "But, more importantly, your letter. How would you like to begin?"

He pressed his lips together and exhaled slowly before he spoke. "To Sybil and Bennet of Marshdown."

Natalie's quill hovered above the paper as she knitted her brow. "You call them by their names?"

"No, but a letter feels like it should be formal."

"Not this letter," she smiled. "Let them hear your voice. What do you call them?"

He frowned and sat forward on the chair. "Ma and Papa?"

"Better." Warmth pooled in Natalie's heart as her pen scratched against the parchment. She wrote in large, clear letters, to give their reader a better chance of understanding. "Go on."

Brandon took a long breath and clasped his hands together, pinning them between his knees. "It's been too long since I saw you. I miss you." He paused to allow her to catch up. "I hope you're both well, and happy."

Natalie's heart skipped as he leaned forward and brushed his lips at the skin below her ear. She smiled as she scolded him. "You're distracting me."

"Well, you're distracting me too, so it's only fair."

She gently swatted him away. "I'm simply sitting here, Sir."

"And it's distracting." He chuckled, but waited until her pen stilled before continuing to dictate. His throat bobbed as he swallowed. "Perhaps you have heard that I haven't been doing so well in the Tourneys of late. Please don't fret. I will keep sending money for the healer, and I will always send it, no matter what."

Natalie pressed her lips together as she wrote. His sudden vulnerability gave her pause. "Brandon..."

"The truth is," he continued. His voice dropped lower, barely a whisper as his eyes turned glossy. "I've never been as happy as I am now. Some days I'm so happy I can't contain it. My heart feels like it's bursting."

Her blush deepened, tightening her cheeks. The touch of his hand on her arm drew her attention away from the parchment.

"I can't tell them why," he muttered. His eyes were downcast. "I don't want them to worry about money or medicine."

"I understand." She offered him a smile, but it sat weakly on her lips, unable to convince the rest of her face.

"I want to tell them. I want to tell them that their son is in love. That he feels giddy and reckless and luckier than any man has any right to be."

She glanced at the closed door, her ears straining to confirm the silence beyond it. She leaned towards him and stole another kiss. Her heart cartwheeled at the brief touch of his lips.

When she broke away, the candlelight shone gold in the pools forming in his eyes. "I wish I could tell them about you."

She tried to swallow the lump forming in her throat. "I'm sure they'll be overjoyed just to hear you're happy."

He nodded slowly and wiped his eyes with the cuff of his sleeve. "Perhaps one day we could go up there, to Marshdown. They'd adore you, whether I introduce you as my friend or my love."

"I'd like that." Natalie reached over and placed her ink-stained, aching hand over his. "I promise we'll go, as soon as we're able."

He brightened a little at her words, and his eyes turned back to the parchment on her desk. His eyes scanned back and forth, following the lines of the letter. "What was the last thing you wrote?"

Natalie turned back to the page. She fought back a smile as she read aloud. "Some days I'm so happy I can't express it. My heart feels like it's bursting."

"Ah, yes." He sat forwards again, as though he had to speak directly to the page. "I hope to be able to come and visit you soon. Big Lad is doing well. He sends his love."

Natalie chuckled as she wrote. "That's good."

"I send mine too. Your boy, Bran."

"Bran?"

"Aye."

She beamed as she finished off the letter and set her quill on the desk. "I'll have it sent in the morning, with a note to the Lord of Marshdown asking him to read it for them."

"Thank you." He pulled himself up onto stiff legs, groaning and stretching out his back. "How many do you have now?"

She ran her hands across the pile of folded parchment on the desk, each one sealed with wax. "Some thirty, I'd say."

"I'm surprised so many of them had the money to send letters."

"They don't. The messenger will send me a bill."

He bowed down and pressed a brief kiss to the top of her head. "You're wonderful." He ran his hands through her hair, pushing it back over her shoulders. "This means a lot to so many of them. It's hard for the younger ones to be away from their families."

"It's the least I can do."

His next kiss found her lips. Her soft moan of pleasure was echoed by his own as his thumb caressed her jaw.

"Lock the door," he whispered. "I'll tell them you held me prisoner and I was helpless to resist."

"I'm sure they'd believe it."

He chuckled as he lowered his lips back to hers.

A sharp knock at the door sent them both darting back from each other.

"Lady Blackmere? Brandon?" the Guild Master's voice called to them from the corridor.

Brandon leapt to his feet at the sound. He tugged down his tunic, ran his fingers through his hair and strode towards the door.

Natalie straightened her pile of letters, pressing her lips

into the sweetest smile she could manage as Brandon opened the door and greeted the Guild Master.

"You kept me waiting," the Guild Master grumbled. "I shouldn't have to come and find you."

"Forgive me, sir. Thank you for your services, Lady Blackmere," Brandon bowed as he left the room, casting her a last, knowing look.

She smiled and added Brandon's letter to the pile. "It was my pleasure."

TWENTY-SIX

The Guild was a hive of organized chaos.

Carts were loaded with equipment, suits of armor and weapons were polished until they mirrored the sunlight, and squires and champions alike hurried through the keep, double checking they had everything prepared for their departure in the morning.

By the afternoon, a sense of calm descended on the Guild. There was little left to do but train.

Natalie leaned against the wall as Brandon and Darius sparred. She chewed her lip as she watched him, marveling that a man so large could move with such speed. Every strike hit with the force of a charging bull, yet even in the heat of battle Brandon remained calm, winning each bout with a quiet confidence.

Darius laughed between hard-fought breaths. "By the Goddess, Sweet Bear. Have you discovered some secret fount of strength down there on the beach?"

Brandon's blade clanged against Darius's breastplate.

He panted and pulled off his helmet, gulping down the balmy ocean breeze. "Something like that, aye."

Natalie hid her smile behind her knuckles. Their hurried tryst that morning had been a welcome reward for her practice. She could still feel the pressure of him pressed against her, the chill of the rock at her back. A shiver ran through her body, and an ache gripped her thighs.

In the morning they would ride to Westgarden, along with the other participants in the Midsummer Melee and their squires. It would be a three-day ride to the city; three days and two nights without a moment of privacy.

"Nervous about tonight?" Darius grinned. "I've no doubt there will be songs about you."

Brandon chuckled. "There always is, but I've survived my fair share of Rufflings."

"Rufflings?" Natalie asked.

Darius's grin widened. "He didn't tell you? The Rufflings are nights where we ruffle each other's feathers before a contest. We feast and drink and pay the bard to sing songs about ourselves and our opponents."

Brandon turned a shade of crimson as he turned to her. "Those songs about me... you know... they come from the Guild. The champions pay for them, and the best ones— usually the bawdiest—get spread around."

Darius threw his head back and laughed, clapping his iron clad hands together. *"Brandon the Bear, strong and brave and fair..."* Fierce concentration narrowed his eyes. He looked to Natalie for assistance.

"Taller than two men and twice as strong," she laughed.

Brandon's cheeks reddened and a broad grin erupted across his face.

Darius and Natalie continued together, clapping in time with the words. *"Blessed is his blade, beware you wicked knaves, he's bigger than two men and twice as long!"*

Natalie's cheeks grew hot and tight as she pressed her lips together, stifling her laughter.

"Alright!" Brandon groaned as he hid his eyes behind his hand. "I'll admit it was a mistake to pay for that one. I was young and foolish."

"Wait," Natalie laughed. "*You* paid for it?"

Brandon scuffed his boot through the sand and sighed. "Aye. Wasn't cheap either."

Darius chuckled. "Well I look forward to seeing what atrocity you commission now that you're old and foolish."

"I haven't paid for any songs tonight. I need every penny I have." Brandon took a deep swig of his water, he tossed Darius's blade back to him. "Time for one more?"

"You work me so hard," Darius grumbled, rolling his eyes dramatically, as he bent over to pick his sword from the dirt. "You'd be a tough Guild Master."

A chuff of laughter shook Brandon's shoulders. He glanced towards Natalie and shook his head dismissively. "Just shut up and raise your blade."

The impending Ruffling sent Natalie's heart into a nervous canter, but the champions were gleeful, even in the face of possible ridicule and humiliation. The noise coming from their wing of the keep echoed through the corridors as she passed after practice, bidding farewell to Brandon with a fleeting squeeze of his fingers.

She returned to her room, washed in the basin and dressed in the clothes provided for her; a billowing white chemise, and a pale blue cotton overdress which laced at her sides. As the dinner bell tolled, she gave up on the attempt to braid her own hair, letting it spill over her shoulders in loose coppery waves. Excitement, and nerves, rising, she made her way to the banquet hall.

Brandon waited in the corridor outside the hall, his eyes tracing the length of her figure as she approached. The sight of him reignited her yearning for him. He wore a midnight blue doublet, embroidered with silver vines around his collar and sleeves, and cream-colored breeches which clung tight to his legs, showing off the muscles in his calves and thighs.

His hair and beard were groomed and neat, and the air around him was sweet with the scent of cinnamon.

She grazed her teeth across her bottom lip as she smiled. "My champion."

"My lady." He blushed beneath her approving stare. "Shall we?"

The distance between them was agonizing as they entered the hall.

There were three long tables, as opposed to the usual

two, each one topped with all manner of meats and vegetables, fruit, bread and pies. The mouthwatering, savory aroma of the food was tinged with the sour scent of ale.

Natalie cast a parting look at Brandon and made to walk over to her usual seat at the squire's table.

"Not tonight," he smiled, threading his hand through the crook of her elbow and pulling her gently towards him. "We sit together tonight."

Natalie felt as though she was glowing as he led her to the central table. They found Genevieve and Darius and squeezed onto the bench opposite them. Heat rose to Natalie's cheeks as Brandon's thigh pressed against hers beneath the table.

"Good evening, Lady Blackmere," Joss, Darius's squire greeted her. Since Natalie had broken the news of the passing of her aunt, the squire had warmed to her, and that acceptance had spread to the others.

Further along the table, more squires waved eagerly, greeting her with wide smiles. She recognized them all from the time she had spent with them reading and writing letters. Months ago, they would barely have given her a second look, assuming she was just as cold and lofty as their own nobility.

She bowed her head and raised her cup in greeting. "Good evening everyone."

"Do you think my letter's arrived yet?" Genevieve's squire asked, for perhaps the fiftieth time since she'd sent it.

Natalie smiled. "I'm sure it has."

"Where's Henry?" Brandon whispered as he peered down the table. "Goddess, don't tell me he's dropped out."

Natalie joined him in his search, craning her neck to peer down the tables. Henry was nowhere to be seen among the ranks of excited champions.

Brandon's disappointment was palpable. His body seemed to shrink a little as he filled his cup with water. His throat bobbed as he took deep gulps.

"Water?" Darius scoffed. "Since when does Brandon the Bear drink water at a party?"

He shrugged. "I want to be at my best."

"You've three days until the competition. Plenty of time to get it out of your system."

Brandon refilled his cup with water, still scanning the banquet hall for Henry. "I'm just thirsty."

"Perhaps he's late." Natalie offered him a reassuring smile. "I'm not sure you can get rid of him so easily."

"I hope not," Brandon grumbled, setting his cup on the table. He reached across the table and began to fill his plate with food. "I've hardly seen him since..." His words trailed off as he gestured to his scarred eyebrow. "That day."

Darius's broad grin spread as he chewed on a roll of bread. "He did you a favor. The scar makes you look even beastlier." He gave a dramatic shudder. "Even more... dangerous."

Brandon arched an eyebrow. "Don't think flattery will stop me kicking your arse when we get into that arena."

Darius laughed and placed his hand over his heart. "Stop, you're giving me chills."

Natalie chuckled in agreement, but a soft, tickling sensation beneath the table rendered her silent. Shielded from the eyes of their friends by the pile of food in the center of the table, Brandon stroked her from her knee to the top of her thigh. The bold, possessive touch stole her breath.

Genevieve rolled her eyes at Darius's flirtation. The whites of her eyes were already turning a pale shade of pink from the quantity of ale she was quaffing. "I'll kick all your arses."

Brandon's barking laugh drowned out Natalie's shuddering breath as his fingers teased the crease between her thighs. "I may as well forfeit now."

"Please do." Henry's voice slithered into the conversation, swiping the smiles from their faces. "It'll make things far easier. Though it would give me great pleasure to humiliate you publicly."

The Dragon was dressed in deep crimson silk, his black hair swept back and slick with oil. Beside him, Sara watched them with cool indifference, her silver tunic siphoning what little coloring she had.

Natalie reached out below the table and placed her hand on Brandon's. The muscles in his arm flinched, as though preparing to reach across the table to grasp his enemy.

Henry's glare settled on Brandon. His eyes narrowed and his lips quirked in faint amusement. "What a shambles this Guild has become."

"Keep walking, little man," Genevieve snarled above her cup. "There's nowhere here for you to sit."

"I wouldn't debase myself by sharing a table with such company," Henry said.

Natalie swallowed hard as his accusatory eyes raked across her face.

"I do hope you enjoy the songs tonight, Lady Blackmere. I expect you'll be hearing them again when you return to your hovel."

"I'm sure I will." She smiled sweetly, hoping he did not hear the tremble in her voice. "And I'll ensure our troubadours sing loudest and most frequently of your defeat. Perhaps I'll even commission some songs of my own."

Color rose in his cheeks, and the vein in his forehead fattened. "Watch your step, squire."

Brandon stiffened at her side. His fist tightened around the fork in his hand, and there was no doubt in Natalie's mind he was capable of wielding it with as much force as he did his blade.

She took a deep breath and addressed Henry calmly. "I am not *your* squire. And since you refuse to be civil, from now on, when you address me, you will address me as Lady Blackmere. You have less authority over me than a cockroach."

Across the table, Genevieve grinned at her. Darius and the squires sat stiff and straight-backed, with their eyes downcast. Sara's lip curled in disgust behind them.

Henry opened his mouth to retaliate, but was silenced by a round of rapturous applause, as the bard bounded into the banquet hall.

The performer danced between the tables, a streak of emerald green and gold silk, wielding his wooden lute like a battle hammer, feigning attacks on the cheering champions. As the cheers continued, the bard ran to the head of the dining hall and bowed, folding himself completely in half, so that his face was pressed to his knees. The Guild Master followed close behind, dressed in a fine golden tunic, decorated with embroidered black serpents.

Natalie joined in with the applause as Henry turned from her to find a seat. The hall was packed, and the air pulsed with heat and excitement, as every person working in the Guild, squire, champion and servant alike, sat around the tables. Natalie felt woozy, even without the ale. Brandon's hand on her thigh only added to her dizziness.

Under the cover of applause, he leaned towards her ear. "You're ferocious tonight, my lion."

His breath was hot, tickling the sensitive skin beneath her ears. She longed for his lips to follow.

"My champions!" The bard held out his arms in greeting as he stood at the top of the hall. "My dear little squires!"

Silence descended on the hall as the Guild Master held his hand aloft. "Champions and squires, tomorrow, those of you competing in the Midsummer Melee will depart for Westgarden. By our traditions, tonight will be a celebration of your impending battles, and a chance for you to really get under each other's skin. The Ruffling is as much a part of our traditions as the contests." He gestured towards the Bard. "Garrett has memorized songs commissioned by you. Some of them are about your friends, some, your rivals. Others among you may feel it necessary to write about yourselves."

The Bard clapped his hands and gave a sharp laugh.

"Aye, and we can always tell which ones those are because they're usually about the size of your weapons."

Laughter rippled around the room. Darius leaned forward and gave Brandon's arm a jovial punch.

"It's not that bad," Brandon groaned.

Natalie pressed her lips together, stifling her laughter. The warmth in her cheeks rose as Brandon's fingers resumed their dance across her thigh, tracing swirling patterns which dipped agonizingly close to where she longed to feel his touch.

At the head of the hall, the Guild Master continued, "I will leave it to our esteemed bard, Garrett, to entertain you this evening. You've spent months preening your feathers, now... let's get them ruffled."

A smattering of applause travelled around the room, missing Natalie as she focused all her effort into breathing. The thin fabric of her skirts only heightened the sensation as Brandon continued to touch her. It seemed not to affect him at all, as he casually ate his meal with the other hand.

"Now," Garrett grinned with a flourish of his hands. "For the first ditty of the evening." He pulled his lute across his body and gave it a gentle strum as he cast a predatory glance across the gathering. "Who shall be our first great hero immortalized in song?"

Silence, punctured by nervous laughter, descended on the hall.

Natalie hid her smile behind her cup as Brandon lifted his hand from her thigh and rested it on the table.

His breath was short and sharp, and his back stiffened as the bard approached. "Oh...Goddess, no."

"My dearest Bear," Garret smiled. "We meet again."

Darius howled with laughter, clapping his hands together as he reveled in his friend's discomfort.

"Excuse me," Garett pardoned himself before stepping onto the bench between Natalie and Brandon, climbing up to stand in the center of the table, straddling the food.

Natalie buried her face in her hands, hiding her laughter as much as the color rising to her cheeks.

Garrett addressed the room. "I've composed so many songs about Brandon the Bear, I sing them in my sleep. What's a few more to add to my repertoire?"

"A few?" Brandon's eyes widened. He turned to Natalie in despair.Natalie bit back a grin. "I didn't commission him."

"I did," Darius beamed, raising his cup.

The bard raised his arms, clapping a quick rhythm which caught on around the hall. He cleared his throat and began to sing.

"Oh there's no one else like Brandon

In this, or any land.

He'll find your fairest maiden

And take her by the hand.

Her senses she'll abandon,

She won't be fit to stand

'Cause our bonny, burly Brandon

He's a very hungry man."

A cheer broke out around the hall as Brandon roared with laughter. Darius ducked a projectile chicken bone and leaned across the table to throw his arms around his friend.

"My Sweet Bear, will you ever forgive me?"

"Never."

Natalie pressed her knuckles to her lips and fought back her laughter. Her cheeks were on fire. Even Genevieve covered her mouth as she stared wide-eyed towards Brandon.

Undaunted, he raised his cup to Darius. "It was a good one. I'll give you that."

It warmed Natalie's heart to see him so carefree. Brandon was joyous amongst his fellow champions, laughing loudly and taking every instance of gentle teasing in his stride.

As the bard worked his way around the room, singing songs about the various champions, Natalie pressed her arm against Brandon's, as she clapped along with the other songs. Ale and wine flowed freely, and the champions' giddiness and distraction afforded Natalie and Brandon a little more freedom with their discretion. He smiled as he leaned towards her, and for a moment, she thought he was going to kiss her.

"Every word of that song was true," he whispered against her ear. "You are the fairest maiden, and I am hungry."

A wave of heat rolled through her body, breaking between her thighs as her anticipation mounted.

His gaze lowered to her lips. "There's somewhere we can go tonight."

"Tonight?"

"Aye."

She all but swooned as his fingers caressed her once more, edging agonizingly close to her inner thigh. Moistening her lips with her tongue, she tried to breathe steady. "Where?"

"Just wait and see."

She sank her teeth into her lower lip and let her gaze linger. No matter how often she saw him, she was always mesmerized; his warm brown eyes, the silver shining at his temples, his addictive lips surrounded by the softness of his beard. It took all her effort not to pounce on him right there at the dining table.

She sipped her water and looked towards the very end of the table. Henry glared at them; his blue eyes were chips of sharp, jagged ice. Beside him, Tommy sat miserably picking at his food, and Sara and her squire sat beside them, their mouths downturned while others around him laughed and reveled.

"Sara and Henry are spending a lot of time together of late," Darius whispered, following her gaze. His words slurred a little. "I wouldn't be surprised if they form an alliance for the next Tourney."

"Why would anyone ally with him?"

Darius gave a nonchalant shrug. "He's skilled, beloved by the crowd—mainly because they don't have to spend any time with him—and he looks pretty. Of course it depends, though, on whether he thinks himself beatable."

Henry's cold eyes stared back at her, radiating intense hatred, as though a look alone could drive her from the hall. She smiled at Tommy.

At the young lad's nervous wave, Henry's eyes turned from her.

"Well, well." Garrett's voice shot a spike of panic through her body. The bard stood directly behind her, his fingers resting around Brandon's broad shoulder. "It seems there is another song about you, Sir Brandon, though this one, I believe, is from a rival."

A hiss of anticipation went around the room. At the end of the table, Henry's lips flickered into a smile.

Brandon's shoulder shook as he chuckled. "Very well, do your worst, Bard."

"I apologize in advance." Garrett shook his head and struck up a melancholy melody on his lute.

"Oh Bear! Oh Bear!

What happened dear Bear?

Has your last great battle been fought?

Oh Bear! Oh Bear!

Once so strong and fair,

But not half the man that we thought.

Those muscles most mighty have long turned to fat,

A sad, faded boar where a hero once sat.

Oh Boar! Oh Boar!

It's tragic old Boar.

It's time to relinquish your rule.

Oh Boar! Oh Boar!

Save us all, we implore,

From watching you become a fool."

A polite ripple of applause crept around the room as the melody ended. Natalie's heart hung heavy as she pressed her arm against Brandon's. Henry sneered and broke into joyful applause.

Brandon clapped along with them. He smiled and raised his cup towards Henry. "We'll soon see, won't we?"

"Oh, I have a feeling you'll be experiencing public shame, in one way or another," Henry snickered down the table. His eyes travelled between Brandon and Natalie.

Her guts coiled as Brandon shrunk back and tensed at her side. The threat was loud enough for the entire hall to hear, yet the tipsy champions did not seem to catch on.

Natalie did not allow herself to falter as she stared her enemy down. Her jaw clenched.

It was Henry's turn to flinch as the Bard strode towards him and gripped his shoulder.

"Our mighty Dragon," Garrett announced as Henry's cheeks reddened. "The most recent victor of the Grand Tourney. A hero to so many. You assisted with the rescue of the people of Blackmere, did you not?"

"I did," Henry smirked. "Though it was hardly worth the effort."

The proclamation roiled Natalie, sending white hot jolts of fury through her veins. His arrogance, his cold indifference to the lives lost in Blackmere enraged her. She shot to her feet, ignoring Brandon's wide-eyed stare, and the trill of the lute as Garrett began to sing.

"The Dragon sits on a pile of gold,

His only worth, in the world, I'm told.

And when he fights, he cheats to win,

The ghosts of so many follow him.

Though he may travel to many lands,

He'll never escape the blood on his hands.

For above us all, he seeks to soar,

But he bathes in the blood of the Ironclaw."

The room fell silent as the bard struck his final chord. Natalie stood still, her back an iron rod as Henry's eyes fixed her in place. The intensity of his rage could have shattered the glass in the windows.

CHAPTER

TWENTY-SEVEN

The Guild Master stood at the head of the silent banquet hall. His face twisted into furious outrage, teeth bared, eyes wildly searching the faces who stared back at him. "Who commissioned the song?"

Henry twisted in his seat, pulling himself to his feet. He gripped the bard by the lapels of his emerald green jacket. "Who was it?" He snarled. "Which one of these curs?"

Garrett stiffened, the bottom of his lute thumping against the stones as he struggled to keep his balance. "Let go of me." His breath shook as he brought his hand up to Henry's in an attempt to loosen the iron grip. "It... it was anonymous."

"Henry!" The Guild Master's voice boomed from the head of the hall. "Unhand him."

The Dragon's eyes remained fixed on the bard as he raised his finger to point at Natalie. "It was *her* wasn't it? You all heard it. These same, ludicrous accusations about

Blackmere." Henry's eyes were wide and savage as his features distorted with rage. "She told me earlier she would have songs written about me, and this is what she meant. Blatant slander."

Natalie forced a breath from her stony lungs. "Me?"

Brandon stood beside her. His hand at her back was cool against the inferno blazing across her skin. Her throat clamped shut as every pair of eyes fell to her.

The Guild Master rubbed his brow. "Lady Blackmere, did you commission the song?"

"No." She shook her head as her pulse thumped in her throat. "No."

"The accusations implied by the song are severe. Henry's name was cleared when you came to the Guild, and I expect you to respect my decision. If it was you, then you leave me no choice but to have you banished from the Guild, nobility or not."

"No." The sweat on her back turned cold. "I swear, it wasn't me."

Henry snarled. "It was you, you foul, deceitful harlot."

"You speak to her like that again, and it'll be the last time you speak," Brandon growled beside her.

Bitter laughter burst from Henry. "You see how he threatens me?"

Brandon huffed a breath. "This is ridiculous. It's just a song, like the one you commissioned about me. If you can give it out, then you can take it too."

Garrett stumbled back as Henry's fingers unfurled. Natalie longed to follow him as he retreated from the table. Her eyes burned with tears as she froze in the intensity of

Henry's anger. His lip curled as he looked Brandon up and down.

"It is *nothing* like the song I commissioned about you, fool." His eyes narrowed as he raised a finger to point at Brandon. "It was you, wasn't it?"

"Do you really think I have money to waste on songs?"

"I think there's no limit to what you'll do to besmirch my name. Well, perhaps I should commission a song about you swiving your s—"

"It was me."

All eyes turned to Genevieve as she raised her cup to her lips and gulped her wine. The world fell out from under Natalie's feet as Genevieve stood and turned towards the Guild Master. "I commissioned the song."

Henry's mouth opened and closed, his throat bobbing as he fought to restrain himself.

"Viv." The Guild Master shook his head, cringing as he uttered her name, as though it physically pained him.

"I'll see my own way out." Genevieve drained her cup and slammed it onto the table. "I don't wish to keep company with murderers and sycophants anyway."

The champion offered Natalie a brittle smile, held together with hope. Natalie's eyes fell to the letter clutched in Genevieve's trembling hand.

Brandon took a step, as if to follow her. "Viv..."

"I hope to see you again soon, my friends." She climbed over the bench and bowed towards Natalie and Brandon. "Good luck in the Melee." Her eyes dropped towards her squire. "I'm sorry."

Tears spilled down Natalie's cheeks as Genevieve began her journey out of the hall.

"You betrayed me," Henry's voice broke as he watched her leave. "After all we went through."

Genevieve turned back towards them as she reached the door. "No. You betrayed the Guild. You betrayed every one of us. And I will betray my conscience no longer. I'm done."

She turned on her heel and walked away.

Murmurs spread around the hall, growing louder and more fevered with every passing moment. The Guild Master leapt from his seat, striding after Genevieve, his echoing pleas growing ever more distant.

Natalie sunk down on the bench, her pulse racing as she reached for her water. Genevieve was gone.

Across the table, Darius's eyes were wide, his mouth agape. "Well," he picked up his spoon and resumed his feast. "I think we've all been well and truly ruffled."

TWENTY-EIGHT

The moon was an orb of silver, bathing Natalie and Brandon in a steely glow as they tiptoed across the courtyard. Back in the keep, the party was still in full swing, the shock of losing Genevieve drowned by the champions' consumption of ale. The boisterous song from the dining hall reached them even so far from the keep, accompanied by the rhythmic pounding of fists and cups on tables. Away from the heat, Natalie felt her skin prickle in the cool evening air.

"By the Goddess," she muttered as she threaded her fingers with his and huddled beside him as they walked. "This night..."

"Aye."

"Did you know Viv was going to do that?"

"No," he sighed, and a cloud of steam danced through the air. "She confided in me this evening and told me she was leaving, but I didn't realize it was going to be so sudden... or dramatic."

Natalie could not help but smile. Genevieve's departure seemed like a dream. Some part of her was half convinced she would see the formidable warrior at breakfast the next day, but Natalie hoped she was already on her way back to Blackmere. Back to Jenny. It was difficult to be saddened by her leaving when she was following her heart.

Natalie smiled to herself as warmth pooled in her stomach. She looked to the stars and wished the women well.

"In here," Brandon whispered as he led her towards a shadow shrouded building.

The dusty sweetness of hay permeated the night air.

"The stables?"

"Aye, everyone's in the hall celebrating." He lifted the latch on the stable door. "They won't be back to work until morning. We have the whole place to ourselves."

Natalie's heart beat harder at the thought. Casting one final glance across the dark, empty courtyard, Natalie bolted into the stables after him. The air inside was ripe and warm, scented with straw and the musk of horses. Other than the whisper of rustling hay, and short puffs of equine breath, the stable was silent.

In the darkness she could make out the hulking shape of Brandon's frame.

His hand gripped hers. "Be careful."

He led her through the stables, through a seemingly endless maze of dark stalls until at last he placed her hand on the wooden frame of a ladder. "Go on up."

"What if I fall?" she breathed.

"Then I'll catch you."

She smiled as she placed a foot on the first rung. "And if you fall?"

"Then leave me lying here and tell them I passed out drunk. It wouldn't be the first time."

Climbing the ladder, Natalie stifled a laugh, sinking her teeth into her lower lip. By the time she reached the top and stepped into the hayloft she was breathless. Moonlight streamed in from an open hatch in the roof, illuminating the rafters and the stacked bales of fresh hay in pale blue light.

"Will they catch us?" she asked as Brandon reached the top to stand beside her.

"It's worth the risk." He took a step towards her, reaching out to caress her cheek. "I've missed you too much."

He took another small step towards her, pressing his body against hers. Though it was only a few days from midsummer, the ocean breeze cooled the night air. Brandon's warmth took away the chill but did nothing to stop the tingle of goosebumps spreading along her arms.

"I missed you too," she whispered as she leaned into the touch of his broad, rough hands. Months of rigorous training had hardened him. The coarse grain of his toughened palms rasped against the tender skin of her cheek. She ran her hand across the swell of his bicep, thicker and harder than before. His muscles twitched at her touch, his breath hitching in his throat as his eyes, black in the moonlight, feasted on the sight of her.

Natalie wondered if he blushed as she did, if his chest was flushed pink beneath the dark blue of his doublet. She longed to look at him fully. If only the moon was a little brighter, a little lower in the sky. If only they could light candles.

For six months their trysts had been hurried, bursts of passion against the rocks. He never left her unsatisfied, but the encounters had been as brief as they were intense. Now she wanted to take her time, to spend hours rediscovering the body which had been locked away behind layers of steel and leather.

He smiled as though he shared her frustration and bowed his head to press his forehead to hers. Their breaths shuddered together as he grazed the tip of her nose with his.

"Let's forget all the unpleasantness of tonight," he whispered. "The rest of the world is of little importance when I have you."

Natalie's heart thrummed beneath her breast as she nodded.

The anticipation of his kiss tightened her nipples and sent heat flooding between her thighs. The air grew silent as they both held their breath.

"I love you," she whispered. It felt like a release to admit it aloud.

He swallowed and smiled. "I love you. Though those words hardly seem grand enough."

Unable to resist anymore she tilted her chin up, brushing her lips against his. He held her to him with a strength and ferocity which stole her breath. At the touch of his lips she was home. It no longer mattered if she was at the Guild, or Blackmere, or an abandoned cottage in the woods surrounded by bandits. Her home was with him.

His tongue slid against hers, sending tingling need

pulsing through her body. When she broke away, breathless and lightheaded, she was grateful for the tight grip around her waist pinning her against him and keeping her upright.

He brushed his fingers back through her hair and smiled. "I have something for you."

"For me?"

His grin flashed through the dim light as he stepped back. "Aye, come here." He took her hand in his and led her across the hayloft. Sitting on a bale, he pulled her down onto his lap. She was facing him, straddling his thick thighs.

Natalie leaned forward and buried her face against his neck as he rummaged beneath his doublet. A growl rumbled in his chest as she nipped at his throat with her teeth, tracing each bite with the tip of her tongue.

"My lady, if you keep that up, it'll all be over before I even find your present."

She smiled against his neck, breathing in the salt and cinnamon scent of his skin. Beneath the gentle aroma of the spiced soap, he smelled of the ocean, of battle and leather. It took all her self-control not to begin nibbling at him again.

Something tickled against her neck, soft and silken, flashing pale blue in the moonlight. A sleek white feather.

He smiled as she arched her neck against the touch. "As much as I know you don't mind wearing the old one, it may raise some eyebrows in Westgarden." He traced the outline of her face with the feather. "It took me a while to find one pretty enough."

Her breath sharpened as he reached her chin and trailed his touch back down her throat. She leaned forward and kissed him, her fingers resting against the neckline of his jacket. "It's lovely. Perfect."

"Good. Then it suits you."

Her hands wandered down his body, finding the hem at his hips. She buried them beneath the fabric, pressing into the warmth and softness of his stomach.

He flinched at her touch, "Goddess, your hands are cold."

"Then warm me up."

"With pleasure."

His strong arms wound around her waist, pulling her towards him. As he kissed her, he hummed his approval, teasing her lips with his teeth. Pulling on the knotted laces at her hips, he loosened the dress and lifted it over her head, leaving her in the flimsy cotton chemise.

He tugged loose the tie at the neck of the garment, leaving it to hang loose around her shoulders. Slowly, he pulled the chemise down, exposing her breasts, and stomach, and letting the cotton bundle around her hips. The cool night air hardened her nipples and pebbled her skin.

He leaned back and drank in the sight of her. His breath hitched. "So beautiful."

A lump formed in Natalie's throat as she met his eyes. There was reverence in his gaze, as though she was some celestial being, worthy of breathless awe. Her nerves rattled in her chest.

She was used to lying flat beneath him or standing, crushed between the rocks and his body, but sitting across his lap, she could not help but compare her body to those of the champions. Despite months of training, Natalie's stomach was more cushioned, sculpted by a comfortable noble life. The flesh at her sides formed soft rolls as she straddled his lap. As her mind taunted her, she brought up her hands to cover her breasts and abdomen.

"Don't," he whispered, gently lowering the hand covering her stomach. "You're perfect. I've never seen anything so beautiful."

He took the feather in his free hand and fluttered it against the ticklish skin around her navel. She gasped, at the sensation, biting down on her bottom lip.

"That's cruel," she laughed.

"Is it?" He arched an eyebrow. "Would you like me to stop?"

Her breath shuddered as he trailed the feather up her abdomen and swept it across her nipple. "No."

The sensation was so light, so maddeningly gentle. Every touch heightened the ache between her legs until she could bear it no more. She rocked her hips, grinding against his thighs as he continued to tease her.

Lips parted, he watched her, his eyes hungry black abysses in the moonlight. He forced an exhale and whispered. "My lady."

A desperate moan escaped her lips as he teased the underside of her breasts with the feather. Heat and pressure built up between her thighs as she arched her back, pressing herself harder against him. With a broken sigh, he reached his hand beneath her skirts, tangling his fingers in the cotton layers.

She stood, sliding her skirts down over her hips, her

buttocks, and down her thighs, until she waited before him naked, her bare flesh licked by the night air.

"You're so beautiful," he whispered as he wound his arm around her thighs.

She laughed a little as he pulled her towards him, so that she stood straddling his thighs, and pressed his face against her stomach.

He kissed the soft skin, his hands gliding over the curve of her backside. His thighs kept her legs parted, exposed to him. She could barely breathe as he slipped his fingers into the slick, throbbing heat between her thighs.

"Brandon—" She gasped as he teased her clitoris with the soft tip of the feather. Her legs threatened to give way, wavering beneath her as her pleasure grew. Bracing her hands on his shoulders, she arched her neck and lost herself in the sensation.

A low growl of approval escaped Brandon's lips. His own breath was as heavy as hers. "How does it feel?"

"Good. So good," she whispered between breaths. "Don't stop."

He flashed that cocky smile, knowing full well how good he made her feel. "I told you I would pleasure you as many times as you wanted me to."

She whimpered as he sucked her nipple into his mouth, teeth grazing over the sensitive peak. His moan vibrated against her breast, as he exchanged the feather for a finger, and ran it through her slick folds.

Raking her fingers through his hair, she tilted her pelvis towards him, longing for more. The more she insisted, the slower he moved. He loved to draw it out, to take his time, and relish her pleasure. It was maddening, and exquisite.

Her toes curled against the floorboards, and her thighs shuddered, threatening to collapse beneath her as he stroked her, building her pleasure with every caress. When she was close to climax, agonizingly close, he withdrew his hand. She almost cried out in disappointment as she lowered her face to scowl at him.

With unwavering eye contact, he brought his fingers to his lips. They were glistening with her arousal. His lips quirked into a self-assured grin as he put his fingers one by one into his mouth and sucked the taste of her from each one. Natalie could only watch, lips parted, chest aching with need.

"I've dreamed about the taste of you every night for six months," Brandon growled.

Lightheaded with desire, Natalie let out a breathless, "oh."

He grinned, cupping her backside in his rough, warm hands, and leaned back against the hay pulling her with him, until her knees rested on his shoulders. She cried out, delirious with pleasure as he pressed his mouth to her.

The silken softness of his tongue explored her, hungry for the taste of her, coaxing stifled moans from her, as she gripped fistfuls of straw.

She came undone against his mouth, tangling her fingers in his hair, with her thighs shaking against the sides of his head. As the waves of pleasure subsided, she climbed down, straddling his thighs once more and nestled her face against his chest.

The thundering rhythm of his heart pounded against her ear as she caught her breath, basking in warm, tingling pleasure. Her fingers drifted towards the fastenings of his doublet.

She smiled as he kissed the top of her head, and trailed his hand along the curve of her hip.

"I wish I could do that every day," he sighed.

She raised her head to look at him. His eyes were closed, his face serene. The ebb and flow of his breath steadied as he tightened his embrace.

"I wish you could too."

His chest shook as he quietly chuckled.

"Let's stay here tonight," she sighed. "Together, in each other's arms."

His chest billowed as he drew a deep breath. "I'd like that."

Her fingers fumbled with a clasp on his doublet until she worked it free. She pressed a kiss to the downy, scarred skin of his chest, as his heart leapt beneath her lips.

She worked open the rest of the fastenings, opening the doublet to reveal the body she so desperately craved. Slowly, she ran her fingernails across his chest, relishing the bristling hair beneath her touch.

He exhaled heavily as she let her hands drift down, over the gentle sloping mound of his stomach.

The white feather lay on the hay beside him, stark and bright in the moonlight. She picked it up, and let it flutter against one of his nipples.

Her lips quirked at his sharp intake of breath.

He invited her touch, raising his arms above his head,

and settling back against the hay. Pressing her teeth into her lower lip, she trailed the feather across his body, tracing each hill and valley, every scar and bruise. He shifted beneath her, arching his back to press his hips closer to her, desperate for release.

"I am yours, my lady," he moaned, his eyelids fluttering closed as she bowed her head and let her tongue flicker against the sensitive bud of his nipple. His cock strained against her thigh, locked inside the confines of his breeches. A moan escaped his lips as she grazed his nipple with her teeth. Laughing, she covered his mouth with her palm as he gasped and growled.

"You'll alert the whole Guild," she chuckled.

"Let them hear." He sat upright, cupping his hand at the back of her head and pulling her to his lips. As he broke away, he bowed his head. "After this year, after the next Grand Tourney, I'll retire, no matter the outcome. I need to be with you. I'll find some other way to provide for my family, but I want to come with you, back to Blackmere."

"You're certain?"

"I've never been more certain of anything. I'll find a way to make everyone happy."

Joy swelled in her chest. Leaning towards her, his tongue slipped between her lips, and the musky taste of her own arousal drew a shuddering sigh. Desperate for him, she reached down, unlaced his breeches and slipped her hand into the dense patch of dark curls. Her fingertips grazed against his cock.

"Not yet," he whispered, brushing the hair back from

her face. His smile returned to his lips. "I have a reputation to live up to."

She stifled a laugh against his neck as he rocked forward, laid her back on the floor, and hooked her legs over his broad, burly shoulders. He gazed down at her with adoration, his tunic open to reveal his chest and rounded stomach. His throat bobbed as he swallowed, and the tip of his tongue flashed pink against his lower lip. Kissing a trail along her thighs, he settled between them, arms pinning apart her legs, his breath blowing against her sensitive flesh.

"Again?" Her breath quickened beneath the intensity of his hunger for her. At any moment she would combust.

"Aye. Well, you've heard the songs."

Back arching, she gasped as his tongue slid across her clitoris once more, stroking her with long teasing licks. It was almost too slow, keeping her on the precipice of pleasure for as long as possible. There was no doubt he would happily spend all night between her thighs, until she was too exhausted to move.

Natalie tangled her fingers in his hair as her toes curled against his thighs. "Brandon?" She could barely breathe.

"Hm?" The vibration against her drew a gasp.

"I—want you."

He quickened his rhythm in response, gently holding back the hood of her clitoris to expose her fully to his tongue. She came silently, almost weeping as he licked and licked her over-stimulated skin, drawing out every last throbbing beat of her pleasure.

When her thighs stopped trembling, he raised his head.

His lips were glossed with her arousal as he flashed that cocky grin. "As my lady wishes."

Through heavy lidded eyes, she could not help but admire his body as he raised onto his knees and pulled his breeches down to his knees. She hooked her feet around his backside, pulling him closer with a lazy grin, until the head of his cock pressed against her entrance.

His gentle laughter faded as he entered her. His body shivered, and his eyes screwed shut as he mouthed, "Oh, Goddess."

Natalie groaned as he pressed himself into her, holding her ankles to his shoulders, and igniting a new sensation of pleasure deep in the pit of her stomach. He thrust slowly, letting her feel every inch of him, almost withdrawing completely, before pushing back into her. His eyes feasted on the sight of her body, focusing on her breasts as her soft flesh rippled with every thrust.

"You're so beautiful," he whispered, biting his lower lip as he quickened his pace. "My Nat."

She held her breath as his steady rhythm quickened. He pounded against her, lowering his body until her knees pressed to her chest.

His back arched as he came, his growls riding on puffs of steaming breath, as his pace stuttered. Spent, he unhitched her legs from his shoulders and collapsed on top of her, lying his head between her breasts. His fingers brushed against her shoulders.

For the first time in months, she was truly content, holding the person she loved in her arms, basking in the glow of their passion. They were together, two souls bound by love. He was her sanctuary from every doubt she had about herself and the world.

"Am I crushing you?" His voice was sleepy and distant.

She drew in a labored breath, her chest aching beneath the weight of him. Stroking his hair with one hand and wrapping the other arm around his shoulders she smiled. "No. Don't move."

They held each other until the first birds began to sing. Before the sun rose, they dressed and hurried back to the keep, returning to their separate wings of the castle to sleep until it was time to depart the Champion's Guild.

CHAPTER

TWENTY-NINE

The champions and squires rode for two days, making steady progress towards Westgarden. Garett the bard accompanied them, singing the songs the champions had commissioned, as well as some of his own. He did not sing Genevieve's song.

The landscape transformed around them, from craggy coastal roads and rolling moorlands, to ancient forests and towering mountains. As sore as she was from the saddle, Natalie could not help but stare in awe at the beauty of Aldland. The first night they slept beneath the stars, gathered around a crackling campfire.

As their companions drifted off to sleep, Brandon brushed the tips of his fingers against hers, loving caresses, both innocent and dangerous.

Despite the need to be discrete, Natalie's heart was full. In just six months they would be together, without anything to stand between them.

On the second night, their party stopped at a quaint inn,

The Ivory Rose, less than three hours ride from Westgarden. Lady Luray had already paid for rooms and food for her champions and had left instruction that their squires be allowed to sleep on the tavern floor, once the champions left for bed.

Brandon had not left her willingly, protesting to the landlord that Natalie should be permitted to sleep above with the champions.

"She's a noble lady," he insisted to the barkeep. "You can't have her sleeping on the ground."

"I'm a squire, Sir Brandon," she had reminded him, hoping her veneer of cheeriness might soothe the creases between his eyebrows. "Besides, I'm so exhausted from the ride, I'm sure I'll be asleep in moments."

How wrong she had been.

Natalie lay with her back pressed to the stone floor, sweating from the stifling heat. She breathed through her mouth to lessen the overpowering sickly stench of stale ale. The snores of the squires rattled through the balmy Midsummer air. Flinging the coarse wool blanket from her body, she shuddered, and raised her arms above her head.

She stared at the ceiling, wondering if Brandon slept soundly above. The urge to go up there and find him tormented her, but then she would not know which room he slept in, nor who patrolled the corridors. She pushed the urge aside and closed her eyes.

Every creak of the floorboards, every clatter of hoofbeats on the road outside snatched her from the outskirts of sleep. In the morning they would ride to Westgarden, and Natalie would stand before a crowd and compete against the other squires—squires who had trained for competition for years.

She placed her hands on her stomach as her guts slithered. Her own competition was not the only source of her worry. Brandon would, most likely, have to fight through many rounds to even reach his rival, and as much as she believed in him, there was no doubt Henry was formidable, strong, and most worryingly of all, angry. Every one of the champions was strong, their bodies young, lean and swift.

She ground the heel of her hand against her eye sockets and sighed.

"Can't sleep either?" a familiar voice whispered.

Natalie rolled onto her stomach and raised herself onto her elbows. Tommy lay on his back, staring wide-eyed at the ceiling.

She shook her head. "I'm so nervous."

"So am I." He swallowed and placed his hands on his forehead. "I don't even know if I want him to win or not."

"Henry?"

"Aye. On the one hand, if he does, it'll put me in good stead to become a champion myself next year. But on the other, I don't want him to feel the satisfaction." A bitter huff of laughter jolted his chest. "This is the first year I've squired for him. At first it was an honor—he won the Grand Tourney last year, as you know—but now... this is the first time I've ever considered quitting the Guild."

"I'm sorry, it can't be easy."

"It's not."

"Don't quit."

He smiled. "I won't. Becoming a champion is my dream. I've wanted this all my life."

Natalie peered down, running her fingernail along a crack in the stone slabs of the floor. She chuckled quietly. "Mine too."

Tommy turned over to lay on his stomach. His eyebrows knitted together. "Really? But you're a noble lady."

"Aye. I used to dream about running away to join the Guild when I was younger."

"Well in that case, good luck to you tomorrow. I hope one of us gets our dream."

"I don't stand a chance."

A broad smile cracked his anxious expression. "Is the Guild everything you dreamed it would be?"

She smiled and sighed. "It's more."

"Ah, but you get to squire for Brandon, lucky. I'd give anything to have him be my champion. I was sure he was going to be this year; I could feel it. But then you came along—which I'm very thankful for—but..." he shrugged a shoulder and rested his chin on his arm. "This sounds ridiculous, but he's... well, almost like a father. I wish he was."

"Brandon?"

"Aye, a lot of us see him like a dad, especially the younger ones. He's a good man."

"He is." Natalie smiled. It filled her with pride to know that Brandon was loved by so many. But the pride came with sadness. If he was to leave the Guild, it would be a loss to so many of the squires.

Tommy's eyes fluttered closed. He took a deep breath

and closed his eyes. "I can't wait until he's the Guild Master."

Her breath snagged in her throat as she frowned. "What?"

The lad's eyes flickered open for a moment. "Oh. You haven't heard yet? There's been rumors for a while, but the Guild Master officially offered him the position before we left..." His voice began to fade as he slipped into sleep. "I can't wait... Hopefully by then I'll be a champion, and he'll train me..."

The world dropped from beneath Natalie. Her mind raced.

Brandon had been offered the position of Guild Master?

If what Tommy said was true, taking the position would ensure Brandon had the money to help his family for their entire lives, and have enough that he could be comfortable long after his eventual retirement, but he would have to remain at the Guild until then, never leaving the walls of the castle.

Weeks ago, on the evening she received her letter from Jenny, Genevieve had mentioned that Brandon was making sacrifices for their love. Now she knew the meaning behind those words.

Suddenly, the idea of them spending their life together, was a distant dream. She had only known Brandon for six months, and though she loved him, she could not ask him to give up the safety of his family, and the opportunity to dedicate his life to the Guild he loved so much. Abandoning the life of a champion was one thing; his income was never guaranteed, and as the years went by, victories would be harder, but the Guild Master's position offered safety and stability.

Nausea rose in her throat. For the welfare of Brandon's family, and for the future of the Guild, as much as it pained her, she might have to let him go.

She rolled onto her back, tears stinging her eyes, and waited for the dawn birdsong.

THIRTY

The short ride to Westgarden was more uncomfortable than the previous two days added together.

Sore, exhausted, and riddled with guilt, Natalie rode beside Brandon, an internal battle raging beneath her enthusiastic façade. She hid her sorrow behind laughter, riding proudly beside the man she loved. It was not the time for difficult conversations. For Brandon, she would be strong. She had to be.

The eight boisterous champions goaded each other along the way, insulting everything from their prowess in the ring, to their stamina in the bedroom. The squires riding alongside their champions laughed nervously at the jokes they were yet too young to understand.

At the back of the procession, draft horses pulled three large carts laden with chests. The champions' weapons and armor were stored safely within, along with the simple weapons and armor for the squires' contest.

Henry rode at the head of the pack, straight-backed, his focus unbreakable as squabbles broke out throughout the group.

"I will put you in the dirt within three seconds," Darius asserted to a white-haired champion, dressed in grey silk. "And you can wipe your tears on that ridiculous mop you call hair."

Brandon chuckled at Natalie's side. They were in the back of the group, with little privacy to discuss anything other than the impending contest. Big Lad dwarfed the rest of the horses, his silver coat gleaming, and his dark mane brushed until it shone.

The news of Brandon's promotion rattled in the back of Natalie's mind even as she pushed it away. The lack of sleep left her eyes raw and her brain fuzzy. She glanced down her chest, ensuring the tattered black feather and the sleek white one were both securely in place behind the ram's head brooch.

"You look tired," he said. His voice was laced with concern. "I knew I should've argued harder for them to let you sleep upstairs."

She chanced a lingering look at him. He was stunning in a teal silk tunic, his beard and hair trimmed and perfectly coiffed. His clothing had been stored in a chest with sachets of lilac and mint, and their gentle perfume wafted through the morning air. Her throat dried out as the urge to run her fingers through his hair overwhelmed her.

"I'm well," she assured him, smoothing down her matching tunic. "Just a little nervous." She clutched her horse's reins tightly so he would not see how her fingers trembled. "Did you get enough rest?"

"Aye," he smiled. "I think so."

Darius turned in his saddle. "I hope everybody heard that. My Sweet Bear is well-rested, he's unbeatable. You may as well go home now."

"You realize that means you won't be able to beat him either?" Sara sighed up ahead.

"It would be an honor to have my arse kicked by such a man."

Brandon's deep laughter brought a smile to Natalie's face, despite her inner turmoil. Darius broke into song, bellowing his song, *"There's No-One Else Like Brandon"*, at the top of his lungs. At the head of the party, Garratt accompanied him on his lute. The song had become a favorite among the group, and would no doubt catch on in the taverns.

When he had finished his rendition, Darius laughed and shook his head. "Oh, the women of Westgarden don't know what's coming to them. Some sweet creature is waking this morning, unaware that she's going to have the best night of her life with Brandon the Bear, victor of the Midsummer Melee, buried between her legs."

"Stop it," Brandon dismissed him with a shake of his head.

From the corner of her eye Natalie saw him glance towards her, but her vision glazed over as they began to climb the sloping road, the final stretch towards Westgarden. The voice in the back of her mind taunted her, reminding her she was unworthy of his sacrifice. It was not worth severing his connections to the Guild to come with her to dreary Blackmere.

His sacrifice meant not only giving up his lifestyle, his home in the grand castle by the ocean, but the family he had found among the ranks of the Guild. As the Guild's Master, he would go down in legend, not just as a great champion, but as a man who helped to train a generation of Aldland's finest fighters.

A sharp burst of laughter burst from Henry. "Brandon? The victor? I very much doubt that."

Darius chuckled. "Ah, you think you'll win?"

"I know I will," Henry smirked. "That's a given. And I doubt Brandon will be spending the night with anyone from Westgarden."

Natalie stiffened in the saddle. The air hung heavy around her and Brandon.

Darius scoffed. "Oh, shut up, Dragon. You know nothing."

Sara chimed in, twisting around in her saddle to face Brandon. "Well the last time the champions came to Westgarden, it didn't end so well for you, did it, old man?"

"Indeed," Henry laughed. "By the time you left everyone knew about your sad little cock."

A ringing tone started in Natalie's ears as heat crawled across her face. She clamped her mouth shut, and stared straight ahead, hoping none of the other champions noticed the color rising in her cheeks. Brandon's hands dropped to Big Lad's mane. He took a handful of the ebony strands of hair and began to braid them.

Darius turned towards Brandon, his mouth wide in indignation. "Are you going to sit there and take this?"

Brandon shrugged. "If he wants to obsess over my cock, let him."

The champions broke into riotous laughter as Henry turned away. His ears were crimson beneath the black of his oil-slicked hair.

Darius leaned to the side and plucked a pink azalea blossom from a shrub in the hedgerow, twirling it between his fingers before tucking it behind his horse's grey ear. "Well I know for a fact there are hundreds of women in Westgarden just dreaming of spending the night with Bonny Brandon. And, if her letters are to be believed, Lady Luray is among them."

The name coiled Natalie's gut. She had quite forgotten the letters she had found in Brandon's room in Blackmere's tavern. Lady Luray was from a great family and was lovelier than any rose in Westgarden. Her letters made no secret of the fact she lusted after Brandon, and if he won, it would not be unexpected for her to request an audience with him.

Brandon released an exasperated breath as he began the next braid in Big Lad's mane. "Will you all please stop discussing my sex life? You lot think about it more than I do."

"Yes," Darius chuckled. "Because we have to listen to the moans coming from your room at night." The champion threw back his head and gasped. "*My lady, oh, my lady. Don't play coy with us, Sweet Bear.*"

Brandon's ears turned red to match Henry's. Natalie could barely breathe as cold fear washed over her. She lowered her head and focused on the rhythmic movement of her horse's shoulders, drowning out the banter between the champions.

A glint of copper flashed in the corner of her eye as Brandon turned the coin over between his fingers. Her heart ached at the sight of it. He loved her, and she loved him, but after the contest, she would shatter both their hearts.

She kept her head down until they drew closer to the city, and the crackle of distant applause met them.

Brandon took a deep breath and sat upright in his saddle. Big Lad's mane was covered in intricate braids. "Here we go."

Natalie straightened and pinned back her shoulders as they reached the cheering crowd. At the front of the pack, Henry sat aloof, facing dead ahead, even as crimson banners bearing his dragon sigil were frantically fluttered towards him by excited admirers, and declarations of love were screamed from all sides.

There were almost as many purple lightning bolt flags flying for Darius, representing his sigil of The Storm, and a few grey wolves, blades of silver, and golden stags for the other champions. A handful of flags bearing thorny red roses waved back and forth, as word had not yet reached them of Genevieve's resignation from the Guild.

Natalie's heart sunk as she scanned the crowd. There were no bears on any of the flags or banners.

"Is that Brandon the Boar?" A man jeered as he leaned out of an upstairs window. "Give up! You're past it man, go home!"

Natalie's jaw tightened as heat flooded her face. As far as the crowd were concerned, Brandon was all but finished, a bastion of faded glory.

Brandon waved calmly as the crowd cried out for the other champions. The insults did not seem to bother him.

The sun beat against them, reflected from the freshly painted white walls of houses and shops. Many of the walls were covered in climbing roses, their white and pink blooms larger and brighter than any roses Natalie had ever seen.

They followed the sparkling blue waters of the serpentine river, until they could make their way across the glistening white bridge towards the more affluent side of the city. A procession of spectators followed, cheering the champions along on their journey to the contest arena. Looming above them, perched on a grassy hill, was Westgarden Tower. The round structure, topped by a conical blue roof was surrounded on all sides by rose bushes, with only a narrow white brick walkway towards the entrance breaking the field of delicate flowers.

Natalie took a deep breath of the floral, perfumed air. Her body trembled with dread and excitement all at once. Ever since she was a child, she had fantasized about the roar of the crowd, of becoming a champion and fighting in an arena like the one at Westgarden. Now, as her dream drew ever closer, and the beating of drums echoed the frantic rhythm of her heart, she clung to her horse's reins with trembling fingers.

Brandon reached across, and briefly squeezed her hand. "I'm at your side," he smiled. "Whatever happens."

She took a deep breath, and set her jaw.

Ahead of them the path disappeared into the yawning gateway of an enormous amphitheater, crafted from blocks of shimmering white marble. The earth-shaking applause of the spectators swelled, growing with every step as Henry's and Tommy's horses broke into a trot at the head of the group and one by one, the pairs of champions and squires followed their lead. As each pair reached the amphitheater's gates, the riders raised their blades, and sped into a gallop.

Every breath was a monumental effort as Natalie's horse jolted beneath her.

Riding at her side, Brandon's eyes lit up with excitement as they approached the gates. "Let's go, my Lioness of Blackmere."

At his signal, they tapped their horses' flanks, and charged side-by-side into the arena.

CHAPTER

THIRTY-ONE

Pounding drums matched the rhythm of the horse's hooves as they rode around the arena through a shower of white rose petals. Natalie could hardly breathe. The crowd was enormous, easily ten times the entire population of Blackmere, and louder than anything she had ever heard. They stood on marble tiers, flying the banners of their favorite champions.

It was glorious.

Riding at Brandon's side, she forgot her fear. Nothing mattered but the drums, the roar of the crowd, the thunder of hooves, and him.

The sand beneath them was littered with silk scarves and handkerchiefs; tokens thrown by spectators to the champions who rode ahead of them, trampled into the dirt by the hooves of their mounts.

As they rounded the arena, the box reserved for Westgarden's nobility came into view. Flowing white silks fluttered gently in the breeze around the gazebo. Lady

Catherine Luray stood before her throne, a mass of auburn curls tumbling over the white silk of her dress as she clapped her hands. Her council members sat behind her, draped in silks, each wearing a gold circlet about their head.

Natalie and Brandon slowed their horses to a trot and joined the other teams who stood in a line before Lady Luray. When all eight teams had gathered, the champions took a step forward, leaving their squires in a row behind them. Their brightly colored outfits stood out like jewels against the white marble and silk of the arena.

In the corner of Natalie's eye, Darius craned his neck, attempting to catch Brandon's attention. His broad grin flashed along the line as he tilted his head towards the noblewoman standing before them.

There was no denying her beauty. Even from that distance, Natalie could see the generous, silk-draped curves of her voluptuous body, the brilliance and warmth of her smile.

"My fearless champions!" Lady Luray greeted them with her arms outspread. "Welcome to Westgarden."

A cheer erupted around the amphitheater, pulsing against Natalie's ears and rattling her heart against her breastbone. Natalie's blood ran cold as she imagined them jeering at her failure.

Lady Luray continued. "It is my great honor to host the Midsummer Melee, a tournament of strength and skill, to determine who among you is this year's Melee Victor."

The champions raised their blades in unison, and their steeds raised their front right leg in salute.

Once again, a cheer went up from the crowd, and a

fresh wave of white rose petals fluttered down from the top of the arena. Lady Luray's smile widened as she clapped in delight.

"My champions," Lady Luray purred. "Prepare yourselves for battle."

The squires moved in unison. Natalie nudged her horse forwards, stopping beside Brandon for a moment as they awaited their turn to depart. One by one, each team set off, charging towards Lady Luray to head through a dark gateway beneath her stand.

Natalie held her breath as they left the roar of the crowd behind them and descended a sloping tunnel into the belly of the arena. Torches flickered along the walls as they passed, casting an amber glow around the arching passageway.

"She is beautiful!" Darius cackled as he reached the bottom and dismounted his chestnut mare. "This whole city is beautiful."

"If this is what their Midsummer Melee is like, imagine the Grand Tourney," another champion laughed.

Natalie groaned as she swung her stiff legs over the saddle and stepped down from her mount, taking stock of the large subterranean chamber. The air was cool, but already bristling with excitement. Torchlight flickered on the stone walls, illuminating eight large dressing stalls, one for each of the champions. At the far end of the chamber, a door led to a small surgery, a sobering reminder of the danger Brandon and the other champions faced.

Workers from Westgarden led the horses away and brought forth the chests containing the weapons and arms of each champion. There was little time to stand and gape. Natalie joined the rest of the squires as they sorted through them. She was relieved to see Brandon's bear-crested chest had made the journey safely.

Heart pounding, she gripped the handles and lifted the chest, the muscles throughout her body straining from the effort.

"Allow me," Brandon said gently at her side.

The sound of his voice, so calm and steady in the midst of the excitement and anxiety, soothed her. Lifting the chest cost him no effort at all as he hoisted it from her arms and carried it over to one of the booths for dressing.

A slim, bald-headed man stepped into the center of the chamber as the champions and squires settled in their booths. He unfurled a scroll and took a moment to read it to himself.

Satisfied, he tilted his chin and addressed the champions. "The Council of Westgarden have pre-determined the order in which we would like to see you fight." He chuckled to himself. "We hope to get the least anticipated bouts over with as quickly as possible for the first round, and have the contest accumulate in a spectacular battle between your finest warriors."

"Sounds good to me," Darius grinned as his squire, Joss, worked on attaching his greaves.

"With that in mind, we've selected The Bear, and The Silver Wolf for the first bout."

Henry's snickering laughter filled the armory. "Spectacular."

The white-haired champion that Darius had squabbled

with on the road reeled with an indignant look on his face. "I should've just stayed at home."

Brandon bowed in thanks to the announcer and took a steady breath. "That's good. I hate waiting."

Darius chuckled across from them. "Oh, Sweet Bear, it appears you lost Lady Luray's favor."

"Aye."

Natalie bit down her frustration as she looked to Brandon. He remained unmoved by the slight, as he always did. Still, she longed to hold him, to assuage any doubts which ran deeper beneath the surface. He was a true champion —*her* champion.

Her heart splintered at the thought of what she had to do.

She opened the chest and removed the pieces of armor, inspecting and accounting for each one. His new bear's head helmet snarled at her from the chest, its ferocious maw demanding battle. Satisfied that all the pieces of his armor were there, she began her work. The rest of the champions began to dress as they were assigned an opponent and a slot for their first battle.

"They're underestimating you," Natalie whispered as she stepped up to face Brandon. "Use it to your advantage."

He smiled, all too familiar with tactics. "Aye. I will."

Slowly, he unbuttoned his tunic, inching his way down. His intense stare set her alight as he peeled back the silk to reveal his body. His muscular biceps, shoulders and chest flexed as he pulled his arms free of the sleeves, and for a moment, that cock-sure grin played across his lips. The adrenaline, the thrill of the upcoming fight, shone in his eyes.

Her breath staggered from her as her desire for him momentarily overrode her worry. "Come back to me in one piece."

"I will." He curled his fingers around the copper coin in his hand. He lowered his head as he shrugged on the thick canvas jacket. "I always will."

But not if you become the Guild Master.

She pressed her lips together and began strapping his armor to him. Now was not the time to discuss her fears. He needed her to be strong, efficient, and calm—or at least, to appear calm.

Despite the mask of tranquility which she wore as she dressed him, her mind still whirred, clutching at any plan, any way they could stay together. The Guild Master's words, forgotten over the months, returned to her now in full horrifying clarity; he had been unable to leave the castle for thirty years.

The thought occurred to her, that she could simply give up Blackmere, and let it fall into the eager hands of one of her nieces or nephews. But then, if she abandoned her life, her family, and remained with Brandon at the Guild, their relationship would still have to remain a secret until the day he left the keep. Their love would exist only in short bursts, stolen moments and longing glances.

She shook off her crawling dread and stepped back to admire her work. Brandon was resplendent in his armor, torchlight gleaming on the shining steel. There was nothing left to put on but his armored gloves and the helmet. She handed him the left gauntlet, unwilling to look away from his eyes.

He was still hers, even if just for one more day.

As he held out his hand for the final gauntlet, she took the coin from his palm and clutched it in her own. He said nothing but arched his eyebrow at the theft.

She plucked the two feathers from her brooch and tucked them behind his breastplate. "A token," she smiled, she kept her voice low, her words only for his ears. "For luck. I've carried the black one by my heart for the past six months, and the white one... well... that one just feels lucky."

He chuckled, and his eyes drifted down to her lips. "Thank you."

"Whatever happens, I'm proud of you."

"It seems a waste of time to even bother getting in your armor, Brandon," Henry sneered as Tommy tied off his pauldrons. "If this is anything like Blackmere, it'll all be over for you in moments."

Brandon chuckled dryly. "It's funny, I don't remember you being this smug at the Guild when I kicked your arse. In fact, I remember you hiding for weeks afterwards."

Henry's lip curled.

Natalie stifled her laugh against the palm of her hand as Darius cackled from his stall.

Brandon's cheeks reddened and his armor clanked as he shrugged. "It had to be said."

The announcer's voice echoed down the tunnel. "First competitors!"

Brandon took a sharp breath and cast Natalie a sideways glance. His easy smile was at odds with her thundering pulse, and the sharp tang of acid on her tongue.

Brandon's first opponent, the Silver Wolf, stalked to his side. His wolf's head helmet bared its teeth at Brandon's bear. "Come on, Old Man. We've a rabble to entertain."

THIRTY-TWO

Brandon's hulking shape blocked her view of the amphitheater as she followed him out towards the end of the tunnel. The steady rhythm of impatient applause grew louder, rattling against her breastbone. The champions stood silhouetted against the brilliant sunlight.

The Silver Wolf at Brandon's side banged his ironclad fist against his breastplate. "Goddess smile on you, Bear."

Brandon lowered his head, and briefly pressed his palm to his heart. "And also, on you."

The edges of the coin dug into Natalie's palm as she clutched it to her chest. A queasy sensation forced her to keep swallowing, lest she empty the meager contents of her stomach all over the arena floor.

"People of Westgarden!" The announcer's voice boomed above them, amplified by the shape of the arena. "It is my great honor to present to you, the first of your great champions."

Applause burst through the air. The crowd shifted as one, rising to their feet and waving their banners.

Horns blasted out a fanfare as the announcer continued. "Please welcome to the arena, Mateus, The Silver Wolf, and Brandon, the Bear!"

Natalie felt as though she had been dunked in ice water as Brandon and his opponent charged into the ring. She raised her hand to shield her eyes as sunlight glared, reflected from their armor.

The roar of the crowd was ear-splitting, as Brandon and the Silver Wolf stepped into the center of the arena. They raised their blades, saluting Lady Luray, before turning to face each other, their ferocious helmets snarling.

Natalie closed her eyes, silently praying for Brandon's safety, and his victory. Her mind played tricks on her, telling her that his breastplate was not tight enough, that she had forgotten to tie the pauldrons securely to his shoulder, that she was somehow entirely responsible for his inevitable injuries.

At the clash of steel, her eyelids sprang open.

She pressed her fingertips to her lips, holding back the cry swelling in her chest. Brandon staggered, forced back by the Silver Wolf's blade, left to defend himself against an unforgiving onslaught of blows from the younger champion.

Howls erupted among the crowd as they fluttered their flags in support.

"Hurry up and get this over with!" Someone heckled from the seats above. "Get the old man off!"

Anger simmered on Natalie's tongue, but was quelled as Brandon broke the Silver Wolf's barrage, forcing him back with a mighty blow of his blade. The younger champion hopped back, narrowly avoiding the thrust towards his breastplate as the crowd hissed.

A steady clank of metal armor sounded behind Natalie as Darius approached. "How's he doing? Do you think he can win?"

Natalie dared not tear her eyes from Brandon as she answered. "He has to."

The crowd jeered as Brandon advanced, pushing the Silver Wolf back, exhausting him, forcing him to block blow after bone-shattering blow.

"Fight back!" a voice called from the crowd. "Come on Wolf!"

Undeterred by the boos and insults, Brandon fought on, striking his opponent with unmatchable force. For years, Natalie had dreamed of watching the legendary Brandon the Bear face his opponents in the arena. She had imagined the raw power, and the unrivaled skill of such a renowned warrior.

The chance had been stolen from her at Blackmere.

But as with everything she had ever expected of him, he surpassed her wildest imaginings.

Darius chuckled at Natalie's side. "Goddess, help the rest of us, this isn't a second wind." His armor gleamed in the corner of her eye as he pressed his fingers to his lips. "It's as though his glory days were just the warmup. He's fighting *for* something now, something greater than fame."

Natalie flinched as the Silver Wolf's blade darted towards Brandon's side. He deflected it, pushing back against the attack. Her breath flowed a little easier. "He fights for his family," she said, her heart filled with pride. "And for everything he lost at Blackmere."

Darius made a non-committal sound and continued to watch. The roar of the crowd reached fever pitch as the champions fought on.

"Brandon!" A man cried out in support. "Brandon the Bear!"

"*Bear! Bear! Bear!*" A chant began above them. It was a mere flicker of light in the endless abyss of taunts, but it was enough to spark hope in Natalie's heart.

"*Bear!*"

He threw his weight behind each blow, forcing the Silver Wolf back, back across the ring. More and more voices joined in with the chant.

"*Bear!*"

Natalie's heart slammed against her palm as she held the copper coin to her chest.

"*Bear! Bear! Bear!*"

The clang of Brandon's blade against the Silver Wolf's breastplate echoed around the arena. Relief all but swept Natalie into Darius's arms as the audience erupted into cheers.

Beside her Darius cried out, victorious. "He's done it!"

She held onto the cheering champion's arm, anchoring herself to the tunnel as the urge to run to Brandon overwhelmed her.

The champions in the arena bowed to Lady Luray, and then to the audience, before the Silver Wolf returned to the tunnel.

"Good fight, Mateus!" Darius clapped the loser on the

shoulder as he descended into the dark to change. When he was out of earshot he added. "Poor sod. He'll be sore for days."

Natalie only had eyes for Brandon as he strode towards them. Tears blurred her vision, and her throat knotted as he approached.

He pulled off his helmet and his bright pink cheeks swelled above the curve of his grin.

"By the Goddess, Sweet Bear," Darius wrapped his arms around Brandon and pounded his steel-covered back with an armored fist. For the first time Natalie noticed his armor was engraved with swirling clouds, and silver lightning bolts adorned the sides of his helmet. "I've honestly never been so aroused in my life."

Brandon laughed. His eyes fixed on Natalie as she battled the urge to leap into his arms. The fight faded from his eyes and was replaced by warmth and softness.

"Well fought, Sir Brandon," she beamed.

"My lady," he dipped his head and ran his fingers through his hair, pushing it back from his forehead.

The announcer above announced the next pairing, and the trio stepped aside to allow two new champions to charge into the arena.

"Come on," Darius grinned. "There are three bouts before your next round. You need to rest those old bones of yours."

Brandon cursed him, chuckling as they made their way into the armory.

THIRTY-THREE

The rush of adrenaline which followed Brandon's victory soon ebbed. Natalie's fingers trembled as she waited for the results of the other battles.

Darius's name was chanted above them as he fought his opponent, a golden-haired, muscular swordsman on his fourth melee season. The Storm versus the Stag, both beloved by the crowd.

"Come on Darius," Brandon whispered as he watched from the tunnel. Natalie stood behind him, pressing her shoulder to his back as she peered around him. Their closeness brought her comfort.

After Darius's fight, there was only one more battle left in the round, before they moved on to the semi-finals. Henry had been scheduled to fight against Genevieve, but after informing the Westgarden council of her departure from the Guild, her replacement had been added to the roster. Natalie suspected the order of the tournament had been carefully planned to make it highly likely Henry and

Darius would face each other in the final; a spectacular showdown of the two most favored champions. They had not counted on Brandon's strength.

Natalie brushed her fingertips against the blade at her belt, and a fresh wave of nausea rolled through her. After Henry's battle, she would compete in the squire contest. Her throat clenched at the thought.

Darius's victory rang throughout the arena. He threw his arms up in celebration, and, ever the showman, began blowing kisses towards the crowd.

The golden-haired Stag lumbered past them, muttering beneath his breath as his squire chased after him.

"Well fought Eugene," Brandon called after him.

Despite her nerves, Natalie could not help but smile. Brandon was lively—almost giddy—with the excitement of the contest, the thrill of victory. He had to win just one more fight, and he would be through to the final round.

As Darius bounded over, he opened his arms wide to embrace Brandon. "My Sweet Bear, hold me, I'm exhausted."

"You've another round to go, at least." Brandon chuckled, pinning Darius to his chest. "Go rest, drink some water."

"And miss Lady Blackmere's contest debut? I wouldn't dream of it."

Darius's words struck both fear and warmth into her heart. A nervous laugh escaped her lips.

The announcer above cut short the conversation. "People of Westgarden, it is my honor to present to you, the final fight of the first round of the Midsummer Melee. Let the Goddess hear your voices, as we bring to the arena, Henry Percille, The Dragon!"

Something hard and heavy cracked against Natalie's shoulder, shoving her against Brandon's chest. He wrapped his arms around her waist, holding her to him as Henry charged into the arena. The crowd screamed so loud the Goddess was likely covering her ears.

Natalie scowled after Henry as he raised his arms to the sky, basking in the cheers and adoration. Amorous screams erupted around the arena as he removed his ferocious, dragon's head helmet and flashed a wide grin towards Lady Luray.

"Are you hurt?" Brandon asked, his lips close to Natalie's ears. His face was etched with concern as he placed a hand over her shoulder.

Natalie looked up into his eyes—eyes she would never get tired of seeing. Her face warmed as she realized one hand still rested on her waist. "No, he just startled me."

The announcer continued above them. "And fighting The Dragon in the first round, please welcome, Lucille, The Charging Bull."

Natalie turned to applaud the warrior as she thundered into the arena, wielding twin blades, the copper horns on her helmet shining in the sunlight.

Close behind, sticking to the shadows, Joss approached Darius. The young squire flashed a crooked smile at Natalie as she clutched a cup of water in her hands.

Darius raised his eyebrows and accepted a cup from his squire. "So, tell me, Darling Bear, who do you hope wins this fight?"

Brandon stiffened a little before releasing a frustrated breath. "I honestly don't know. Part of me hopes he suffers the embarrassment of being knocked out in the first round."

"Liar," Darius grinned.

Natalie's heart leapt as Lucille gracefully spun on the ball of her foot. Her blades clattered against Henry's as he blocked each strike. The Dragon's strength and precision were both terrifying and impressive. The part of Natalie which loved the drama and the sport of the Tourneys almost enjoyed watching him fight.

"You know..." Darius placed his hand on Brandon's forearm. "You could just have him thrown from the Guild when you become Guild Master."

Her back stiffened as Brandon fell silent. The rumor was true, and there was no hiding the fact that she knew. The walls of the tunnel closed in around Natalie as the high-pitched ringing in her ears blocked out the roar of the crowd.

She had to let him go.

Henry's victory barely stirred a reaction from Brandon. He clapped politely, clearing his throat, as though a thousand unspoken words kept it closed.

Defeated, Lucille returned to the tunnel, and the clatter of ironclad palms on her backplate echoed around the darkness as Natalie stared ahead. In the center of the arena, Henry stood, his arms outstretched as a shower of white rose petals fluttered down onto him.

"Look at him, the cocky bastard," Darius laughed, unaware of the maelstrom he had conjured between

Natalie and Brandon. "They're acting as if he's already won."

"Aye. Well, good luck to you," Brandon sighed at last. The sound of his voice allowed Natalie to breathe once more. "You fight him next."

"Good luck to me? Does that mean you want me to beat him?"

"Of course."

"Liar." Darius snorted. "One of us will end this day disappointed, but let's not let it come between us. Love often demands sacrifice."

"Aye," Brandon replied. "That it does."

Natalie turned to face them, her heart heavy with the burden of knowing what she had to do. The light had left Brandon's eyes, and where once he had glowed with the thrill of the contest, he seemed to fade under the weight of the challenges before him. She forced a smile, and hoped it was enough to give him courage. She would never blame him for choosing the Guild over her, for putting his mother's health over their reckless, newfound love, no matter how much it pained her to let him go.

Giving him a single, determined nod she steadied her nerve. "Well now. I believe it's time for my public humiliation."

CHAPTER

THIRTY-FOUR

The champions who had been knocked out of the contest sat on a marble bench beneath Lady Luray's throne. Their good-natured cheers greeted the squires as they filed out of the tunnel. Still, the arena was only half as full as it had been for the champions' bouts as Natalie and seven other squires stepped out into the bright light.

The contest was the furthest thing from her mind.

Her fingers trembled as they brushed against the hilt of the blade at her hip, but it was not for the eyes watching her, nor for the fear of failure.

As far as Natalie was concerned, she had already lost.

The squires split into predetermined pairs, with each one assigned a quarter of the arena floor. Four pairs of squires prepared for battle, each one of them determined to win, to be considered for promotion and to become a champion.

Natalie faced her opponent; The Stag's squire, nineteen

years of age and built like a brick outhouse. He had never come to her with letters, and his slow smirk told her he saw her as an inconvenience rather than a real opponent. She faced certain defeat, but her heart beat steady, numbed by the certainty of what she had to do when the contest was over.

To cling to Brandon, was to drag him underwater, and with him, the people he was helping to keep afloat.

For a few moments at least, she would fight and find release in the thrill of the contest.

"Squires!" the announcer bellowed. "At my signal... fight!"

She raised her blade, blocking the squire's first strike, then the second, then the third. Each blow shot jarring pain through her arm.

Her opponent was a strong lad, but slow. She ducked beneath his arm as he lunged towards her, spun around to face him and sprung, tapping her blade on his breastplate.

"Point! Lady Blackmere!" the announcer declared.

A polite smattering of applause rippled around the arena.

"What?" Natalie gasped. Her grip on the blade loosened. There had to be some mistake.

"Good fight," her opponent panted, before trotting out of the arena back down the tunnel towards the armory.

In the center of the ring, Tommy and Joss stood waiting, already victorious in their own battles. They beckoned Natalie over, both laughing in delight.

"You did well," Tommy beamed as she approached. "Brandon's a good teacher."

"Aye," she panted.

"Hopefully not too good. You fight me next."

The thought of facing Henry's squire, a lad she thought so fondly of, cooled her blood. The fourth and final squire through to the semifinals joined them, a younger boy, who could not have been older than fourteen. He faced Joss; his sword comically large for his small frame.

"You can do it, Nat!" Brandon called from the tunnel. The sound of his voice filled her with as much sadness as courage.

She took a deep breath and closed her eyes. An image haunted her in the darkness, the image of herself laying before the fire, back in the cottage at Blackmere. Brandon was beside her, smiling as he brushed the strands of her hair back from her face. He lifted her hand and brought her knuckles to his lips and let the heat of his breath melt the chill from her fingertips. She was calm, and content, curled against him as he traced the curves of her body with loving touches.

The bandits had not torn them apart, nor had the rules of the Guild.

No matter what happened, they had shared so much love, so much passion and pleasure, but for the sake of those dearest to him, for his own sake, she had to let him go.

Love would drive a wedge where hate and fear could not.

"Squires," the announcer called. "At my signal... fight."

Natalie opened her eyes and exhaled slowly. She raised her arm, bracing herself as Tommy charged towards her. His first blow hit like a bolt of lightning, the shock pulsing agony through her muscles. His style mirrored Henry's, unrelenting vicious attacks, each blow almost tearing her own blade from her hands. As good-hearted and sweet as he was, he was not going easy on her.

Fire poured through her veins, feeding the muscles in her arm. Brandon had taught her to block, to protect herself against these onslaughts. Her lips pulled back as she bared her teeth.

She was no longer Lady Blackmere.

In the face of the onslaught, she forgot the contest, forgot the cheering crowd. She forgot her aching heart and the impossible choice she faced with Brandon.

Terror and exhilaration guided her arm and filled her with a strength she had not known she possessed. Every training session, every step climbed up the cliffside made sense. She was strong, stronger than she had ever felt in her life, and for a moment she allowed herself to believe that perhaps she could become a champion.

But the tap of his blade on her breastplate brought her dream crashing around her.

CHAPTER

THIRTY-FIVE

The wind was knocked from her lungs as the squire pounced on her, wrapping his arms around her and cheering with the crowd. Moments later Joss joined them, tackling Natalie and Tommy with a ferocious, somewhat painful hug. Natalie was lost in a tangled forest of arms, cheers and congratulations.

The disappointment of her defeat was shaken away by their boisterous celebrations, by the wide, beaming smile spread across Tommy's face.

"By the Goddess, Lady Blackmere," Joss laughed. "For an amateur that was amazing."

"Thank you." Natalie smiled, even as tears stung her eyes.

The squires stepped back, and at last she was able to breathe. The relief was momentary, as a pair of infinitely strong, ironclad arms crushed her against a vast wall of unyielding metal.

"You're incredible," Brandon whispered against her ear, sending shivers through her flesh. She clung to him, the tips of her fingers paling against the cold metal. Savoring every moment that he held her, she closed her eyes and let her breath stagger from her lungs.

"I lost," was all she managed to say.

"Aye, but you've only been fighting for a couple of months." He led her to the edge of the arena, so that Tommy and Joss could battle for the title. "I couldn't be prouder."

"You're too kind."

She could not take her eyes from him as the battle between Tommy and Joss commenced. His keen eyes followed every blow and block. He took a deep breath, the muscles of his jaw twitching as he turned to look at her.

He reached up a hand to rake his fingers through his hair. "My lady, when we get a moment, I need to speak with you."

This was it. It gave her some hope to know that Brandon would be the first to broach the subject. Perhaps he would be the one to call off their relationship, to choose their love as the unavoidable sacrifice.

She opened her mouth to speak but was rendered silent by Darius's approach. "Lady Blackmere, noblewoman and mistress of the blade." He held out his arms and wrapped her in a painful, but welcome embrace. "You did wonderfully."

The silver blockade of Darius's armor obscured Natalie's view of Brandon, a fact she was entirely glad of. It was too painful to look at him.

Behind her the audience erupted into cheers. The squire's contest was over.

"Ah," Darius said, more than a little disappointed as he released Natalie from his arms. "I did so hope Joss would win."

"There's always next year. She's still young. Tommy's got a lot of promise." Brandon said as he applauded the fight. "He'll make a fine champion, and so will Joss one day."

Darius chuckled, clapping his friend on the back. "Spoken like a true Guild Master."

The words hit Natalie like an arrow to the heart, but she had little time to dwell on it.

"Squires!" The announcer cried out. "Please approach Lady Luray to receive your prizes."

"That's you," Darius chuckled, jostling Natalie's shoulder. "Don't keep her waiting. You know how these nobles are."

Natalie nodded her head and forced a laugh. Heart racing, she stepped back out into the light, shielding her eyes from the sun as the crowd cheered. The scent of roasted meat wafted through the air as the audience members returned from procuring refreshments. There were fewer empty seats around the arena as the people prepared to watch the semi-finals of the champion's melee.

Lady Luray's eyes followed Natalie as she joined her fellow squires to stand before the hosting noblewoman and her council. The Lady of Westgarden's auburn curls shimmered in the breeze, as white silks fluttered around her. She was ethereal in her beauty, and as her eyes raked across

Natalie, in her drab clothing and bedraggled hair, she felt herself wilt.

"A noble lady turned squire." Lady Luray's lips quirked in amusement as she glanced at Natalie's tunic. The last time they had met was more than a decade ago; a yuletide feast in the capital when both women had been dressed in their finery.

Natalie bowed and smiled. "Sadly, just until the winter. I owe a great debt to the champions for their aid at Blackmere."

"So we've heard. It was rather a thrilling tale. And now you squire for Brandon." She gave a musical laugh. "I must say, we thought he was past his best, but he surprised us in the first round of the contest."

"He continues to surprise me," Natalie said, pride filling her heart. "His already limitless strength and kindness grow greater still with every passing day, and... it's been my honor to stand beside him. Men like Brandon are rare indeed, and I will not leave his side happily." Her throat closed. "When I return to Blackmere, that is."

A ripple of polite applause traveled around the arena. Lady Luray raised her hand, rendering the people silent. "There's one thing I must know, Lady Blackmere. The stories say you fought by his side at Blackmere. Are they true?"

Natalie lowered her head. "I did. I did what I had to do, to save my people. And Brandon fought bravely, putting his life on the line for people he had never met before. He's not just a champion, but a hero to so many."

"How very..." Lady Luray's smile broadened as her gaze

shifted towards the yawning darkness of the tunnel where Brandon waited. "Stirring." A flash of pearly teeth briefly pressed against the petal-pink of her lips.

Her curiosity satisfied, the noblewoman took the first of three finely made swords from a cushion and held it aloft. "In any case, the third prize in the squire's melee combat, goes to Lady Natalie Blackmere, squire to Sir Brandon."

The world dropped from beneath Natalie as her mouth gaped. They had to be mistaken.

Searching the smiling faces of the squires, who urged her forward to take her prize, her eyes filled with tears. "Me? Are you sure?"

"You scored the third highest," Lady Luray chuckled as she held out the blade. "I believe that's how this works."

Natalie wrapped her fingers around the handle, gripping the leather as though her life depended on it. Her own blade. The scabbard was made of rich reddish-brown leather, and the steel of the cross-guard was engraved with tangled vines of roses.

Lady Luray raised her hand for silence. "The second prize goes to Jocelyn, squire to Darius."

Joss beamed as she took her weapon from Lady Luray. Her cheeks reddened as the crowd cheered for her.

"And the first-place prize goes to Thomas, squire to Henry Percille," Lady Luray announced.

Natalie thought her heart might burst as Tommy received his grand prize, a finely crafted sword, the pommel inlaid with sparkling sapphires. The stones alone were worth a small fortune.

With the prizes distributed, Lady Luray returned to her

throne. Her curious gaze lingered on Natalie as she handed the ceremony back to the announcer.

"Squires!" His voice boomed around the arena. "Return to your champions and help them prepare for the semi-finals of the Midsummer Melee."

Tommy laughed all the way back to the armory, his cheeks rosy with excitement. He turned the sword over and over in his hands, as though he feared at any moment it would vanish.

"Look at this thing," he beamed.

Natalie shared his excitement. "It's very well deserved."

His eyes shone with the overwhelming force of his excitement and relief. "This'll put me in good stead to become a champion."

"Then you'd better start planning your alias." Brandon approached, stealing the air from Natalie's lungs. His presence sent an ache through Natalie's body, a longing to be held, to raise onto the tips of her toes and kiss him. "I'm proud of you, both of you," he grinned, ruffling his fingers through Tommy's hair. His eyes drifted towards Natalie. "Might I speak to you a moment?"

She could only nod.

The remaining three champions prepared themselves for the next round and the atmosphere hung heavy around them. Sara and Henry whispered amongst themselves, their eyes raking across Natalie and Brandon as they passed by.

"Congratulations," Darius grinned to Joss as he admired her blade. "Next year, you'll be unstoppable."

But every shred of pride in the squires, every drop of

excitement for the victories was washed away by the cold, creeping dread of losing Brandon.

When they reached a darkened corner, and relative privacy, Brandon turned to her and brushed his fingers against her arm. "I'm not taking it."

She froze. "What?"

"You heard what Darius said, about me taking up the position of Guild Master, and it's true. The Guild Master mentioned it a couple of weeks ago and officially made the offer just before we left."

"I know." Her lips trembled as she whispered. "As much as it hurts me to say, I think you should take it. Knowing that I'm the reason the people who love you are suffering... Brandon, I couldn't live with myself."

"Well you'll have to."

"Brandon..."

"I'll tell him no. This year is my last at the Guild."

Tears stung at her eyes, both from relief and panic. "But what about your family? A position like that would ensure you have more than enough money to help them."

"Aye it would, but at what cost? I'd never be able to leave the Guild. I'd never even be able to see my family again. I don't want that. I'd rather work hard somewhere else, and still have the freedom to leave." Curling his fingers around her palm, he held it low down by her hip so they would not be seen. He lowered his voice even further. "And no matter how much money they'd give me, no matter how comfortable my life, it would always be empty without you."

His dark eyes, so full of strength and kindness filled with tears.

Her heart shattered "But what about those who love you here? The champions and squires? You becoming the Guild Master would mean so much to them."

"They'll find someone else. There are good people, lots of them, who would be better than I at the role." His eyes creased as he smiled. "I'm not changing my mind, Nat. I made my decision; I just haven't told the rest of them yet. I thought it might get under Henry's skin."

She could only nod her head as relief overwhelmed her. "Are you certain? That's truly what you want?"

"*You* are what I want." His smile was fleeting but hit Natalie with the force of a battering ram. He ran his thumb across the back of her hand and sent her heart soaring. "I just have two more fights to win. I face Sara in the next round, and then either Darius or Henry. The prize money from this will give me time to think about what I do next. If I'm careful, I can make it last four years. In the winter I'll fight in the Grand Tourney. If I can win that, and this time not fritter all my winnings on drink and... Goddess knows what... I'll find a way to make it all work, I promise. But I'm not losing you."

It took all her effort not to wrap her arms around him. "You're so strong."

"Every ounce of my strength comes because you remind me of it. Every blow I strike, and every one I block, brings us closer together. If I have to, I'll keep fighting until I draw my last breath."

He gave her hand a parting squeeze, and together they

walked back to his booth to take up his weapon. Natalie could not help but smile through the tears blurring her vision.

She was his, and he was hers, and nothing could tear them apart.

THIRTY-SIX

The battle between Brandon and Sara raged on, the Snow Fox's twin blades whirring against the Bear's indomitable longsword. Sara was fast, agile, and skilled, but Brandon shattered her defense.

Brandon was unstoppable.

The crowd chanted, pumping their fists into the air. *Bear! Bear! Bear!*

Natalie held her breath as Sara leapt through the air, her blades aimed true. Brandon deflected her blow, sweeping around to tap the tip of his blade against her breastplate.

The crowd erupted into feral howls.

Darius roared at Natalie's side. "He's done it! Goddess he's through to the final!"

Natalie was bursting, her heart filled with pride, love and hope. He was a champion, *her* champion, and no matter what happened, they would find a way to stay together. Their love would overcome any obstacle.

Sara stormed by them, her eyes dark and her knuckles bone white as she gripped the hilt of her blade. "This is ridiculous," she spat. "He's cheating. He has to be."

Darius chuckled as she disappeared into the shadows beneath the arena. "Sore loser."

Silk handkerchiefs and tokens of allegiance rained down onto the arena sand as Brandon bowed before the audience.

"They love him," Natalie beamed.

"Who can blame them?" Darius rested his hand on her shoulder. "Some of that love comes in part from your testimony of his bravery at Blackmere. The people love an underdog, and they love someone who fights for people like them. Brandon is both."

"I'm surprised the news of what happened traveled this far. Blackmere is little more than a swamp compared to Westgarden."

Darius chuckled. "A champion fighting beside a noble lady to defend her castle? It's romantic. They lap it up." His eyes lit up as Brandon ran towards them, scrunched bouquets of silk scarves and handkerchiefs clutched in his fists. "It does help, of course, that he's absurdly handsome."

Natalie silently agreed as Brandon approached. She took his blade and held it dutifully. "Just one more fight to go."

"Aye," he panted. His eyes were bright once more. "Depending on the outcome of the next fight, it's either Henry, or this posturing little peacock."

Darius tapped the point of his blade against Brandon's chest, his eyes narrow and lips tight in mock indignation. "It *will* be me. I need that prize money just as badly as you, Sweet Bear. Don't think my love for you will stop me from trying to kick your delightful bottom." He thrust his helmet on and took a deep breath. "I sent my squire to fetch me some lunch. Victory does tend to make me ravenous." He arched an eyebrow. "For many things."

Brandon chuckled as he stepped aside, allowing Darius to enter the arena. "Fight well."

Natalie pressed her teeth into her lower lip as Darius began to spin his blade gracefully for the benefit of the spectators. The smile faded from her lips as Henry approached from the darkness to stand beside her.

The menthol tang of the oil the champions used to soothe their aching muscles stung Natalie's nose. Henry was drenched in it.

He smirked as he fixed his eyes on Darius. "I'm honestly thrilled you're through to the final, Brandon. It'll make your humiliation all the more satisfying."

Natalie clamped her jaw shut. Beside her, Brandon stared straight ahead, undeterred by Henry's taunting.

"I have a proposition for you," The Dragon sneered in response to their silence. "One which I think you'll find most attractive."

"Another marriage proposal?" Natalie said, keeping her voice firm and level. "Wasn't one rejection enough for you?"

"Sadly, I'm not that desperate. The Guild Master believed me, trusted my innocence, and welcomed me back to the fold with open arms. There was no need for me to settle for a life at Blackmere, nor to hide behind the protection of a noble wife—if only in name." He smiled slowly, knowing his words meant nothing. No one would believe them if they accused him of arranging the attack at Blackmere again. It was their word against his. "Besides, I'm rather enjoying this season. It's tremendous fun to watch this lummox's ego inflate again. We all know how hard it plummeted once it grew too large."

"Whatever it is, we're not interested." Brandon sighed. "I'm tired of your weaseling. Just face your battles like a champion."

"Rather rich coming from a man flouting the Guild's rules at every chance he gets." Henry held Brandon's gaze, his eyes cold above the curve of his smile. He pulled on his helmet and turned to face the arena. "I'll speak to you after my victory."

The announcer called his name, and Henry charged forward into the arena, leaving Natalie and Brandon alone.

"Prick," Natalie spat. The curse lifted some of the tension in her muscles.

"Aye."

She turned back to face the shadows, and found Brandon smiling at her. The creases at the corners of his eyes curved upwards, and the sunlight glimmered on the silver at his temples.

The armory behind them was empty, the shadows comforting.

Natalie and Brandon were shrouded in darkness. The urge to kiss him, even briefly, pulled at her. It had been days since they had the luxury of holding each other.

His gaze drifted across her features, lingering on her lips, as though the sound of clashing blades in the arena was the least important thing in the world. Nothing else mattered, Henry's taunts and provocation washed over her.

Lips parted, Brandon stepped towards her.

Her chest tightened, and her breath hitched as he pressed himself against her. Brandon—her Brandon, a mountain of strength and steel, pushing her against the cold stone wall of the tunnel. When he looked at her, his eyes dark with hunger, the rules and traditions forced upon them were meaningless.

She raised onto her tiptoes and wrapped her arms around his neck, pulling him into a kiss. At the touch of his lips she was home. Visions of their future played out before her, of waking up beside him in the mornings, and holding him as they fell asleep. They would ride up to Marshdown together and meet his family, ride to Caer Austwick to meet her father, and one day, one day when they truly knew each other, when he had seen everything of the world that the Guild had kept hidden from him, he might ask her to be his wife.

Her knees threatened to buckle beneath her as his tongue teased hers. His cold metal fingers cooled the heat flaring on her cheeks.

"I'm going to win this," he whispered against her lips. "We'll be together, and nothing will take you from me. I won't let it."

She reached up, brushing the loose strands of hair back from his forehead, trailing her hand down to cup his cheek. Something swelled against the confines of her ribs, something between a bubble of laughter and a squeal of delight.

She suppressed it with a fragmented breath. "I love you, with all that I am."

"And I love you." He took her hand in his and kissed her knuckles, letting the warmth of his breath tingle against her skin. "My lady."

His smile was shattered by the movement in the darkness.

Tommy stood frozen in the shadows. His wide eyes scoured Brandon's face.

"Oh, Goddess." Brandon jumped back away from Natalie. His gasping breath echoed in the tunnel. "Tommy. I didn't know you were there."

Heart pounding, Natalie stood against the wall, pressing her back to the stones in the hopes that they would swallow her. Thoughts rushed through her mind. Perhaps he had not seen them, perhaps he could be convinced to keep their secret, perhaps—

Perhaps she had caused Brandon to lose everything.

"Tommy?" Brandon took a step towards the squire.

The audience cried out in shrill unison, but Natalie dared not turn around to see who had claimed victory of the round. The rise and fall of her chest grew faster with every passing moment. The silence inside the tunnel was agony.

She worked her tongue around the arid cavern of her mouth before speaking. "Tommy... please—"

"*Get the physician!*" The command rang out across the arena, pulling their attention to a small cluster of people in the center of the arena, crouched around a lifeless figure.

"No." Brandon charged into the dazzling afternoon sun.

Natalie was less than a heartbeat behind him, and

Tommy soon overtook her. The sand shifted beneath her feet, every step taking twice the effort. By the time she reached the gathering, she was breathless.

Henry stood a few feet away, gripping his blade in one hand, the fingers of his other buried in his hair. Natalie's vision darkened. Wine-red spots stained the sand and coated the tip of Henry's blade.

"What have you done?" Brandon bellowed.

Henry stared, wide-eyed and open mouthed. "Oh Goddess, is he alright?"

Natalie was frozen in place. The blood on the sand, the stillness and silence in the once frenzied arena emptied her heart.

Brandon pushed his way into the gathering of people. "Not again." His voice cracked as he sunk to his knees and gripped Darius's hand. "Please, Goddess, no. No. Not again. Not again."

The crowd was silent.

THIRTY-SEVEN

Natalie's uselessness tormented her.

The sharp rise and fall of Darius's chest was both a blessing and a cause for worry. He was alive, but the severity of his wound was still unknown. She stood by Brandon's side, resting her hand on the back of his neck, hoping he drew some comfort from her.

Henry stood back, silently observing, unnoticed by all but Natalie as they awaited the physician's verdict. The Dragon's concern had been replaced by calm and stillness, as he stared at the tip of the sword in his hand. Slowly, his lips curled into a smile.

Horror emptied Natalie's heart. Henry was proud, whether the injury was deliberate or not. His eyes snapped to hers, and the smile was gone, leaving Natalie with a chill coursing through her veins.

The physician—an elderly man with a thin, hooked nose—inspected the wound, pressing his fingers into a puncture in Darius's armpit, his expression unreadable. "The wound is fairly deep, though not, I hope, unfixable. He'll live."

Brandon's shoulders slouched beneath Natalie's palm as his breath broke free. "Thank the Goddess."

Relief surged in Natalie's chest. Darius's eyelids flickered a little as the wound was packed to stem the flow of blood.

"He'll need to be stitched." The physician instructed his assistants.

"It's so like him to be dramatic," Henry chuckled.

Brandon bolted upright. His eyes, normally so warm and kind, were dark, filled with anger. Hands curling into fists, he faced Henry.

Natalie's pulse raced. Her own anger simmered in the pit of her stomach. That smile, the slow, satisfied smirk as Henry looked down at the blood-coated tip of his blade, haunted her.

"You did it on purpose," she said. Her voice sounded distant to her ears, lost beneath the muffled pounding of her pulse.

Henry snickered, and his face twisted in incredulous indignation. "What?" He held out his blade for Tommy to take. "Based on what evidence?"

Tommy stepped back, gripping the blade. The young squire's eyes hardened as they drifted over Natalie and Brandon. "You don't know that. You didn't even see what happened."

Henry whirred around to face his squire. "I do not need you to defend me, boy. I'm used to them throwing baseless accusations at me by now. Go and clean my blade."

The squire lowered his head and turned to head back to the armory. Natalie's body trembled as Henry's sneer returned.

Horns blasted around the arena, rendering them silent. They followed the direction of the sound, to see Lady Luray walking towards them. Her servants walked before her, placing a path of straw mats before her feet, keeping her from spoiling her silk slippers on the sandy arena floor. Silk billowed in the breeze as she drew closer, and the air filled with the scent of honeysuckle. Gold strands in her hair glistened in the afternoon sun.

Brandon and Henry lowered their heads and placed their right hand across their chests. Natalie gave a slight bow of her head. Lady Luray was radiant in silks, whilst Natalie sweated in leather and armor, but they were still equals.

Lady Luray dipped her head to Natalie as she stood before her. "Are his injuries severe?"

Natalie glanced over her shoulder. The physician's assistants lifted Darius from the arena floor and carried him carefully back towards the armory.

"The doctor says he'll live," Natalie tried to make her voice as assuring as possible, hoping to assuage her own doubts. There was so much blood on the sand. "He's strong. He should pull through."

"I'm glad to hear it." Lady Luray's eyes drifted towards Brandon, and her generous lips curved into a smile. "Brandon the Bear."

"My lady," he greeted her. The muscle in his cheek flexed as she held out her hand towards him. Gently, he took her fingers in his, and grazed his lips against her knuckles.

"You seem to be winning the hearts of everyone in Westgarden."

"Aye, I'm honored."

"It's marvelous to watch you return to your full strength." She chuckled softly before inclining her head and stepping towards him, blocking Natalie from the conversation. "I wrote to you, many times. Did you receive my letters?"

Natalie held her breath as Brandon pressed his lips together. The crease between his eyebrows deepened. "I did, my lady."

"You never did write back." Her tongue lapped at the cushion of her lower lip, followed by a white flash of teeth. "What did you think of them?"

"Sadly, being a commoner, I'm unable to read." Brandon took a deep breath before adding, "My lady."

Natalie's heart thundered. The noble lady's flirtations sent liquid fire pulsing through her veins, burning at the back of her neck. The letters Lady Luray sent had been explicit in her desire for Brandon.

Lady Luray's lips quirked once more as she held out a hand to touch the steel vambrace covering his forearm. "Oh, well that's a pity." She rocked up onto her tiptoes, and whispered, her lips close to his ear, "If you come to the keep tonight, after the contest, I'll recite what I remember by heart."

The sensation of being coated in hot wax consumed

Natalie. Heat rolled down her body as her vision blurred and her muscles tightened, frozen in panic.

Brandon shifted uncomfortably. "That's very kind of you, but unfortunately I'm... I can't..."

"Oh, come now," Henry laughed, clapping Brandon on the shoulder. "Whatever you have planned for tonight can surely be put off."

"I'm afraid not, Lady Luray," Brandon smiled courteously. "I must decline, with the greatest of respect."

The noblewoman's cheeks reddened as she took a step back, withdrawing her fingers from Brandon's arm.

Henry scoffed. "What could surely be more important that you would turn down the invitation of such an esteemed noble lady?" His eyes snapped towards Natalie as he grinned, relishing the discomfort. "Set your champion right, Lady Blackmere. Surely, he cannot deny the hospitality of the radiant Lady Luray? To do so would be an insult most dire."

Natalie's throat clamped as her heart kicked against her ribs. Her whole body cringed as she tried to navigate the awkward situation. "I—" She looked at Brandon. Through his nervous laughter, his eyes pleaded with her. She steeled her nerve. "I always feel such decisions should be enthusiastically agreed upon by both parties, don't you think, Catherine?" She turned to Lady Luray, hoping the informality would warm her to Natalie. "Brandon has as much right to say no to your advances as any woman should to a noble lord."

She held her breath, awaiting Lady Luray's response. Henry's face hardened in the corner of her eye.

"No, you're quite right, Natalie." Lady Luray bowed. Her cheeks were flushed, the same shade of pink as the roses surrounding her castle. "Forgive me, Sir Brandon." She cast a sharp glance towards Henry. "It was never my intent to cause you discomfort."

"It's quite alright, my lady," Brandon's expression brightened as his breaths came easier. "I am truly flattered."

Henry cleared his throat and used the side of his foot to swipe sand over the bloodstain on the ground.

Natalie pitied Lady Luray. She was flirtatious, yes, but she had not pressed the issue. It was Henry, goading her in his desire to see Natalie and Brandon suffer. She hated him with every fiber of her being.

Lady Luray smiled warmly. "Although I would understand your hesitancy to continue the contest, I do hope we shall see the final round."

Natalie's body tensed as Brandon and Henry looked to each other. In the flurry of panic and tension, she had almost forgotten there was still one round left.

Brandon took a deep breath nodding slowly. "Aye, my lady. We'll fight the final round."

"Let's get this over with," Henry muttered.

Undeterred by Henry's cold demeanor, Lady Luray turned and held out her hands to her subjects. "People of Westgarden, it is my delight to announce that the final will be fought between Henry Percille, the Dragon, and Sir Brandon the Bear."

Applause erupted around the arena as Natalie's blood ran cold. Henry's eyes blazed into Brandon's, filled with loathing and determination.

"Return to the armory," Lady Luray instructed them. "Prepare yourselves but take your time. Ensure your friend is well. I'll have entertainers keep the crowd warm."

"You're too kind, my lady," Brandon bowed. "Thank you for your understanding, in all matters."

As they turned and walked back to the armory, the arena seemed to pulse around Natalie. Her jaw was clenched, and her body tense as she glanced at Henry. "I suppose this is all highly amusing to you?"

"Oh, Lady Blackmere, I'm just warming up." Henry snickered and strode ahead, holding his head high as he disappeared into the shadows.

CHAPTER

THIRTY-EIGHT

Darius lay on a bench in a small room off to the side of the armory. His wound had been stitched with silk, and a salve applied to fight off infection. Natalie pressed her back to the rough stone wall of the surgery, the color draining from her face as the doctor cleaned the dried blood from his skin.

"It'll be awhile before he can use the arm again." The physician wiped his bloodied fingers on a cloth. "And longer still before he regains the strength he had. But he's alive, and his lungs are mercifully intact."

"Thank you," Brandon said, as he sat by Darius's side. He cupped one of Darius's hands in his. "A thousand times, thank you."

The doctor gave a bitter bark of laughter. "What you people are willing to do for fame and riches; I'll never understand it. You risk your lives for sport, you sterilize yourselves and abandon family and love, and for what? Gold?"

Natalie half expected Brandon to protest, but as with everything, he absorbed the physician's grumbling and buried it within him. Still muttering beneath his breath, the doctor sidled out of the room, leaving the three of them alone. Brandon released a labored sigh.

"I'm alright," Darius muttered from the table. He raised his other arm, wound his fingers around Brandon's and gave him a weak smile. "I could take on one hundred Dragons, right now. Just put my blade in my hand."

Natalie smiled, folding her arms across her chest. "Thank the Goddess there's only one Dragon."

Darius laughed. He winced, sucking the breath through his teeth. "I'll let you fight him for me, Sweet Bear."

"That's very kind of you," Brandon smiled.

"Please, don't let him get away with it."

"I won't." Brandon tightened his grip around Darius's hand and held it to his chest. "You should stay in here and get some rest."

A bitter chuckle escaped his lips. "You have to be kidding. I want to watch this. I want to see you crush him. Give me a moment to dress."

Brandon shook his head. "Darius..."

"Out. Before you see something that'll really throw you off kilter."

With a chuckle, Brandon stood and turned. Together he and Natalie headed out of the room, closing the door behind them.

Once they were alone, he sighed and held Natalie's gaze. "I don't believe for a moment it was an accident."

"Neither do I." Natalie reached out to caress the silver

at his temples, a brief smile breaking through the darkness as he leaned into her touch. There was little need for discretion. Henry and Tommy were the only two remaining in the armory, and they both knew.

"He's going to pay for this, Nat. For Darius, for Robert, and for us."

"Please be careful." Her heart hammered as her eyes drifted towards the scar cleaving his eyebrow in two.

They walked back through the shadows to the main room of the armory. Henry sat in his booth, inspecting his blade as Tommy stood before him. All the color had drained from the squire's face, and he winced as Natalie and Brandon approached, as though the mere sight of them hurt him.

"My squire informs me he did not witness my victory." Henry rose to his feet and a satisfied smirk crossed his lips. "He's altogether too traumatized by what he witnessed while you two thought you were alone; the people he respected, flouting the rules of the Guild who raised him."

Tommy was shaking, his eyes ringed red and downcast. His face was marked with dark pink blotches, four along one side of his jaw, and one on the other.

The hairs on the back of Natalie's neck raised as Brandon took a step towards Henry. "This has gone too far."

"You're quite right, which is why, as I mentioned earlier, even before all this unpleasantness, I have a proposal for you."

"And I told you, I'm not interested."

"You should be. Your reputation, and Lady Blackmere's is on the line. Remember, I have a witness to your tryst, a very trustworthy young man. I'm sure even you would not stoop so low as to tarnish dear Tommy's name by calling him a liar."

Brandon's shoulders slumped as the fight ebbed from his heart.

"I thought not." Henry grinned. "Your family depends on you, Brandon." He tutted, tapping the tip of his blade against Brandon's breastplate. "How can you be so heartless?"

Brandon inhaled slowly, closing his eyes. "What do you want?"

"I want many things." Henry chuckled and wrapped his arm around Tommy's shoulder. Natalie's body tensed as the young squire flinched. "I want it all. Victory, the promise of my family name, the destiny I was born to, and for you to realize you can't have it all, not again. You had your glory days, and you let them slip through your fingers. You were a paragon of champions, now look at you, a disgrace, flouting the rules of the very Guild you owe your life to."

The room throbbed around them in rhythm with Natalie's pulse. Tears pricked at her eyes. "Oh, stop this nonsense Henry. What do you want from us?"

Her guts squirmed as The Dragon took a step towards them. He stood before Brandon and tilted his face to look him in the eyes. "Send *her* away from the Guild, and then lose the contest. If you don't, the Guild Master will discover your secret and you lose everything."

Natalie scoffed in disbelief. "You don't even need the prize money. You won four times that amount in Blackmere."

"You don't get a say in this." Henry turned to her. "You came here threatening my livelihood, laying the blame for my friends' deaths at my feet. You, a noblewoman with more power than I might ever possess, accused me of murder, and tried to take everything from me."

"I don't think you murdered anyone, Henry. Not by your own hand, at least," Brandon muttered. "I just think your ambition has reached a point where you no longer care if people die."

Tommy lowered his head and pressed his lips into a hard line. Beyond the tunnel, the audience began a slow, impatient clap.

"Your choice is simple, and non-negotiable," Henry snarled, snatching his helmet from Tommy's hands. "Come out there, fight me and lose the contest, or lose everything. You've had everything for far too long. And believe me, Boar, when you're forced out of the Guild and your titles stripped, your family will know why their money suddenly stopped. They'll know their son chose to follow the whims of his cock, over love and honor."

Brandon stood staring at the ground. Tears stung Natalie's eyes as she watched him crumble beneath the threat.

"I'll leave." Natalie's voice startled her as it echoed around the chamber. "I'll leave now if you wish it, but don't force him to lose. His family needs the money."

A bitter laugh cracked the air. "I've told you what I want. No compromises, no bargains."

"Very well." Brandon's answer was almost a whisper. "You win. I'll throw the contest."

Henry's smirk sent a wave of nausea through Natalie's

body. "Excellent. Make it a good fight and I'll consider giving you half the prize money, boar. If you beg me for it, that is." He turned on his heel and strode out towards the tunnel and the howling of the rapturous crowd.

Natalie released a breath and looked to Brandon. He stared at the floor, his lips parted and brow creased. The world which just minutes ago had been filled with love and hope, was now crushing. They had lost.

Tommy's lip quavered, his resolve collapsing under the weight of all that had happened. "I'm... sorry."

Brandon stepped forward and enveloped Tommy in his arms, holding the lad as he broke into sobs. Natalie held Brandon's gaze as he tightened his embrace. "It's alright. It wasn't your secret to keep."

"He said he'd have me thrown out unless I told him what happened. He took my sword and said if I kept another secret from him, he'd break it in two. He knew something had happened. I'm sorry, I couldn't hide it."

Natalie's heart hung heavy in her chest. "We should've been more careful. You shouldn't have been put in this position."

Tommy wiped his eyes on his sleeve and sniffed, breaking free of Brandon's embrace. "I don't want you to go, Lady Blackmere."

"Don't worry yourself." Brandon offered him a gentle smile, looking into his eyes as he squeezed Tommy's shoulder. "We'll get it put right. Would you help Darius back up to the arena? See that he's comfortable."

"Yes sir," Tommy smiled weakly.

"You've done nothing wrong."

"Thank you." Tommy nodded and hurried over to the side room. As he disappeared through the door, Brandon slumped on the bench in Henry's booth. He leaned forward and buried his face in his hands.

Natalie dropped to her knees before him, wrapping her arms around the cold metal of his shoulders. She breathed in deeply, savoring the scent of leather and oil, the warmth of his skin at his neck. "I'm sorry."

He shook his head and inhaled, filling his chest. A vein throbbed in his throat, as his eyes turned glossy.

Desperate for the comfort of his touch, she took his hand, and eased off his gauntlet, placing it on the ground by his feet. She laced her fingers with his and kissed his knuckles as tears spilled down her cheeks. Her lips trembled as she closed her eyes and bowed her head. "I'll wait for you in Blackmere."

"You don't have to."

"I do, and I will, no matter how long it takes."

Six months, six beautiful months of love and passion, of feeling safe in the fleeting moments he held her. He was not just her lover, he was her best friend, the person she allowed to see every part of her and having him torn from her was as agonizing as ripping out her heart at the root.

He shifted a little, and the armory filled with the sound of metal grinding against metal. "Since we returned from Blackmere, everything has changed. I want to fight; I want to be the strongest, the greatest—"

"And you are, Brandon, you're incredible. You win the heart of everyone you meet, you're better now than you ever were, and I can't take you from this. I can't—" Her throat clamped shut as she held back a sob. The slow, distant clapping of the crowd marked the seconds they had left together. "You have to fight, and yes, this time, you have to lose. But you can still win the Grand Tourney, and every competition after that. Fight for your family, for Robert, for everything you've lost."

She lifted her face to look at him. He held the black and white feathers between his fingers. "You know the reason I've found my passion for this again?" He took his ungloved hand and caressed the side of her face. "It isn't revenge for what happened at Blackmere, and it isn't a desire to see Henry lose."

Her breath hitched as he brushed his thumb across her lower lip.

"You make me want to be a better man," he whispered. "I fight for you. I want to be the champion you deserve. And I will never stop fighting to be with you, for as long as you'll have me."

Her heart lifted as a smile tugged at her lips. "Forever. I want you forever."

"Then who am I to deny my lady?" He stood, offering her his hand to help lift her from the ground. Once she was on her feet, he pulled her to his chest and pressed his lips to her hair. "I'm yours, forever, no matter what. I can't live with these constant threats and secrecy. I'm done with the Guild."

She was dizzy, blood rushing to her head as her mind raced. He wanted her and was willing to choose her above the Guild. "What about your family?"

He stepped back and wrapped his fingers around the

handle of his sword. He filled his lungs and exhaled sharply. "Well, I suppose I'd better get that prize money before we go."

She picked up the gauntlet from the ground by his feet and held it out for him. He slipped his hand inside, flexing his fingers until it sat snug. Pride swelled in her chest as she stepped back to look at him, her champion. "What will you do about Henry?"

He placed the feathers back beneath his breastplate and took a deep breath, turning his face towards the light at the mouth of the tunnel. "What I should've done the moment I returned to the Guild."

CHAPTER

THIRTY-NINE

Rose petals rained down onto the arena floor, no longer white, but scarlet. Henry stood in the center, basking in the applause of thousands of spectators.

Brandon's breaths were heavy, each one shuddering from his chest as he stood in the mouth of the tunnel. He glanced up as the first raindrops began to fall.

The dusty scent of rain on hot sand clouded Natalie's breaths as she tightened her fingers around Brandon's. She kept to the shadows, her back pressed against the rough grain of the stonework. She curled her other hand around the grip of her new sword, comforted by its presence at her hip.

"Are you certain about this?" Her words rattled from the dry chamber of her throat. "I wouldn't blame you if you changed your mind. You're giving up so much."

"Never." His eyes softened as he looked at her. "I would

give up the throne of Aldland if it meant I could be with you."

She longed for his kiss, and her lips parted in anticipation. "Fight well, my champion."

"I will. Harder than I've ever fought, for you, my lady. For us."

He ran his thumb across her knuckles and gave her hand a parting squeeze. As he stepped into the light, rain spattering on the shining steel of his armor, Natalie's chest tightened. Her fingers flexed, longing to cling to him as he walked towards the fight.

The roar of the crowd swelled as he entered the arena, pulsing against her ears. Chants of *"Bear! Bear! Bear!"* soared, growing louder and more frenzied.

Natalie took a deep breath and steadied her nerve. She stood alone, with the dark clawing at her back.

Brandon stopped a few feet from Henry and drew his blade. He held his hand up to the crowd in thanks for their applause.

Perched in her box, Lady Luray sat straight-backed on the edge of her seat. A row of champions and squires sat below, their fists pounding the marble barrier before them. At the end of the row, Tommy sat beside Darius, both of them wearing grim expressions.

Henry's lips curled into a pleased smirk as he dipped his head to Brandon. The men exchanged words, lost to Natalie's ears in the roar of the crowd, before pulling on their helmets; the Bear and the Dragon, snarling, teeth bared.

The announcer cried out, "Let the final battle commence!"

The crowd's frenzied screams were painful to her ears.

Swords clashed, steel bit steel. Every muscle in Natalie's body tensed. Brandon staggered beneath the strain of Henry's blow but managed to push him off and away. The Dragon regained his balance and struck again.

This time, Brandon deflected Henry's sword, as effortlessly as swatting a fly. Henry's confusion, and anger were palpable.

Brandon began his advance. Every strike rang around the arena, quaking Natalie's bones. His strength and ferocity would have been terrifying if she did not know the gentle heart which lay beneath the shell of steel.

Natalie's throat clamped shut as Henry swept his leg beneath Brandon's, and dropped him to his knees, using his size against him. She placed her hand on her chest and willed herself to breathe.

The blades met again and again. Henry advanced, relentlessly attacking from above, whilst Brandon's defense remained unbreakable. The rain did nothing to dampen the enthusiasm of the crowd. Some booed and jeered at Henry, others cheered and commanded him to take Brandon down.

The Dragon stepped back to catch his breath, giving Brandon the chance to get back on his feet. Once standing, he retreated a few steps, and gave himself time to breathe as he circled his opponent. Their feet churned the earth, a mass of brown sand and scarlet petals, clinging to wet steel.

"Please," Natalie whispered against her knuckles. "Let him have this."

"It's over." Henry snarled, from within his dragon's maw helmet. He roared in fury and determination as he thundered towards Brandon, his blade drawn back in preparation to strike. Brandon blocked the blow, and swept his leg outwards, tripping the Dragon and sending him crashing to the ground.

Joy surged in Natalie's chest. Her knuckles paled as she gripped the hilt of her blade, squeezing as tight as she could to expel some of the excited energy swelling inside her. She held her breath as Brandon loomed above his enemy.

Their blades clashed again and again, until at last, Brandon broke through Henry's defense, and the tip of his blade struck the breastplate.

Elation soared in Natalie's chest. He had won, for her, for his family, and everything he loved. He cast his sword aside and held up his hands in celebration.

Her vision blurred as tears stung her eyes,

"Brandon the Bear is the victor of the Midsummer Melee!" the announcer bellowed to the delight of the crowd.

Henry's feral roar, and the clash of steel sent ice through Natalie's heart. The world was pulled into sharp focus as Brandon cried out in pain. Henry was back on his feet, thrashing Brandon's body with his blade.

The crowd erupted into boos and protests as the fight continued with Brandon unarmed. Lady Luray rose to her feet, indignation twisting her features. "Stop this!"

Brandon was helpless, deflecting each blow with the steel vambrace covering his forearm. Henry thrashed him again and again.

"Stop!" Lady Luray cried.

Brandon fell, crumpled to the floor beneath the force of Henry's attack. The audience's shrieks echoed around the arena. Henry was not going to stop until it was too late.

There was no time to think.

Natalie's feet moved of their own volition, carrying her out into the rain, across the arena floor. She pulled her sword from its sheath as she ran and charged with every ounce of strength she had. Wet sand sucked her down, attempting to hinder her, but she pushed through, fighting for every inch. Every blow Henry struck gave her more speed, more strength.

There was nothing Brandon could do but protect his face from the furious onslaught. He was helpless, unarmed, alone.

She snatched his discarded sword from the sand and gripped both blades in white-knuckled fists. If Brandon was willing to fight for her, then she would fight for him.

As Henry drew back his arm to strike Brandon once more, she summoned every shred of her courage, raised the blades, and charged between the champions.

FORTY

Pain rattled through Natalie's arms, pooling in her chest as she blocked Henry's blade with the crossed blades. She gripped the hilts as though her life depended on it, and threw her weight behind both swords, pushing the champion back just enough to slow his onslaught.

"Stop!" Her roar gave Henry pause. Her breath rushed from her in sharp, unsatisfying gasps. "Enough."

"Out of my way," he snarled.

"No." She raised her blades, ready to defend his attack. "If you want Brandon, you'll have to cut me down."

"Don't think for a moment I won't."

"Do it then, in front of all these people."

The Dragon snarled, raising his sword.

She could barely hear above the pounding of her heart. Every muscle in her body, every primal instinct told her to flee. "Is this your legacy? You would commit murder in front of thousands of witnesses. All because you lost at the Melee?"

"I've lost so much more than the Melee." He ripped off his helmet and threw it to the ground. Tears pooled in his eyes. His gaze drifted down to Brandon, and slowly his lips parted. His shoulders slouched, as he lowered his blade. "This was supposed to be my time. My chance to become what I was born to be. He has everything..."

She dared not take her eyes from him, kept her swords raised. Her knuckles were bone-white against the brown leather hilts. The clank and groan of armor sounded at her back as Brandon got to his feet. Cautiously, she held her left arm behind her, neither daring to blink nor lower her guard as she waited for Brandon's touch.

Steel fingers gripped hers, releasing the barricade in her chest and allowing her to take a deep breath. Brandon took his sword from her hand and stood by her side. Henry's eyes darted between the two of them as they faced him, their blades poised to defend.

"Henry..." Brandon took a step forward. He held out his hand, placing Henry's blade on the apex between his thumb and forefinger. "It's not too late to stop, as far as anyone else knows, this is part of the show."

Natalie tensed, waiting for Henry to pounce. The realization that thousands of eyes were upon her was a distant and insignificant thought.

The Dragon's ferocity shattered as he relinquished his hold on the blade. He dropped to his knees, holding his head in his hand, his heavy breaths breaking through the silence in the arena.

The other champions ran towards them. They surrounded Henry, gripping his arms, and pulling him back. Only then did Natalie lower her blade.

Brandon turned to face her and pulled off his helmet. His armor was dented but he did not appear hurt. His eyes were wide as they darted over her. "You...Nat..." He took her hand and held it to his chest. "You saved me. You stood between us."

Her emotions toppled onto her, flooding her all at once as she sheathed her blade and fell into his embrace. Laughter sent tears spilling down her cheeks, and her hands began to tremble. How she wished she could press her body through his armor, feel his heartbeat beneath her fingertips, and know with certainty that he was safe.

He enveloped her in his arms as she sought solace in the warmth of his neck. She pressed her body against the cold, wet, unyielding wall of steel and breathed in the scent of him.

"I love you." He was trembling against her. "So much."

"You see, they're together," Henry cried as the champions held him. "They've been together since Blackmere, and he had the audacity to bring his wench to the Guild. He holds no regard for our order, and yet, you all want him as Guild Master."

Brandon's hold on her loosened. His throat twitched above the steel of his gorget, and his eyes lowered to Natalie's. The air grew heavy between them. His nod was barely perceptible.

Natalie took a deep breath as she looked at him. "Are you certain?"

"Aye, more certain than I've ever been in my life."

"Brandon?" Darius stood before them, his eyes scouring both Brandon and Natalie. "Is it true?"

He turned towards his fellow champions and bowed his head. "Aye. It's true."

Henry's sharp burst of triumphant laughter echoed around the amphitheater. He broke free of the champions' hold and pointed a trembling finger towards Brandon. "You—"

His eyes widened as he looked over Brandon's shoulder.

Natalie followed his gaze. Lady Luray stood behind them on her straw mats, as her servants held a canopy above her to protect her from the rain. She was flanked by four guards, each armed with polearms.

"Arrest him," Henry commanded the guards. His finger still pointed at Brandon.

Lady Luray's soft laughter greeted his demand. "On what grounds?"

"He broke the Guild's rules."

"This is not the Guild." Lady Luray shook her head. "However, it is against our laws here in Westgarden to assault an unarmed man."

Henry clamped his lips together and shrunk back into the group of champions gathered around him.

Darius lowered his eyes and shook his head slowly. When at last he looked to Brandon, his heart was breaking. "Sweet Bear, think about what you're doing."

Brandon took a step towards Natalie. "I have, and as much as I love the Guild, and as dear to me as you all are, I have to follow my heart."

He pressed his hand against her waist, and the firm touch spread throughout her body. She took a deep breath and looked to Darius. "I love him, and he loves me."

People in the crowd shifted restlessly, their movements rippling like blades of grass blowing in the wind. Their murmurs filled the amphitheater.

Henry turned and held his arms out towards the audience. "Listen to me," he bellowed. "Listen."

Natalie's thundering pulse drowned out the sound of the crowd. She tightened her grip on Brandon's hand. Behind her, his breaths came sharp and shallow.

Satisfied he held the crowd's attention, Henry continued. "The Champion's Guild is an ancient and proud order, and every champion among us must abide by the Guild's rules. We are forbidden from falling in love, so we can dedicate our lives and our hearts to the Champion's Guild. That is the sacrifice we make, and we make it for you good people." He stood, slowly nodding his head, to allow his words to sink in, before baring his teeth to speak again. "But Brandon has broken our rules, and he has the audacity to enter this arena, and parade his... his..." He turned to curl his lip at Natalie. "*Slut.*"

Heat fanned across Natalie's cheeks as Brandon lunged a step forward. The crowd surged, rising to their feet, jeering and booing.

Lady Luray's guards surrounded Natalie, blocking her from view, standing between her and Brandon.

"Let me pass," she begged. "Please."

Lady Luray's voice called to her above the din. "You must stay safe, Lady Blackmere."

Natalie was shielded from the champions and the crowd, but Brandon was not. She would not leave him to be picked over. Finding no way to push through the guards, she crouched and searched for a gap between the guards' legs.

Brandon stood face to face with Henry, as the other champions attempted to pull them apart. Darius stood off to the side, too injured to join in the fray. The champions' voices melded together, an indiscernible racket amongst the jeering of the crowd. The spectators were furious, screaming their disapproval at the champions, at her.

She covered her ears as a high-pitched whistling drowned them all out. Heat flooded her veins, and the blood rushed from her head.

The slick swish of drawn steel spurred the frantic pounding of her heart.

"Stop this!" She hurled herself forward, darting through a gap between two guards' legs. Wet sand clung to her, coating her hands, soaking through the cloth of her breeches. "Stop!"

Lady Luray held her hand aloft, commanding her people to listen. Silence descended on the audience.

Natalie looked to her, grateful for her assistance as she pulled herself to her feet. The champions' argument faded as they grew aware of the stillness.

At once, she was back at the Mid-Winter feast, trying to recount the verses of The Ballad of Barthalow, for an audience, shame and fear clawing at her, turning her blood to ice.

"It's true." She swallowed, trying in vain to wipe the sand from her hands. "I should not have come to the Guild.

The champions have always meant so much to me, and I should've respected your rules."

The sadness and hurt in Brandon's eyes drove her on.

"But... I..." Her words faded as her vision shook. The sight of him anchored her. She had to be with him, no matter the cost. She breathed deeply and looked into his eyes. "I love Brandon, recklessly, and completely."

Brandon's lips curved into a smile as he stepped towards her.

"And love defies rules." She leaned into his touch as he cupped her cheek in his hand, wiping her tears with his thumb.

He lowered his head and pressed his brow to hers. "I've fought all my life, and nothing is so worth fighting for as you."

She smiled as he crooked his finger beneath her chin and tilted her face to meet his lips.

When he kissed her there was no crowd, no champions, no noblewoman nor her soldiers. There was only him, his lips, his pulse pounding at her fingertips as they rested on the heat of his neck.

She was no longer Lady Blackmere, and he was no longer a champion. She was Natalie, and he was Brandon. They were back at the beach, the roar of the ocean drowning out the rest of the world. She melted against his lips as he crouched, never breaking their kiss, and hooked his arm beneath her knees, lifting her from the ground and pinning her to him.

He made her breathless.

As she broke away the world slowly resumed its turning, but the roar of the ocean did not stop. She clung to him, her arms around his shoulders as his breath blew hot against her temples.

The roar came from the people in the crowd, and they were cheering. They were cheering for her and Brandon.

"Let's just go," Brandon said. He pressed his lips to her hair as he carried her, leaving his blade and his fellow champions behind.

Natalie kept her eyes on him, not daring to look at the thousands of people watching them, screaming for them.

"Stop them," Henry bellowed, his voice fading behind them, drowning amongst the racket of the crowd. "They can't do this."

Lady Luray laughed. "I am the Lady of Westgarden, they are within my jurisdiction, and I say they can. They are under my protection and are free to leave. You, however, are not."

Henry's protests as the guards seized him, were swallowed by the cheers of the crowd.

Darius hurried to Brandon's side, gripping his arm and gritting his teeth against the pain in his chest. "My dear friend, the Guild Master will not welcome you back."

"Nor should he," Sara hissed behind him.

"Your life with us might still be salvaged," Darius pressed, casting a dismissive look towards Sara. "Don't go."

Brandon's chest swelled against Natalie as his hold on her tightened. "I've given enough years of my life to the Guild. If you have any love for me, you'll understand why I have to follow my heart."

Darius took a deep breath and his brow stitched

together. The turmoil in his heart shone in his eyes, but he reached out towards Natalie, and briefly squeezed her fingers. "Take care of him."

Natalie's heart filled as she laced her fingers with Darius's and offered him a reassuring smile. "Always."

Brandon smiled at her and carried her back to the shadows of the armory beneath a shower of rain and rose petals. She peered above Brandon's shoulder, meeting Lady Luray's gaze as the noblewoman escorted them with her guards.

"Quite the finale," Lady Luray chuckled. "You'll be the talk of Aldland."

CHAPTER

FORTY-ONE

Natalie awoke naked, in a soft, enormous bed in Westgarden's castle. The steady rhythm of Brandon's heartbeat drummed against her ear as she lay with her head on his bare chest. Songbirds trilled outside the window, as a gentle breeze blew through the silk curtains. She peered through her eyelashes at the warm afternoon light and took a deep breath.

Her sword was propped against the wall beneath the window, and beside it, a small wooden chest, containing Brandon's prize of forty gold coins.

Four days had passed since the Midsummer Melee. At Lady Luray's insistence, they had taken a room in the castle, whilst her guards provided them with both security and privacy. Having the notorious lovers who had stood in defiance of the Guild, afforded Lady Luray an added layer of notoriety. Scandal was gold dust to nobles and sheltering them meant she too was coated in glitter. It was a small price to pay for peace.

Natalie strained her ears to listen for the crowd of people who had taken to waiting outside. There was nothing but the birdsong, the rustle of the breeze through the trees, and the rhythm of the heart she loved so completely. It seemed, after four days, the people had given up on trying to catch a glimpse of the couple.

A smile tugged at the corners of her lips.

She nuzzled the softness of his stomach beneath her cheek and stroked her arm across his hips. Brandon stirred beneath her, his belly hollowing as he yawned and stretched.

He stroked his fingers through her hair. "I dreamed of you."

Natalie chuckled and pressed a kiss above his heart. The sight of him, relaxed, content, and bathed in the golden glow of the afternoon filled her with warmth. "Good things?"

"Wonderful things," he smiled. He opened his eyes to look at her. "But none so wonderful as waking up with you." He took a deep breath, his chest rising and falling beneath her cheek. "Did you sleep well?"

"I did," she smiled.

"Do I make a good pillow?"

"You do. I don't remember a time I slept so soundly."

"I'm glad." He wound his arm around her waist, trailing his fingertips across her back. "I was afraid my usefulness would wear thin."

She ran her fingers through his chest hair. "Never. I can think of many uses for you."

"Oh, can you?" His gentle smile widened into a grin. "Like fetching things from high shelves?"

"And moving heavy furniture, yes." She pressed her teeth into her lower lip and let her fingers skate across his chest.

His body twitched at her light touch. He caught her hand and brought it to his lips. "I'll do anything you ask of me."

Content, she sighed and stretched, straightening out until her face was level with his. She pulled the white silk sheets over them, shielding them from the world.

"I think we missed breakfast," she whispered, leaving a fleeting kiss on his lips.

"I think, if I remember correctly, you *were* breakfast."

"Aye, and dinner and lunch, and breakfast yesterday," she chuckled. "And as much as I would love to spend the rest of our lives in this bed, we do need to leave the room eventually. I fear we're taking advantage of Lady Luray's hospitality."

Brandon growled and gripped her shoulders, rolling over until he pinned her beneath him. She laughed against his lips as he showered her with kisses.

He held her hands by her head, resting his weight on his forearms as he nudged her knees open with his thighs. "She's probably forgotten we're even here."

The sensation of being pinned beneath him, fully willing but at his mercy, stoked the fire in her blood. Her breaths were shallow and unsatisfying as her desire built. No matter how long they stayed hidden in the room, no matter how many times she lay with him, it would never be enough.

"I doubt it." She moistened her lips and lifted her head to kiss his neck. "There's probably a line of people waiting to speak to us when we emerge."

"Let them wait." Brandon all but purred as she grazed his throat with her teeth.

"Might we at least take a bath?"

He paused, raising an eyebrow as he shook his head free of the blankets. Natalie stifled a laugh as he peered towards the large copper tub at the opposite end of the room.

"Hm." He pondered. "Do you think we can both fit in there?"

"I believe so, though we'd have to press very close together."

"Then yes." He planted a kiss on the tip of her nose and climbed out of bed. "I'll ask them to bring us hot water."

Natalie sat back against the pillows, admiring the thick, shapely curves of his backside, and the toned muscles of his thighs as he pulled on his clothes.

His lips quirked as he knotted the laces of his breeches and turned his head towards her. "You're ogling."

"Yes?"

He chuckled as he headed towards the door. "I'll be back soon."

Alone in the bed chamber, Natalie turned her face towards the warmth and light streaming through the window and listened to the birdsong. The balminess of Westgarden reminded her of her childhood, of summers in Caer Austwick.

The thought of returning to Blackmere, to the cold and damp, the dreariness of administration and managing her land, filled her with dread. And facing that place again... the place where...

She distracted herself with the glinting blade leaning against the wall, used only once in defense of the man she loved. There was a small nick in the steel, a souvenir from Henry's attack, and a reminder of her potential.

She would likely never use the blade again.

She tried not to think too hard about what might happen in the following six months. It was a time for them to enjoy, to discover each other fully. She and Brandon were together, more in love than she had ever dreamed, and blessed with months of freedom from duties, that neither of them had ever experienced.

She could not help but smile as she ran her fingers across her collarbones. His touch, the sensation of his kiss, lingered on her skin.

The rattle of the door's latch roused her from her thoughts. Though he was gone just a few minutes, the sight of him returning to her made her heart leap.

He dropped a bundle of folded sheets and wound scrolls of parchment on the bed and pressed his lips together. "We are, apparently, in demand."

Natalie sat upright and took the bundle. The letters were each fastened with a colorful wax seal, some she recognized, others were unfamiliar. She took the first one from the pile, sealed in blue wax and embossed with a swallow.

"Lady Luray said she's taken deliveries every day."

Brandon sat, staring at the pile of letters as though they might bite him. "Do you think they're angry?"

"I don't know." Her heart thundered as she broke open the seal. As she unfolded the parchment a scrap of white silk and ribbon slipped out from the paper.

"Goddess!" Natalie reeled back. "Is that underwear?"

Brandon laughed as she flicked the garment from the bed.

When the scrap of silk lay on the white marble floor, Natalie shook her head. "Why would someone send underwear?"

He gave a shrug, still chuckling. "Well it depends if it's been worn or not."

A disgusted sigh burst from her lips. "Well then this must be for you. People don't send me underwear." She took a breath before reading. "*My dearest Lady Blackmere... oh... no... I heard about your performance at the Midsummer Melee and felt compelled to write. We hear you bravely stood between the man you love, and the villain who sought to destroy him, then made passionate love on the arena floor. Rarely has any story conjured such a stir at Wenlock Castle. The enclosed gift is for you and your lover to enjoy.*"

Brandon laughed quietly and picked up the garment by the tip of one of the ribbons. "Scandalous."

She chuckled and shook her head as she continued to scan the page. "It's from Lord Wenlock. He invites us to stay at his castle and attend a masked ball."

"Are we going?"

"Absolutely not, the man's an ass." She glanced at the

underwear, which Brandon held aloft by the ribbons. "Burn those."

"You don't think I'd look pretty in them?"

Natalie dropped the letter onto the bed. His arched eyebrow drew a laugh from her. "You'd look ravishing, but I don't trust where they've been."

"I doubt they'd fit anyway," he teased, flinging them across the room towards the fireplace. "I dread to think what other rumors are flying around about us."

"Well, I'm sure we'll find out."

Natalie's cheeks reddened as she worked her way through the nobles' letters. Many simply congratulated the couple on the declaration of their love, whilst others went into graphic detail of acts Natalie and Brandon were rumored to have committed before the Westgarden crowd. Some of the bolder nobles even offered to join the couple, should the desire for a third ever occur.

When her throat was tender from reading and laughing, Natalie leaned against Brandon, resting her head on his shoulder. "Let them gossip."

"And what about your parents? Surely the news will have reached Caer Austwick and Blackmere."

"My parents know as well as any of us that whatever scandal is currently stirring the nobles should be watered down to a quarter of its strength."

Smiling to herself, she wondered if the rumor had reached Blackmere, and if so, were Genevieve and Jenny together, laughing at the scandal Natalie and Brandon had caused? There was no doubt she would be subjected to relentless teasing when she was eventually reunited with Jenny.

She spread the remaining letters across the bed, glancing at their seals to determine their origin. There were none from Blackmere, or Caer Austwick. Brandon stiffened at her side as she uncovered a scroll. The Champion's Guild's sword sigil was pressed into the gold wax.

"Oh, Goddess," Brandon whispered.

"Do you want me to read it?"

He stared at the scroll, his throat twitching as the muscle in his cheek leapt. His breath shook as he nodded his head. "Aye. Let's get it over with."

Natalie took the scroll from him, lifting the seal with her thumbnail. She unfurled the parchment and began reading immediately so as not to prolong his suffering. *"In light of the events of the Midsummer Melee, The Guild Master hereby commands that Sir Brandon the Bear and his squire, Lady Natalie Blackmere, return to the Guild without hesitation."*

Brandon's eyes were distant. "There's nothing else?"

"No. Just that they want us to return right away."

He took a deep breath, eyes flickering to the ceiling, as if the answers lay among the roses carved into the rafters. "Goddess only knows what poison Henry's pouring into their ears."

The sound of that name sent bristles along her back. After Lady Luray's guards had arrested him, Henry had been taken back to the Guild to be dealt with as the Guild Master saw fit. They had yet to entirely understand why his ire had been so focused on Brandon. Though she had often awakened in the night, replaying the events of that day, Natalie did not yet fully know whether she wanted to understand the Dragon.

Sensing Brandon's anguish, she reached out, placing her hand on the back of his. "Do you want to go back?"

A quiet rumble sounded at the back of his throat. "I gave so much of my life to the Guild, and though I was happy, I never felt complete until I met you."

His fingers laced with hers, and the creases around his eyes deepened with his smile.

Natalie rolled the Guild Master's scroll. "Does he have the authority to order you back?"

Brandon gave a barely-perceptible shrug. "As much authority as a father does over his son."

"It's your choice," she said, placing the scroll on the bed with the other letters. "If you want to go back there and face him and Henry, I'll be by your side. I know the champions were your life for so long. Are you sure you want to leave the Guild without saying a proper goodbye?"

"I'm sure of only one thing." He closed his eyes and drew near her, his soft lips tugging at hers.

She melted into his kiss, running her fingers through the soft down on his cheeks. His arms snaked around her waist, holding her to him until her head spun, and the room tilted around them.

"You would've made a great champion," he whispered. "Brave, fierce, and beautiful...my Lioness of Blackmere."

She smiled. "More like a plump ginger housecat."

"You dare," he growled in mock outrage, pushing her back onto the bed, the letters crumpling beneath them. He showered her breasts in kisses, working his way lower. "You're perfect," he whispered against her stomach, his lips tickling the sensitive skin beneath her navel.

She stifled her laughter on the back of her arm. She was glowing, alone at last with the man she adored, free to love each other without the Guild breathing down their neck. She was his, wholly, and he was hers, and for the next six months, they had no need to worry about Blackmere. They were free.

He rested his chin on her belly and smiled at her. "Let's bathe, then eat." He stroked his knuckles along the curve of her stomach. "Then we'll thank Lady Luray for her hospitality, and we go wherever we damned well please, whenever we see fit, and we do it together."

She relaxed at his touch, soothed by the gentle caress of his calloused, strong hands.

Natalie tried not to fixate on the Guild Master's summons as Lady Luray's servants filled a large, round tub for her and Brandon. When they were alone once more, he undressed and climbed into the tub, beckoning her over with a crooked finger.

She sighed as she sunk into the steaming water, her back pressed against the warmth of his chest.

His teeth grazed the valley between her neck and shoulder, a deep rumble of approval rolling through his chest, more a growl than a purr. Natalie arched against him, her breath catching in her throat as his arms surrounded her, his thumbs brushing against her nipples.

"Let the Guild Master stamp his feet all he wants,

there's only one command I yield to," he whispered against her ear. "And that is the command of my lady."

"My champion," she smiled.

His lips hovered above her shoulder, and his chest grew still beneath her back. "I'm not a champion anymore."

The hint of sorrow in his voice stopped her heart. She turned to face him, her body sliding against his through the water. "You will always be my champion."

His eyes grew distant before snapping back towards her. His mouth lifted into a smile. "I'm just Brandon now. I'm your Brandon."

She held him close, resting her head on his chest as his pulse beat steadily against her ear. "Do you regret it?"

"Never." He brought up a hand to stroke her hair. "I just... I don't know how to be *just* Brandon. The Guild was my life for so long."

Taking a cake of soap from the side of the tub, she dipped it into the water and worked it into a lather between her palms. She began to spread the suds across his shoulders, her hands sliding across the firm swell of his muscles, caressing and massaging his arms and chest, which were still sore from the contest. The air filled with the sharp, sweet scents of lemon and peppermint. "I don't know what lies ahead, but whatever it is, you don't have to face it alone."

His eyelids closed as she lowered her hands to rest them on his stomach. A chuckle broke loose from his parted lips. "I'm supposed to be the trained warrior, yet you've risked your life to save me twice."

"You're worth it. A thousand times over."

"My lady, I could live a hundred lifetimes, and still never be worth a hair on your head."

She leaned towards him, and the sensation of her bare breasts pressed against the slippery expanse of his chest sent a thrill coursing through her body. Her lips were agonizingly close to his. "Take that back."

"Never."

She flexed her fingers against the soft curve of his belly. "Don't make me tickle you."

His eyes darkened as he gripped her wrists, pulling her back towards him and wrapping her arms around his neck. He flashed that cocky smile which always rendered her helpless and swept aside her senses. "You wouldn't dare, you know I always win."

The firm press of his cock against her stomach left her mouth dry. Four days locked in the room with him, making up for the time they had lost at the Guild, had been blissful, yet her body still burned with desire for him. She doubted she would ever stop craving his touch.

Letting her hands slip below the surface of the water, she caressed his body, drawing a broken sigh from him. She wrapped her hands around his length and slowly began to stroke him.

Brandon leaned back, resting the back of his head against the lip of the tub. His eyelids lowered at the sensation of her touch. "Nat."

"Let me take care of you," she whispered, sliding her body against his. She pressed her teeth into her lower lip as he groaned, cupping her breasts in his broad, rough hands.

A frantic knock at the door brought an abrupt end to their bliss. "*Lady Blackmere?*"

The voice belonged to Lady Luray. Natalie forced the air from her nose and rolled her eyes. "Yes?"

"*I have a message for you, I don't mean to intrude, but it is urgent.*"

Natalie brushed a parting kiss against Brandon's lips as she stood. He sat upright, unwilling to let her go, caressing the outer curves of her thighs with his fingertips.

Her cheeks reddened as his gaze lingered on her body. "Now you're ogling."

"Yes?" His lips quirked into a grin as she wrapped a towel around herself. Watching her, he bit into his lower lip, sending a flood of desire throughout her body.

"*Lady Blackmere?*"

"Coming," she called as she reluctantly stepped out of the tub. His hand on the curve of her backside spread a smile across her lips.

Her feet skipped across the cool marble floor, and by the time she reached the door, she was shivering. She opened the door and was greeted by the sight of Lady Luray.

Westgarden's noblewoman was radiant as always is a bright azure gown, her auburn hair piled high on her head and perfectly coiffed.

Natalie grasped the towel at her chest and bowed her head. "Good morning, Catherine."

Lady Luray's smile widened. "And good afternoon to you, Natalie. I apologize for the intrusion." She held out a scroll of parchment. "This just arrived, with the instruction to deliver it to your hand without hesitation."

Natalie held her breath as she turned the scroll over in her hands. She expected her mother's sigil, but the wax sealing the letter was purple. Regal.

"Is that...?" A crown seal was pressed into the wax. "This is from the palace."

Lady Luray chuckled. "I'll be in my quarters, should you require anything." She turned from the doorway and took a step down the gold-trimmed corridor. "I trust everything has been to your..." The brief press of her lips suppressed a smile. "Satisfaction?"

A mixture of embarrassment and excitement swelled in Natalie's chest. "Immeasurably, thank you."

"I am pleased for you. There's food in the kitchen when you need it, and my people will bring you clean clothing, when you decide it's time to dress."

"You are too kind," Natalie laughed quietly.

As Lady Luray bowed and left the doorway, Natalie gripped the scroll and gently closed the door.

The sloshing sound of the water, and the citrus and mint scent beckoned her as she walked back towards the bathtub. He looked up at her, his skin still slick with soap. She found herself torn, desperate to know the contents of the letter, but craving Brandon's touch and warmth.

"What do you have there?" The sight of him, the pink blush on his chest and cheeks, the dark desire in his eyes, pulled at her.

"We've received a letter," she shrugged as she perched on the lip of the tub, reaching down to swirl a finger through the water. Her nonchalance disguised the frantic pounding of her heart. "From the queen of Aldland."

Brandon's eyebrows raised for a moment, settling back down as he leaned back against the edge of the tub. "We must be in trouble then."

"Surely she'd send guards and not letters if we were?" She broke open the seal, lamenting that she could not save it as a souvenir. Fingers shaking, she opened the letter and read aloud. *"To Lady Blackmere and Sir Brandon, formerly of the Champion's Guild. You are hereby requested to grace us with your presence for the grand feast at The Summer Palace on the evening of...* oh Goddess."

Brandon chuckled. "Your eyes are like saucers."

"It's an invitation from the *queen*, Brandon." Her voice was shrill as the room pulsed around her. "Oh Goddess. If we refuse this my mother will string me to the flagpole when I get back to Blackmere." She sat upright. A grand feast. She had nothing but her muddied tunic to wear and only a week to prepare. "What do we do?"

A startled yelp burst from her lips as she was pulled backwards into the tub, enveloped in warmth and the arms of the man she loved. She clutched the soggy letter in her hands, laughing as Brandon pulled the soaking towel from her body, and threw it onto the floor beside the fire.

When she was naked again, he pulled her against him and smiled down at her. "We do whatever we want."

She brushed her lips against his, savoring the blissful intimacy of being so open, so at ease with their love. The letter fell to the floor as she wrapped her arms around him. "I don't even know how to dance."

"I'll teach you."

Her forehead tightened as her eyebrows raised. A smile

tugged at the corners of her lips "I didn't know you can dance."

"Aye." He traced the curve of her waist with his hands. "There's a lot about each other we still have to discover."

He was right, and for the first time since they met, six months ago in Blackmere's tavern, they were free to discover it all.

Their adventure and their life together were only just beginning.

ACKNOWLEDGMENTS

Ali, thank you so much for your editing, especially your enthusiastic "squeeing" during certain events. Feedback can be daunting, but I always look forward to your comments.

Brandon wouldn't be a romance cover hunk without Naj at Najla Qamber Designs. Your work is nothing short of incredible. Thank you so much!

An enormous thank you to my husband, Jake, my very own champion. You've kept me going even on the darkest days and I love you with all my heart.

Thank you to Jack Harbon for formatting these books and making them so beautiful.

As always, thank you to my lovely patrons over on Patreon, for cheering me on and supporting me. Special thanks to the Vixens for Life: Emily H, Katie B, Melanie, Linda W, Janel A, Deanna S, and D Mayo-Wells.

And thank you to you, if you are reading this. Words can't express how grateful I am to everyone who reads my stories. Thank you, thank you, thank you.

SNEAK PREVIEW

Keep reading for a preview of the first chapter of Hearts of Blackmere Book 3, *Forever His Champion...*

FOREVER HIS CHAMPION

Stifling air pressed against Natalie and the overpowering scent of elaborate floral displays mingled with the spice of expensive perfumes which stung her nose. She wilted inside her gown, cocooned in layers upon layers of storm cloud purple silk and silver pearls.

Every breath was a battle.

The walls of the hallway closed in around her as she waited for her name to be called. Beyond the gilded doorway, muffled chatter and bursts of musical laughter struck panic into her heart. Parties never got any easier, and this was no ordinary party.

Beyond the doorway, the most esteemed nobility of Aldland feasted and mingled, and presiding above them all, was Queen Helena and the queen consort, Isolda.

Drawing a deep breath, Natalie closed her eyes and silently cursed Lady Luray for insisting she wear a gown so heavy and which hugged her figure so unforgivingly. Perspiration beaded on the small of her back. The purple silk, she had been told repeatedly, complemented her pale ivory skin and brought out the copper tinge to her hair.

"How many are there?" Brandon's deep, steady voice calmed her nerves.

She opened her eyes, turning to him for comfort. He was dressed all in black, the leather-capped shoulders of his doublet overhanging just enough to add even more breadth to his already intimidating size. Silver embroidery shimmered as he shifted his weight between his feet. He held himself proudly, head high, enormous shoulders back, all too familiar with the sensation of being put on show. Whereas Natalie's neck warmed as a blush crept across her throat, Brandon's complexion was calm and cool. His beard was neat, the brown and silver bristles combed straight and smoothed with some kind of pine-scented oil. The silver at his temples gleamed against the dark brown of his hair, matching the embroidered vines on his doublet. Despite her nerves, Natalie could not help but yearn for him.

A footman guarding the door lifted his chin in answer to Brandon's question. He was a young man, tall and slim, with dark brown eyes and cool, tawny skin. His impassive expression brightened into a polite smile. "Some three hundred guests, Sir."

The blood drained from Natalie's face. Three hundred. Three hundred pairs of eyes judging and scrutinizing. Three hundred mouths gossiping. Her legs grew weak beneath her. The footman's vivid midnight blue tunic and pristine white hose blurred in front of her.

A low chuckle sounded in Brandon's chest. He raised his eyebrows and said, "Big party."

"Indeed, sir." The footman offered the pair a sympathetic smile. "I know everyone is very excited to see you. There's been talk of little else this past week."

The earth shifted beneath Natalie's feet. Reaching out, she placed a hand on Brandon's forearm, steadying herself against him. "Do you think they'd mind if I stay out here all night?"

The warmth of Brandon's palm on the back of her hand anchored her to the room. "You'll be fine, love. It's just a party."

"I don't like parties," she muttered, though it was impossible to truly be sullen when he held her so tenderly.

Brandon smiled. It was easy for him. He was so used to being admired and watched. His life as a champion, a prize-winning fighter, had made him immune to the embarrassment of having every pair of eyes in a room comb over his body, of whispers behind his back, and the endless questions and prying.

Natalie had only been truly renowned for two weeks and already she wanted to flee from it. Their celebrity had begun back in Westgarden, with a handful of letters, exaggerating and dramatizing the story of how she saved Brandon's life in the Midsummer Melee. At first the admiration had been amusing, but now... now it was suffocating.

Brandon gave her hand a reassuring squeeze. "We'll just go in, eat, drink, dance, answer their questions... it'll be alright. Besides, you're more used to talking with nobles than I."

"I don't think talking to myself counts," she grimaced. "I've spent most of my life avoiding this sort of thing."

"Lady Blackmere," he laughed. "You've faced bandits and champions, fought for your own life and mine, but you're afraid of a room full of toffs?" He glanced at the footman. "Don't tell them I said that."

The footman flashed a wry smile. "Your secret is safe with me, sir."

Natalie lowered her head and focused on her breaths. It was just one night, one uncomfortable night. If she fled now, if she insulted the queen, she would never hear the end of it. Of course, the same could be said if she somehow said the wrong thing... did the wrong thing...

The snug bodice of her gown became unbearable, squeezing the life from her. It was too much.

Brandon's broad hand on the small of her back was the only thing keeping her from collapsing. "Breathe, my love. We can go, if you want to." He turned to her. Heat spread throughout her body as his eyes raked across her. "Though you'd be denying these good people the chance to see the most beautiful woman in the world."

Her cheeks prickled. "Flatterer." She took a deep breath and forced it out. "Alright. I'll do it."

Victorious, Brandon turned back to the footman and grinned. "I'm rather looking forward to dancing with Lady Blackmere."

The footman chuckled. "As you should be, sir. She is radiant this evening."

"She's radiant every evening."

Natalie rolled her eyes, fighting back a laugh. "I said alright. I'm going in."

"I heard." Brandon straightened and held his head high. "But you're still radiant."

Cheeks reddening, she smiled to the footman and glanced up at the domed ceiling. The Summer Palace was unlike any structure she had ever been. Her childhood home, Caer Austwick, was known throughout Aldland for its beauty, but compared to the palace, it was little more than a barn. Above them, strands of crystals hung from the golden domed ceiling, swaying and glittering in the warm air, casting tiny, dancing rainbows all over the walls. The effect was mesmerizing.

A low, churning growl snapped Natalie from her admirations.

The footman's eyes widened for a moment, as he brought his hand to his stomach. "Forgive me."

"There's nothing to forgive. Are you hungry?" Natalie asked.

"It's quite alright. We palace staff dine once the party is over," the footman smiled. "Thank you for your understanding."

"Do you want us to bring you something?"

"What's your name? We can sneak it out to you," Brandon nodded. "It's no trouble."

The footman pressed his lips together, hiding his amusement. "My name is Finch, but it's not necessary. Thank you."

Natalie silently resolved to bring the footman something anyway. Her own stomach was growling despite her nerves and she could not imagine the discomfort of waiting until after midnight to eat. If they were kept from the feast much longer, she would have no choice but to devour everything on sight the moment they stepped into the banquet hall.

Brandon threaded his fingers through hers and cast her a warm and inviting smile. Her breath caught in her throat and her stomach fluttered as he raised her hand to his lips. The gentle brush of his beard against her knuckles, followed by the warmth and softness of his mouth made her heart leap.

Beyond the doors a man's voice spoke loudly. "*It is my honor to present our esteemed guests for the evening, Lady Natalie of Blackmere and Sir Brandon, champion—*"

"Former champion," Brandon sighed through gritted teeth.

"*—of the Guild, knight of Blackmere and six-time winner of the Grand Tourney.*"

"Good luck," Finch bowed as he stepped aside.

Natalie's heart plummeted to her stomach as the doors swung open.

Silence swooped into the corridor as three hundred pairs of eyes stared back at Natalie and Brandon. The guests were seated at long tables, which practically groaned beneath a sumptuous feast.

At the head of the banquet hall, sat on her throne at the center of a long mahogany table, Queen Helena was resplendent in wine-red satin. Beside her, the queen consort, Isolda sat tall and graceful in midnight blue.

It was too much. Natalie's knees locked, refusing to move. She would stand there all night if she had to. "I can't—"

"Yes, you can. Breathe," Brandon whispered beside her. Her heart raced as he offered her his arm and leaned closer, until his lips were a hair's breadth from her ear. "You are the Lioness of Blackmere and you can do this."

She steeled her nerves and gave a determined nod. Stepping into the room, she clung to Brandon's arm, her fingertips pressed tight against the firm swell of his bicep.

Every muscle in her body tensed, waiting for their ridicule, their snide comments about her appearance or character.

Amongst the crowd, Lady Catherine Luray, their host at Westgarden, smiled, raising her chin to remind Natalie to stand tall.

The tap of Natalie's pearl encrusted slippers was the only sound as she and Brandon approached the throne of Queen Helena.

Though her likeness had been pressed into every coin in the land, nothing quite prepared Natalie for the sight of their monarch. She was elegant and pristine, the tight coils of her silver hair, topped with a glittering golden crown. Her warm brown face creased and her full lips curved into a welcoming smile as Aldland's notorious lovers approached. Beside her, her wife sat, her liver-spotted tawny hand resting on the arm of the queen's throne, the white waves of her hair shining like starlight, and her eyes darkened with smudged kohl.

A thousand thoughts raced through Natalie's head. She

felt as though she had never spoken to another human being before, never had to conduct herself in public. The appropriate greetings and formalities drilled into her mind from childhood, abandoned her, rinsed from her mind by the flood of nerves.

As they reached the throne at last, Queen Helena's smile broadened. "Lady Blackmere, Sir Brandon, we are delighted to have you here."

Natalie's throat closed. Her ears rang as she stood before them, mouth slightly agape, blood slowly draining from her face. The lines between the floor tiles blurred, until she stood on nothing but a white and gold pulsing haze, which drew ever closer as her knees weakened.

"The pleasure is ours, your majesties." Brandon's voice was a lifeline in a dark, tumultuous sea.

At the sound of it, Natalie was able to breath steadily. She was not alone.

The queen smiled and stood, offering a hand to Brandon. He brushed his lips against her knuckles and repeated the gesture for Isolda.

Natalie's heart froze as the queen's eyes fixed on her, the creases around them deepening. "We don't bite, my dear."

"Oh," Natalie's face flushed. "No, I... I didn't think you would."

Isolda grinned. "I promise we're less frightening than champions or bandits."

"Or your mother," Helena added.

A bark of laughter burst from Brandon's lips, echoed around the room by the nobles.

"How is the ferocious Lady Austwick?" Isolda chuckled. "We haven't seen her for decades. We've just about recovered."

Their jovial tone let Natalie's heart slow a little. "She's well. Currently residing in Blackmere, fixing my messes."

"I'm sure she does not begrudge her daughter spending time with the man she loves," Queen Helena smiled. She tilted her chin towards a band of musicians at the side of the hall. "Play something for our lovers, won't you?"

Heat crept along Natalie's cheeks as the minstrels broke out into a sweet, melodic tune. Beside her, Brandon smiled and bowed once more to the queens. She would have thought him completely unphased, if not for the slight tinge of pink barely creeping above the black of his collar.

"Sit with us," Queen Helena said, lowering herself back into her throne. She gestured to her servants and raised a goblet from the table before her.

The servants carried two hefty wooden chairs and sat them beside the queen. Natalie could almost hear her mother's admonishments about her posture as she shuffled around the table and sat next to their monarch. The eyes of every guest were on her and Brandon as he sat beside her and thanked the servants as they filled their goblets with red wine.

"A toast," Isolda stood, raising her cup. "To love."

"To love," Natalie replied with the rest of the guests. She took a deep drink, pleasantly surprised by the bold, earthy taste of the wine.

Her attention was pulled towards a man, standing at

one of the long feast tables in the hall. He held his glass aloft in his pale hand, a braid of white hair snaking over his shoulder. The nobleman's eyes were wide, scouring Natalie and Brandon as though he could not believe they were real.

Queen Helena lifted her chin. "Is there a problem, Lord Caine?"

The man smirked. "Tell us, Lady Blackmere, tell us the tale of the Midsummer Melee. Is it true that you made love on the arena floor? There's some discourse about the position."

Natalie's lips parted as her breath escaped her. Beside her, Brandon's fists curled and his jaw clenched.

"Sit down, Lord Caine." Queen Helena's sharp command rang around the silenced banquet hall.

With a chuckle, the lord obeyed and the guests resumed their chatter. The air in the hall began to flow once more. The tension in Natalie's body melted. The hardest part was over. The attention on them would wane completely as the feast began.

"Ignore him. He wouldn't say anything if he didn't have an audience" Brandon's fingers skimmed her thigh, pressing against the layers of silk to offer her a comforting touch. "You did well."

"If not for you, I'd still be standing there in the corridor," she whispered. Their eyes met and her lips quirked into a grateful smile. "You give me strength."

"I just remind you that you already have it, just as you do for me."

The music drifted throughout the banquet hall, gentle and sweet, sharpening her urge to lose herself in Brandon's arms. Dining at the palace was an honor, but Natalie would have happily forsaken it all to take Brandon back upstairs to the room they had been provided for the night. The cramped journey from Westgarden to the capital had taken five days and she looked forward to the end of the party, when at last they could lay together in privacy.

He leaned towards her ear and whispered, "Will you dance with me later?"

"I'm..." Natalie's breath caught as he reached out and brushed a strand of hair back into place. "I'm really terrible at dancing."

He smiled. "Then I won't press the issue, but if you would like to, know that I'm always willing." His lips parted beneath the perfectly groomed shadow of his beard. "My lady, you look so..." His words were cut short as he raised his eyes to look above her head.

Natalie turned. The queen peered at them above the rim of her goblet. "Don't let me stop you. It does my heart good to see you two so in love."

Isolda leaned around her wife to look at the pair. "So, is what they say true?"

"Depends what they say," Brandon said. "They say a lot of things, don't they?"

"That they do." Isolda rolled her eyes, before smiling kindly at Natalie. "But we heard that you single-handedly fought off Henry Percille?"

Brandon gave a low chuckle. "Yes, she did."

"Not quite," Natalie countered, taking another gulp of wine. "I wouldn't call it a fight."

Queen Helena lifted a carafe from the table and filled

Natalie's cup once more. Setting it back down, she leaned her elbow against the rim of the table and rested her cheek against her knuckles. "Well, we have all evening, my dears. Tell us everything, starting with the bandits at Blackmere."

Forever His Champion is available now!

ABOUT MARIE LIPSCOMB

Marie specializes in writing romances with plus sized heroines and plus sized heroes. She is the author of the *Hearts of Blackmere* and *Vixens Rock* series as Marie Lipscomb, and also writes short, bonkers, high-heat romances including *No Getting Ogre You* and *Santa Claus is Going to Town On Me* under the pen name M.L. Eliza.

Originally from Bolton, UK, Marie now lives in North Carolina, USA. When she's not writing, she can usually be found playing the same three video games on a loop (*cough* Dragon Age)

ALSO BY MARIE LIPSCOMB

The *Hearts of Blackmere* Series

The Lady's Champion

Forever His Champion

The Harpy and The Dragon

The *Vixens Rock* Series

Rhythm

Strings

Amped

Writing as M.L. Eliza

No Getting Ogre You

Santa Claus is Going to Town On Me